Praise for *Open*

"Reminiscent of the works of W. G. Sebald, this dreamy, incantatory debut was the most beautiful novel I read this year—the kind of book that remains on your nightstand long after you finish so that you can continue dipping in occasionally as a nighttime consolation."           —*The New Republic*

"A psychological hand grenade." —*The Atlantic,* "Best Books I Read This Year"

"A meditative and startlingly clear-eyed first novel."
                    —*Newsweek*/The Daily Beast "Writers' Favorite Books 2011"

"This year, literary discovery came, for me, in the form of Teju Cole's debut novel, *Open City,* a deceptively meandering first-person narrative about a Nigerian psychiatry resident in New York. The bonhomous flaneur who strolls Manhattan from top to bottom, reveals, in the course of his walking meditations, both more about the city and about himself than we—or indeed he—could possibly anticipate. Cole writes beautifully; his protagonist is unique; and his novel, utterly thrilling."           —*The Globe and Mail*

"On the surface, [it's] the story of a young, foreign psychiatry resident in post-9/11 New York City who searches for the soul of the city by losing himself in extended strolls around teeming Manhattan. But it's really a story about a lost nation struggling to regain a sense of direction after that shattering, disorienting day ten years ago. A quiet, lyrical and profound piece of writing."                    —*Seattle Times,* "32 of the Year's Best Books"

"Lean and mean and bristles with intelligence. The multi-culti characters and streets of New York are sharply observed and feel just right. . . . Toward the end, there's a poignant, unexpected scene in a tailor's shop that's an absolute knockout."           —Salon, "Writers choose their favorite books of 2011"

"I couldn't stop reading Teju Cole's debut novel and was blown away by his ability to capture the human psyche with such beautiful yet subtle prose."
                            —Slate, "Best Books of 2011"

"An unusual accomplishment, *Open City* is a precise and poetic meditation on love, race, identity, friendship, memory, dislocation and Manhattan bird life."           —*The Economist,* "2011 Books of the Year"

# OPEN CITY

# OPEN CITY

A NOVEL

## TEJU COLE

RANDOM HOUSE TRADE PAPERBACKS
NEW YORK

2012 Random House Trade Paperback Edition

Copyright © 2011 by Teju Cole

Published in the United States by Random House Trade Paperbacks, an imprint of The Random House Publishing Group, a division of Random House, Inc., New York.

RANDOM HOUSE TRADE PAPERBACKS and colophon are trademarks of Random House, Inc.

Originally published in hardcover in the United States by Random House, an imprint of The Random House Publishing Group, a division of Random House, Inc., in 2011.

Library of Congress Cataloging-in-Publication Data

Cole, Teju.
Open city: a novel / by Teju Cole.
p.   cm.
ISBN 978-0-8129-8009-7
ebook ISBN 978-0-679-60449-5
1. Nigerians—New York (State)—New York—Fiction.   2. Identity
(Psychology)—Fiction.   3. Race—Fiction.   I. Title.
PR9387.9.C67O64 2010
823'.92—dc22   2010008927

Printed in the United States of America

www.atrandom.com

29  28  27  26  25  24  23  22

Book design by Karin Batten

for Karen
and for Wah-Ming and Beth

## PART 1

*Death is a perfection of the eye*

# ONE

$A$nd so when I began to go on evening walks last fall, I found Morningside Heights an easy place from which to set out into the city. The path that drops down from the Cathedral of St. John the Divine and crosses Morningside Park is only fifteen minutes from Central Park. In the other direction, going west, it is some ten minutes to Sakura Park, and walking northward from there brings you toward Harlem, along the Hudson, though traffic makes the river on the other side of the trees inaudible. These walks, a counterpoint to my busy days at the hospital, steadily lengthened, taking me farther and farther afield each time, so that I often found myself at quite a distance from home late at night, and was compelled to return home by subway. In this way, at the beginning of the final year of my psychiatry fellowship, New York City worked itself into my life at walking pace.

Not long before this aimless wandering began, I had fallen into the habit of watching bird migrations from my apartment, and I wonder now if the two are connected. On the days when I was home early enough from the hospital, I used to look out the window like someone taking auspices, hoping to see the miracle of natural immigration. Each time I caught sight of geese swooping in formation across the sky, I wondered how our life below might look from their perspective, and imagined that, were they ever to indulge in such speculation, the high-rises might seem to them like firs massed in a grove. Often, as I searched the sky, all I saw was rain, or the faint contrail of an airplane bisecting the window, and I doubted in some part of myself whether these birds, with their dark wings and throats, their pale bodies and tireless little hearts, really did exist. So amazed was I by them that I couldn't trust my memory when they weren't there.

Pigeons flew by from time to time, as did sparrows, wrens, orioles, tanagers, and swifts, though it was almost impossible to identify the birds from the tiny, solitary, and mostly colorless specks I saw fizzing across the sky. While I waited for the rare squadrons of geese, I would sometimes listen to the radio. I generally avoided American stations, which had too many commercials for my taste—Beethoven followed by ski jackets, Wagner after artisanal cheese—instead tuning to Internet stations from Canada, Germany, or the Netherlands. And though I often couldn't understand the announcers, my comprehension of their languages being poor, the programming always met my evening mood with great exactness. Much of the music was familiar, as I had by this point been an avid listener to classical radio for more than fourteen years, but some of it was new. There were also rare moments of astonishment, like the first time I heard, on a station broadcasting from Hamburg, a bewitching piece for orchestra and alto solo by Shchedrin (or perhaps it was Ysaÿe) which, to this day, I have been unable to identify.

I liked the murmur of the announcers, the sounds of those voices speaking calmly from thousands of miles away. I turned the computer's speakers low and looked outside, nestled in the comfort provided by those voices, and it wasn't at all difficult to draw the comparison between myself, in my sparse apartment, and the radio host in his or her booth, during what must have been the middle of the night somewhere in Europe. Those disembodied voices remain connected in my mind, even now, with the apparition of migrating geese. Not that I actually saw the migrations more than three or four times in all: most days all I saw were the colors of the sky at dusk, its powder blues, dirty blushes, and russets, all of which gradually gave way to deep shadow. When it became dark, I would pick up a book and read by the light of an old desk lamp I had rescued from one of the dumpsters at the university; its bulb was hooded by a glass bell that cast a greenish light over my hands, the book on my lap, the worn upholstery of the sofa. Sometimes, I even spoke the words in the book out loud to myself, and doing so I noticed the odd way my voice mingled with the murmur of the French, German, or Dutch radio announcers, or with the thin texture of the violin strings of the orchestras, all of this intensified by the fact that whatever it was I was reading had likely been translated out of one of the European languages. That fall, I flitted from book to book: Barthes's *Camera Lucida,* Peter Altenberg's *Telegrams of the Soul,* Tahar Ben Jelloun's *The Last Friend,* among others.

In that sonic fugue, I recalled St. Augustine, and his astonishment at St. Ambrose, who was reputed to have found a way to read without sounding out the words. It does seem an odd thing—it strikes me now as it did then—that we can comprehend words without voicing them. For Augustine, the weight and inner life of sentences were best experienced out loud, but much has changed in our idea of reading since then. We have for too long been taught that the sight of a man speaking to himself is a sign of eccentricity or madness; we are no longer at all habituated to our own voices, except in conversation or from within the safety of a shouting crowd. But a book suggests conversation: one person is speaking to another, and audible sound is, or should be, natural to that exchange. So I read aloud with myself as my audience, and gave voice to another's words.

In any case, these unusual evening hours passed easily, and I often fell asleep right there on the sofa, dragging myself to bed only much later, usually at some point in the middle of the night. Then, after what always seemed mere minutes of sleep, I was jarred awake by the beeping of the alarm clock on my cellphone, which was set to a bizarre marimba-like arrangement of "O Tannenbaum." In these first few moments of consciousness, in the sudden glare of morning light, my mind raced around itself, remembering fragments of dreams or pieces of the book I had been reading before I fell asleep. It was to break the monotony of those evenings that, two or three days each week after work, and on at least one of the weekend days, I went out walking.

At first, I encountered the streets as an incessant loudness, a shock after the day's focus and relative tranquillity, as though someone had shattered the calm of a silent private chapel with the blare of a TV set. I wove my way through crowds of shoppers and workers, through road constructions and the horns of taxicabs. Walking through busy parts of town meant I laid eyes on more people, hundreds more, thousands even, than I was accustomed to seeing in the course of a day, but the impress of these countless faces did nothing to assuage my feelings of isolation; if anything, it intensified them. I became more tired, too, after the walks began, an exhaustion unlike any I had known since the first months of internship, three years earlier. One night, I simply went on and on, walking all the way down to Houston Street, a distance of some seven miles, and found myself in a state of disorienting fatigue, laboring to remain on my feet. That night I took the subway home, and instead of falling asleep immediately, I lay in bed, too tired to release myself from wakefulness, and I rehearsed in the dark the numerous incidents and sights I had encountered while roaming, sorting each encounter like a child playing with wooden blocks, trying to figure out which belonged where, which responded to which. Each neighborhood of the city appeared to be made of a different substance, each seemed to have a different air pressure, a different psychic weight: the bright lights and shuttered shops, the housing projects and luxury hotels, the fire escapes and city parks. My futile task of sorting went on until the forms began to morph into each other and assume abstract shapes unrelated to the real city, and only then did my hectic mind finally show some pity and still itself, only then did dreamless sleep arrive.

The walks met a need: they were a release from the tightly regulated mental environment of work, and once I discovered them as therapy, they became the normal thing, and I forgot what life had been like before I started walking. Work was a regimen of perfection and competence, and it neither allowed improvisation nor tolerated mistakes. As interesting as my research project was—I was conducting a clinical study of affective disorders in the elderly—the level of detail it demanded was of an intricacy that exceeded anything else I had done thus far. The streets served as a welcome opposite to all that. Every decision—where to turn left, how long to remain lost in thought in front of an abandoned building, whether to watch the sun set over New Jersey, or to lope in the shadows on the East Side looking across to Queens—was inconsequential, and was for that reason a reminder of freedom. I covered the city blocks as though measuring them with my stride, and the subway stations served as recurring motives in my aimless progress. The sight of large masses of people hurrying down into underground chambers was perpetually strange to me, and I felt that all of the human race were rushing, pushed by a counterinstinctive death drive, into movable catacombs. Aboveground I was with thousands of others in their solitude, but in the subway, standing close to strangers, jostling them and being jostled by them for space and breathing room, all of us reenacting unacknowledged traumas, the solitude intensified.

———

ONE SUNDAY MORNING IN NOVEMBER, AFTER A TREK THROUGH the relatively quiet streets on the Upper West Side, I arrived at the large, sun-brightened plaza at Columbus Circle. The area had changed recently. It had become a more commercial and tourist destination thanks to the pair of buildings erected for the Time Warner corporation on the site. The buildings, constructed at great speed, had just opened, and were filled with shops selling tailored shirts, designer suits, jewelry, appliances for the gourmet cook, handmade leather accessories, and imported decorative items. On the upper floors were some of the costliest restaurants in the city, advertising truffles, caviar, Kobe beef, and pricey "tasting menus." Above the restaurants were apartments that included the most expensive residence in the city. Curiosity had brought me into the shops on the ground level once or twice before, but the cost of the items, and what I perceived as the generally snobbish atmosphere, had kept me from returning until that Sunday morning.

It was the day of the New York Marathon. I hadn't known. I was taken aback to see the round plaza in front of the glass towers filled with people, a massive, expectant throng setting itself into place close to the marathon's finish line. The crowd lined the street leading away from the plaza toward the east. Nearer the west there was a bandstand, on which two men with guitars were tuning up, calling and responding to the silvery notes on each other's amplified instruments. Banners, signs, posters, flags, and streamers of all kinds flapped in the wind, and mounted police on blindered horses regulated the crowd with cordons, whistles, and hand movements. The cops were in dark blue and wore sunshades. The crowd was brightly attired, and looking at all that green, red, yellow, and white synthetic material in the sun hurt the eyes. To escape the din, which seemed to be mounting, I decided to go into the shopping center. In addition to the Armani and Hugo Boss shops, there was a bookshop on the second floor. In there, I thought, I might catch some quiet and drink a cup of coffee before heading back home. But the entrance was full of the crowd overflow from the street, and cordons made it impossible to get into the towers.

I changed my mind, and decided instead to visit an old teacher of mine who lived in the vicinity, in an apartment less than ten minutes' walk away on Central Park South. Professor Saito was, at eighty-nine, the oldest person I knew. He had taken me under his wing when I was a junior at Maxwell. By that time he was already emeritus, though he continued to come to campus every day. He must have seen something in me that made him think I was someone on whom his rarefied subject (early English literature) would not be wasted. I was a disappointment in this regard, but he was kindhearted and, even after I failed to get a decent grade in his English Literature Before Shakespeare seminar, invited me to meet with him several times in his office. He had, in those days, recently installed an intrusively loud coffee machine, so we drank coffee, and talked: about interpretations of *Beowulf,* and then later on about the classics, the endless labor of scholarship, the various consolations of academia, and of his studies just before the Second World War. This last subject was so total in its distance from my experience that it was perhaps of most interest to me. The war had broken out just as he was finishing his D.Phil, and he was forced to leave England and return to his family in the Pacific Northwest. With them, shortly afterward, he was taken to internment in the Minidoka Camp in Idaho.

In these conversations, as I now recall them, he did almost all the talking. I learned the art of listening from him, and the ability to trace out a story from what was omitted. Rarely did Professor Saito tell me anything about his family, but he did tell me about his life as a scholar, and about how he had responded to important issues of his day. He'd done an annotated translation of *Piers Plowman* in the 1970s, which had turned out to be his most notable academic success. When he mentioned it, he did so with a curious mixture of pride and disappointment. He alluded to another big project (he didn't say on what) that had never been completed. He spoke, too, about departmental politics. I remember one afternoon that was taken up with his recollection of a onetime colleague whose name meant nothing to me when he said it and which I don't remember now. This woman had become famous for her activism during the civil rights era and had, for a moment, been such a campus celebrity that her literature classes overflowed. He described her as an intelligent, sensitive individual but someone with whom he could never agree. He admired and disliked her. It's a puzzle, I remember him saying, she was a good scholar, and she was on the right side of the struggles of the time, but I simply couldn't stand her in person. She was abrasive and egotistical, heaven rest her soul. You can't say a word against her around here, though. She's still considered a saint.

After we became friends, I made it a point to see Professor Saito two or three times each semester, and those meetings became cherished highlights of my last two years at Maxwell. I came to view him as a grandfatherly figure entirely unlike either of my own grandfathers (only one of whom I'd known). I felt I had more in common with him than with the people who happened to be related to me. After graduation, when I left, first for my research stint at Cold Spring Harbor, and then to medical school in Madison, we lost touch with each other. We exchanged one or two letters, but it was hard to have our conversations in that medium, since news and updates were not the real substance of our interaction. But after I returned to the city for internship, I saw him several times. The first, entirely by accident—though it happened on a day when I had been thinking about him—was just outside a grocery store not far from Central Park South, where he had gone out walking with the aid of an assistant. Later on, I showed up unannounced at his apartment, as he had invited me to do, and found that he still maintained the same open-door policy he had back when he had his office at the college. The coffee machine from that office now sat disused in a corner of the room. Professor Saito told me he had prostate cancer. It wasn't entirely debilitating, but he had stopped going to campus, and had

begun to hold court at home. His social interactions had been cur-
tailed to a degree that must have pained him; the number of guests
he welcomed had declined steadily, until most of his visitors were
either nurses or home health aides.

I greeted the doorman in the dark, low-ceilinged foyer and took
the elevator to the third floor. When I entered the apartment, Professor Saito called out. He was seated at the far end of the room, near
large windows, and he beckoned me over to the chair in front of him.
His eyes were weak, but his hearing had remained as sharp as when I
had first met him, back when he was a mere seventy-seven. Now,
bunched up in a soft, large chair, swaddled in blankets, he looked like
someone who had gone deep into the second infancy. But that wasn't
altogether the case: his mind, like his hearing, had remained acute
and, as he smiled, the wrinkles spread all over his face, creasing the
paper-thin skin on his forehead. In that room, into which always
seemed to flow a gentle and cool northern light, he was surrounded
by art from a lifetime of collecting. A half dozen Polynesian masks,
arranged just above his head, formed a large dark halo. In the corner
stood a life-size Papuan ancestor figure with individually carved
wooden teeth and a grass skirt that barely concealed an erect penis.
Referring to this figure, Professor Saito had once said: I adore imaginary monsters, but I am terrified of real ones.

From the windows that ran the length of that side of the room,
the shadowed street was visible. Beyond it was the park, which was
demarcated by an old stone wall. I heard a roar from the street just
as I was sitting down; I quickly got up again and saw a man running
alone through the alley that had been created by the crowd. He wore
a golden shirt, with black gloves that somehow reached up to his el-
bows, like a lady's at a formal dinner, and he had begun to sprint with
renewed energy, buoyed by the cheers. He raced, his energies revived, toward the bandstand, the fervent crowd, the finish line, and
the sun.

Come, sit, sit. Professor Saito coughed as he motioned toward the chair. Tell me how you are doing; you see, I've been sick; it was bad last week, but it's much better now. At my age, one falls sick a lot. Tell me, how are you, how are you? The noise outside rose again, and ebbed. I saw the runners-up dash through, two black men. Kenyans, I guessed. It's like this every year, for almost fifteen years now, Professor Saito said. If I have to go out on the day of the marathon, I use the building's rear entrance. But I don't go out much anymore, not with that attached to me, pinned to me like a tail on a dog. As I settled into the chair, he pointed to the transparent bag hanging on a little metal pole. The bag was half full of urine, and a plastic tube led to it from somewhere under the nest of blankets. Someone brought me persimmons yesterday, lovely, firm persimmons. Would you like some? Really, you should try them. Mary! The nurse-aide, a tall, strongly built, middle-aged woman from St. Lucia whom I had met on previous visits, appeared from the corridor. Mary, would you please bring our guest some persimmons? After she disappeared into the kitchen, he said, I find chewing a bit difficult these days, Julius, so something as rich and available as a persimmon is perfect for me. But enough about this, how are you? How is work?

My presence energized him. I told him a little about my walks, and wanted to tell him more but didn't have quite the right purchase on what it was I was trying to say about the solitary territory my mind had been crisscrossing. So I told him about one of my recent cases. I had had to consult with a family, conservative Christians, Pentecostals, who had been referred by one of the pediatricians at the hospital. Their thirteen-year-old son, their only child, was about to undergo a leukemia treatment that posed a serious later risk of infertility. The pediatrician's advice to them was that they have some of the boy's semen frozen and stored, so that when he became a man and got married, he could artificially inseminate his wife and have children of his own. The parents were open to the idea of sperm storage, and had nothing against artificial insemination, but were resolutely opposed, for religious reasons, to the idea of letting their son masturbate. There was no straightforward surgical solution to the conundrum. The family was in crisis over it. They consulted with me, and after a few sessions, and after much prayer on their part, they decided to risk not having grandchildren. They simply could not let their boy commit what they called the sin of onanism.

Professor Saito shook his head, and I could see that he had enjoyed the story, that its strange and unhappy contours had amused him (and troubled him) in the same way they had me. People choose, he said, people choose, and they choose on behalf of others. And what about outside your work, what are you reading? Mostly medical journals, I said, and then many other interesting things that I begin and am somehow unable to finish. No sooner do I buy a new book than it reproaches me for leaving it unread. I don't read much either, he said, with the state my eyes are in; but I have enough tucked away up here. He motioned to his head. In fact, I'm full. We laughed, and just then Mary brought in the persimmons, in a porcelain saucer. I ate half of one; it was a little oversweet. I ate the other half, and thanked him.

During the war, he said, I committed many poems to memory. I suppose that expectation is gone from the schools now. I saw the change during the time I was at Maxwell, how the later generations that came in had little of this preparation. For them, memorization was a pleasant diversion that came with a specific course; for their forebears of thirty or forty years before, there was a strong connection to the life of poems that came with having memorized several. College freshmen had a corpus of works with which they already had a relationship, even before they stepped into a college-level English literature class. For me, in the forties, memorization was a helpful skill, and I called on it because I couldn't be sure I would see my books again, and anyway, there wasn't much to do at the camp. We were all confused about what was happening; we were American, had always thought ourselves so, and not Japanese. There was all this time of confused waiting, harder for the parents, I think, than for the children, and in that waiting time, I stuffed bits of the *Prelude,* and Shakespeare's sonnets, and large tracts of Yeats into my head. Now I don't remember the exact words of any of them anymore, it's been too long, but I need only the environment created by the poems. Just one or two lines, like a little hook—he demonstrated with his hand— just one or two, and that's enough to snag everything, what the poem says, what it means. Everything follows the hook. *In summer season when soft was the sun, I wore a shroud as I a shepherd were.* Do you recognize it? I don't suppose anyone memorizes anything anymore. It was part of our discipline, just as a good violinist has to have his Bach partitas or Beethoven sonatas by heart. My tutor at Peterhouse was Chadwick, an Aberdonian. He was a great scholar; he'd been taught by Skeat himself. Haven't I ever told you about Chadwick? A grouch through and through, but it was he who first taught me the value of memory, and how to think of it as mental music, a setting to iambs and trochees.

His reverie took him out of the everyday, away from the blankets and the bag of urine. It was the late thirties again, and he was back in Cambridge, breathing the damp air of the fens, enjoying the tranquillity of his youthful scholarship. At times, it seemed as though he was talking more to himself, but he suddenly asked a direct question and, interrupted from my own little train of thought, I scrambled for an answer. We reprised the old relationship, student and teacher, and he continued steadily, regardless of whether my responses were accurate or not, whether I took Chaucer for Langland or Langland for Chaucer. An hour went by quickly, and he asked if we could pause there for the day. I promised to return soon.

When I came out to Central Park South, the wind had become colder, the air brighter, and the cheer from the crowd steady and loud. A great stream of finishers came coasting down the homestretch. As Fifty-ninth Street was cordoned off, I walked down to Fifty-seventh and came back up again to join Broadway. The subway was too congested at Columbus Circle, and so I walked toward Lincoln Center, to catch the train at its next uptown stop. At Sixty-second Street, I fell in with a lithe man with graying sideburns who carried a plastic bag with a tag on it and was visibly exhausted, limping on slightly bowed legs. He wore shorts and black tights, and a blue, long-sleeved fleece jacket. From his features, I guessed he was Mexican or Central American. We walked in silence for a while, not intentionally walking together but finding ourselves moving at the same pace and in the same direction. Eventually, I asked him whether he had just finished the race and, when he nodded and smiled, congratulated him. But, I began to think, after twenty-six miles and 385 yards, he had simply collected his bag, and was walking home. There were no friends or family present to celebrate his achievement. I pitied him, then. Speaking again, deflecting these private thoughts, I asked if it had been a good race. Yes, he said, a good race, the conditions were good for running, not too hot. He had a pleasant but worn face, and must have been about forty-five or fifty. We walked a little farther, for two or three blocks, punctuating our silences with small talk about the weather and the crowds.

At the street crossing in front of the opera houses, I bid him goodbye and began myself to walk faster. I imagined his limping form receding as I pressed ahead, his wiry frame bearing a victory apparent to none but himself. I had bad lungs as a child and have never been a runner, but I instinctively understand that burst of energy a marathoner can usually find at the twenty-fifth mile, so close to the finish. More mysterious is what keeps such people going through the nineteenth, the twentieth, the twenty-first mile. By that point the buildup of ketones would have made the legs rigid, and acidosis would be threatening to quell the will and shut the body down. The first man who ever ran a marathon had died instantly, and small wonder: it is an act of extreme human endurance, still remarkable no matter how many people now do it. And so, turning around to look at my erstwhile companion, and thinking of Phidippides' collapse, I saw the situation more clearly. It was I, no less solitary than he but having made the lesser use of the morning, who was to be pitied.

I soon arrived at the big Tower Records store on the corner of Sixty-sixth Street, and was surprised to see the signs outside which announced that the store as well as the company behind it were going out of business. I had been in the store many times before, had probably spent hundreds of dollars on music there, and it seemed right, if only for old times' sake, to revisit it, before the doors closed for good. I went in, intrigued also by the promise that prices had been slashed on all items, although I didn't particularly feel like buying anything. The escalator took me to the second floor, where the classical section, busier than usual, seemed to have been commandeered in its entirety by old and middle-aged men in drab coats. The men were going through the CD bins with something of the patience of grazing animals, and some of them had red shopping baskets into which they dropped their selections, while others clutched the shiny plastic packages to their chests. The store's stereo was playing Purcell, a rousing anthem I recognized right away as one of the birthday odes for Queen Mary. I usually disliked whatever was being played on a music store's speakers. It spoiled the pleasure of thinking about other music. Record shops, I felt, should be silent spaces; there, more than anywhere else, the mind needed to be clear. In this case, though, because I recognized the piece, and because it was something I loved, I didn't mind.

The next disc they played, though utterly unlike the first, was another I immediately recognized: the opening movement of Mahler's late symphony *Das Lied von der Erde*. I returned to my browsing, moving from bin to bin, from reissues of Shostakovich symphonies played by long-forgotten Soviet regional orchestras to Chopin recitals by fresh-faced Van Cliburn Competition runners-up, feeling that the price reductions were insufficiently sharp, losing any real interest in shopping, and finally beginning to acclimatize to the music playing overhead and to enter the strange hues of its world. It happened subliminally, but before long, I was rapt and might have, for all the world, been swaddled in a private darkness. In this trance, I continued to move from one row of compact discs to another, thumbing through plastic cases, magazines, and printed scores, and listening as one movement of the Viennese chinoiserie succeeded another. On hearing Christa Ludwig's voice, in the second movement, a song about the loneliness of autumn, I recognized the recording as the famous one conducted by Otto Klemperer in 1964. With that awareness came another: that all I had to do was bide my time, and wait for the emotional core of the work, which Mahler had put in the final movement of the symphony. I sat on one of the hard benches near the listening stations, and sank into reverie, and followed Mahler through drunkenness, longing, bombast, youth (with its fading), and beauty (with its fading). Then came the final movement, *"Der Abschied,"* the Farewell, and Mahler, where he would ordinarily indicate the tempo, had marked it *schwer,* difficult.

The birdsong and beauty, the complaints and high-jinks of the preceding movements, had all been supplanted by a different mood, a stronger, surer mood. It was as though the lights had, without warning, come blazing into my eyes. It simply wasn't possible to enter the music fully, not in that public place. I placed the small pile of discs in my hand onto the nearest table and left. I made it into the uptown train just as the doors were closing. By this time, the crowds from the marathon were beginning to thin out. I sat down and leaned back. The five-note figure from *"Der Abschied"* continued on from where I escaped, playing through with such presence that it was as though I were in the store listening to it. I sensed the woodsiness of the clarinets, the resin of the violins and violas, the vibrations of the timpani, and the intelligence that held them all together and drew them endlessly along the musical line. My memory was overwhelmed. The song followed me home.

Mahler's music fell over my activities for the entirety of the following day. There was some new intensity in even the most ordinary things all around the hospital: the gleam on the glass doors at the entrance of the Milstein Building, the examination tables and gurneys down on the ground floor, the stacks of patients' files in the psychiatry department, the light from the windows in the cafeteria, the sunken heads of uptown buildings from that height, as if the precision of the orchestral texture had been transferred to the world of visible things, and every detail had somehow become significant. One of my patients had sat facing me, with his legs crossed, and his raised right foot, which twitched in its polished black shoe, also somehow seemed a part of that intricate musical world.

The sun was setting as I left Columbia Presbyterian, giving the sky the look of tin. I took the subway down to 125th Street and, on my walk up to my neighborhood, feeling much less frayed than I usually did on Monday nights, I took a detour and walked for a while in Harlem. I saw the brisk trade of sidewalk salesmen: the Senegalese cloth merchants, the young men selling bootleg DVDs, the Nation of Islam stalls. There were self-published books, dashikis, posters on black liberation, bundles of incense, vials of perfume and essential oils, djembe drums, and little tourist tchotchkes from Africa. One table displayed enlarged photographs of early-twentieth-century lynchings of African-Americans. Around the corner of St. Nicholas Avenue, the drivers of the black livery cabs gathered, smoking cigarettes and talking, awaiting the fares they could pick up off the clock. Young men in hooded sweatshirts, the denizens of an informal economy, passed messages and small nylon-wrapped packages to each other, enacting a choreography opaque to all but themselves. An old man with an ashen face and bulbous yellow eyes, passing by, raised his head to greet me, and I (thinking for a moment that he was someone I surely knew, or once knew, or had seen before, and quickly abandoning each idea in turn; and then fearing that the speed of these mental disassociations might knock me off my stride) returned his silent greeting. I turned around to see his black cowl melt into an unlit doorway. In the Harlem night, there were no whites.

At the grocery store, I bought bread, eggs, and beer, and next door, at the Jamaican place, I bought goat curry, yellow plantains, and rice and peas to take home. On the other side of the grocery store was a Blockbuster; though I had never rented anything from there, I was startled to see a sign announcing it, too, was going out of business. If Blockbuster couldn't make it in an area full of students and families, it meant that the business model had been fatally damaged, that the desperate efforts they had made recently, and which I now recalled, of lowering rental prices, launching an advertising blitz, and abolishing late fines, had all come too late. I thought of Tower Records—a connection I couldn't help making, given that both companies had for a long time dominated their respective industries. It wasn't that I felt sorry for these faceless national corporations; far from it. They had made their profits and their names by destroying smaller, earlier local businesses. But I was touched not only at the passage of these fixtures in my mental landscape, but also at the swiftness and dispassion with which the market swallowed even the most resilient enterprises. Businesses that had seemed unshakable a few years previously had disappeared in the span, seemingly, of a few weeks. Whatever role they played passed on to other hands, hands that would feel briefly invincible and would, in their turn, be defeated by unforeseen changes. These survivors would also come to be forgotten.

As I approached the apartment building with my bags, I saw someone I knew: the man who lived in the apartment right next to mine. He was coming into the building at the same time, and he held the door open for me. I did not know him well, in fact hardly knew him at all, and I had to think for a moment before I remembered his name. He was in his early fifties, and had moved in the previous year. The name came to me: Seth.

I had spoken briefly with Seth and his wife, Carla, when they first moved in, but hardly at all since. He was a retired social worker, following a lifelong dream to return to school for a second degree, in

Romance languages. I saw him only about once a month, just outside the building or near the mailboxes. Carla, whom I had met only twice after they moved in, was also retired; she had been a school principal in Brooklyn, and they still kept a home there. Once, when my girlfriend, Nadège, and I had a day off together, Seth had knocked on my door to ask if I was playing guitar. When I said that I didn't play, he explained that he was often home in the afternoons, and that the noise from my speakers (it must be your speakers, he said, though it sounds like live music) sometimes disturbed him. But he added, with genuine warmth in his voice, that they were always away on weekends, and that we were free to be loud from Friday afternoons onward if we so wished. I felt bad about it, and apologized. After that, I had made a conscious effort not to trouble them, and the issue hadn't come up again.

Seth held the door open. He, too, had been shopping, and carried plastic bags. Getting cold, he said. His nose and earlobes were pink, and his eyes watered. Yes, yes, it is, in fact I thought about taking a cab from 125th. He nodded, and we stood silently for a while. When the elevator arrived, we got in. We got off on the seventh floor, and as we walked down the hallway, our nylon bags rustling, I asked him if they still got away on the weekends. Oh yes, every weekend, but it's just me now, Julius. Carla died in June, he said. She had a heart attack.

I was stunned into momentary confusion, as if I had just been told something that wasn't possible. I'm so sorry, I said. He tilted his head, and we kept walking down the hallway. I asked if he had been able to take some time off from school. No, he said, I've just continued right through. I placed my hand on his shoulder, for a moment, and said again how sorry I was, and he thanked me. He seemed vaguely embarrassed, having to deal with my belated shock at what, for him, was far more personal but also much older news. Our keys clinked, and he entered apartment twenty-one, and I twenty-two. I closed the door behind me, and heard his close, too. I didn't switch on the light. A woman had died in the room next to mine, she had died on the other side of the wall I was leaning against, and I had known nothing of it. I had known nothing in the weeks when her husband mourned, nothing when I had nodded to him in greeting with headphones in my ears, or when I had folded clothes in the laundry room while he used the washer. I hadn't known him well enough to routinely ask how Carla was, and I had not noticed not seeing her around. That was the worst of it. I had noticed neither her absence nor the change—there must have been a change—in his spirit. It was not possible, even then, to go knock on his door and embrace him, or to speak with him at length. It would have been false intimacy.

I finally switched the light on and moved into my apartment. I imagined Seth tussling with his French and Spanish homework, conjugating verbs, laboring on translations, memorizing vocabulary lists, doing composition exercises. As I put away my groceries, I tried to remember when, exactly, it was that he had knocked on my door to ask if I played guitar. Eventually I satisfied myself that it was before, and not after, his wife's death. I felt a certain sense of relief at this, which was taken over almost immediately by shame. But even that feeling subsided; much too quickly, now that I think of it.

# TWO

I was on the phone with Nadège, a few nights later, when I heard noises from far off, noises that were hardly audible to begin with, but that within a few seconds drew closer and became louder. A single voice, a woman's voice, shouted, and a crowd responded. After this had happened a few times, I could identify the crowd as mostly or entirely female. Several whistles pierced the air, but it was not a festive sound; that much I could tell even before I opened my window and looked out. It was something more serious. There were drums, and as the crowd approached, the drums took on an increasingly martial tone (my mind went to a hunting party flushing rabbits out of their holes). It was late, well past ten. Several of my neighbors across the street had leaned out of their windows; we all craned our necks toward Amsterdam Avenue. The voice leading the crowd became even louder, but the words did not resolve into meaning, and most of the crowd, marching toward us, remained obscured by darkness. Then, as the crowd, all of them young women, passed under the streetlamps, their chanting became clearer. *We have the power, we have the might,* the solitary voice called. The answer came: *The streets are ours, take back the night.*

The crowd, several dozen strong but tightly packed, passed under my window. From several floors above, I watched them, as their faces came in and out of the spotlights of the streetlamps. *Women's bodies, women's lives, we will not be terrorized.* I shut the window. It was only a little bit cooler outside than it was in the apartment. Earlier that evening, I had gone walking in Riverside Park, from 116th Street down to the Nineties and back. It wasn't cold yet, and the entire time I was out in the park—as I watched the dogs and their owners, all of whom seemed to have converged on the same paths as I had, an endless stream of pit bulls, Jack Russells, Alsatians, Weimaraners, mutts—I wondered why it was still so warm in the middle of November.

Coming up the hill to my place, just as I crossed the corner of 121st, I saw my friend. He lived only a few blocks away, and had been out shopping for groceries. I hailed him, and we spoke briefly. He was a young professor in the Earth Sciences Department, four years into the uncertain seven-year journey to tenure. His interests were broader than his professional specialty suggested, and this was part of the basis for our friendship: he had strong opinions about books and films, opinions that often went against mine, and he had lived for two years in Paris, where he'd acquired a taste for fashionable philosophers like Badiou and Serres. In addition, he was an avid chess player, and an affectionate father to a nine-year-old girl who mostly lived with her mother on Staten Island. We both regretted that the demands of work kept us from spending as much time together as we would have liked.

My friend was especially passionate about jazz. Most of the names and styles that he so delighted in meant little to me (there are apparently any number of great jazz musicians from the sixties and seventies with the last name Jones). But I could sense, even from my ignorant distance, the sophistication of his ear. He often said that he would sit down at a piano someday and show me how jazz worked, and that when I finally understood blue notes and swung notes, the heavens would part and my life would be transformed. I more than half-believed him, and would even occasionally worry about why I seemed not to have a strong emotional connection with this most American of musical styles. Too often, it merely sounded sweet to me, cloying even, and I especially disliked it as background music. As my friend and I talked, a homeless man sang just across the street from us, and we caught his voice in the snatches as the wind came over in gusts.

These pleasant thoughts were interrupted by a presentiment of the conversation I would have that evening with Nadège. And how odd it was, hours later, to hear her strained voice, in counterpoint with the protesters down below. She had moved to San Francisco a few weeks before, and we had said we would make an effort to work things out at the distance, but we'd said the words without meaning them.

I tried to imagine her in that crowd, but no image came to mind, nor could I picture her face as it would be if she'd been in the room with me. The voices of the protesters soon faded, as the marchers drifted off with their flags and whistles toward Morningside Park. The heart-altering thump of their martial drum went on, and then that faded too, and I could hear only her diminished voice at the other end of the line. It was painful, this breaking apart, but it surprised neither of us.

THE FOLLOWING EVENING, ON THE 1 TRAIN, I SAW A CRIPPLE dragging his broken leg behind him as he moved from car to car. He adjusted his voice to a reedier tone to make his body seem more frail. I disliked his act and refused to give him money. A few minutes later, when I got on the platform, I saw a blind man. His long white stick ended in a tennis ball, and he swept it in a limited arc in front of him and to his side, and when he came close to falling (so it seemed to me) off the edge of the platform, I went up to him and asked if I could help. Oh no, he said, oh no, I'm just waiting for my train, thank you. I left him and walked the length of the platform, toward the exit. I was confused to see, just at that moment, another blind man, who also carried a long white stick with a tennis ball at its end, and who, ahead of me, climbed the stairs out into the light.

I got the idea that some of the things I was seeing around me were under the aegis of Obatala, the demiurge charged by Olodumare with the formation of humans from clay. Obatala did well at the task until he started drinking. As he drank more and more, he became inebriated, and began to fashion damaged human beings. The Yoruba believe that in this drunken state he made dwarfs, cripples, people missing limbs, and those burdened with debilitating illness. Olodumare had to reclaim the role he had delegated and finish the creation of humankind himself and, as a result, people who suffer from physical infirmities identify themselves as worshippers of Obatala. This is an interesting relationship with a god, one not of affection or praise but of antagonism. They worship Obatala in accusation; it is he who has made them as they are. They wear white, which is his color, and the color of the palm wine he got drunk on.

It had been months since I had last been to a movie. At around ten, I entered a bookshop, one of the famous chains, to kill some time before the film began, and as I went in I remembered a book I had wanted to look at for a long time: a book of historical biography by one of my patients. I found it quickly—*The Monster of New Amsterdam*—and settled in among the quieter stacks to read it. V., an assistant professor at New York University and a member of the Delaware tribe, had based the book on her doctoral dissertation at Columbia. It was the first comprehensive study of Cornelis Van Tienhoven. Van Tienhoven had been notorious as a seventeenth-century *schout* of New Amsterdam, officially empowered to enforce the law among the Dutch colonists of Manhattan Island. He had arrived in 1633, as a secretary for the Dutch East India Company, but as he climbed up the social ladder, he became known for his many brutal acts, notable among them a raid he led to murder Canarsie Indians on Long Island, after which he had brought back the victims' heads on pikes. In another raid, Van Tienhoven had been at the head of a party of men that murdered over a hundred innocent members of the Hackensack tribe. V.'s book made for grim reading. It was full of violent events, and in the endnotes were reprinted the relevant seventeenth-century records. These were written in calm and pious language that presented mass murder as little more than the regrettable side effect of colonizing the land. In its patient recounting of these crimes, *The Monster of New Amsterdam* was like those biographies of Pol Pot, Hitler, or Stalin that almost always did well on the bestseller lists. A sticker on the cover of the copy I was holding indicated that it had been nominated for the National Book Critics Circle Award. The blurbs on the flyleaf, written by leading American historians, were fulsome, praising the book for shedding light on a forgotten chapter in colonial history. From time to time during the previous couple of years, reading the newspaper, I had seen some aspect of this critical acclaim, and for this reason, I had heard V.'s name and had some sense of her professional success before she ever became my patient.

When I began treating her for depression at the beginning of last year, I was surprised by her shy manner and slight frame. She was a little older than I, but appeared much younger, and she was at work on her next project, which, as she explained it, was a broader study of the encounters between the northeastern native groups—the Delaware and Iroquois in particular—and European settlers in the seventeenth century. V.'s depression was partly due to the emotional toll of these studies, which she once described as looking out across a river on a day of heavy rain, so that she couldn't be sure whether the activity on the opposite bank had anything to do with her, or

whether, in fact, there was any activity there at all. Her biography of
Van Tienhoven, pitched though it was to a general readership, came
with all the scholarly apparatus and with much of the emotional distance typical of an academic study. But it was clear, too, from talking
to her that the horrors Native Americans had had to endure at the
hands of the white settlers, the horrors, in her view, that they continued to suffer, affected her on a profound personal level.

I can't pretend it isn't about my life, she said to me once, it is my
life. It's a difficult thing to live in a country that has erased your past.
She fell silent, and the sensation created by her words—I remember
experiencing it as a subtle shift in the air pressure of the room—
deepened in the silence, so that all we could hear was the going and
coming outside my office door. She had closed her eyes for a moment, as though she had fallen asleep. But then she continued, her
shut eyelids now trembling: There are almost no Native Americans
in New York City, and very few in all of the Northeast. It isn't right
that people are not terrified by this because this is a terrifying thing
that happened to a vast population. And it's not in the past, it is still
with us today; at least, it's still with me. She stopped, and then she
opened her eyes, and as I recalled all this sitting on the carpet between those tall shelves at the bookshop, I could picture V.'s curi-
ously serene face that afternoon, on which the only physical signs of
distress were her tear-filled eyes. I got up and went to the counter,
and paid for the book. I knew I would not have time to read all of it,
but I wanted to think more about what she had written, and I also
hoped that the book might, in those moments when it left the strict
historical record and betrayed some subjective analysis, give me further insight into her psychological state.

After paying, I walked the four blocks to the movie theater on
what, I recall, was a warm night. I had my recurrent worry about how
warm it had been all season long. Although I did not enjoy the cold
seasons at their most intense, I had come to agree that there was a
rightness about them, that there was a natural order in such things.

The absence of this order, the absence of cold when it ought to be cold, was something I now sensed as a sudden discomfort. The idea that the weather was changing noticeably bothered me, even if there was as yet no evidence that this warm fall in particular wasn't due to a perfectly normal variation in patterns that stretched across centuries. There had been a natural little ice age in the Low Countries in the sixteenth century, and so, why not a little warm age in our own time, independent of human causes? But I was no longer the global-warming skeptic I had been some years before, even if I still couldn't tolerate the tendency some had of jumping to conclusions based on anecdotal evidence: global warming was a fact, but that did not mean it was the explanation for why a given day was warm. It was careless thinking to draw the link too easily, an invasion of fashionable politics into what should be the ironclad precincts of science.

Still, the way my thoughts returned to the fact that it was the middle of November and I hadn't yet had occasion to wear my coat made me wonder if, already, I was one of those people, the overinterpreters. This was part of my suspicion that there was a mood in the society that pushed people more toward snap judgments and unexamined opinions, an antiscientific mood; to the old problem of mass innumeracy, it seemed to me, was being added a more general inability to assess evidence. This made brisk business for those whose specialty was in the promising of immediate solutions: politicians, or priests of the various religions. It worked particularly well for those who wished to rally people around a cause. The cause itself, whatever it was, hardly mattered. Partisanship was all.

The crowd at the ticket counter of the movie theater was atypical, but this is what I had expected, given the late hour of the film, the fact that it was set in Africa, and the absence of marquee Hollywood names. The ticket buyers were young, many of them black, and dressed in hip clothes. There were some Asians, too, Latinos, immigrant New Yorkers, New Yorkers of indeterminate ethnic background. The last film I'd seen at the same theater, months earlier, had had an audience consisting almost entirely of white-haired white people; many fewer of those were now in attendance. In the great cave of the theater, I sat alone. No, not alone, exactly: in the company of a hundred others, but all strangers to me. The lights went down, and as I slouched in a plush seat, as the film began, I noticed someone else in my row, at its far end: an old man, asleep, his head thrown back and his mouth open, so that he looked more dead than sleeping. He did not stir even when the film began.

The jaunty credit sequence featured music from the right time period, but not from the right part of Africa: what had Mali to do with Kenya? But I had come prepared to like some things about the film, and I expected that some other things would annoy me. Another film I had watched the previous year, about the crimes of large pharmaceutical companies in East Africa, had left me feeling frustrated, not because of its plot, which was plausible, but because of the film's fidelity to the convention of the good white man in Africa. Africa was always waiting, a substrate for the white man's will, a backdrop for his activities. And so, sitting to experience this film, *The Last King of Scotland*, I was prepared to be angry again. I was primed to see a white man, a nobody in his own country, who thought, as usual, that the salvation of Africa was up to him. The king the title referred to was Idi Amin Dada, dictator of Uganda in the 1970s. Decorating himself with spurious titles was only the least grim of his many hobbies.

I knew Idi Amin well, so to speak, because he'd been an indelible part of my childhood mythology. I remembered the many hours I had spent at my cousins' watching a film called *The Rise and Fall of Idi Amin*. In that film, no detail was spared to present the callousness, insanity, and sheer excitement of the man. I was seven or eight at the time, and those images of people being shot and stuffed into car trunks, or decapitated and stored in freezers, stayed with me. The images were genuinely shocking because, unlike the blood-spattered American war movies we also enjoyed during those long school vacations, the victims in *Rise and Fall* looked like our fathers and uncles, with their safari suits, afros, and shiny foreheads. The cities in which this mayhem played out looked like our own city, and the bullet-riddled cars were the same models as the ones we saw around us. But we enjoyed the shock of it, its powerful and stylized realism and each time we had nothing to do, we watched the film again.

*The Last King of Scotland* mostly avoided such gory imagery. Its story was concentrated, instead, on the relationship between Idi Amin and the briefly innocent Scottish doctor, Nicholas Garrigan, whom he pressed into service as his personal physician. This was the story of a man in whom the classic traits of dictatorship had taken the most extreme form. With his extroverted madness—parts anger, fear, insecurity, quicksilver charm—Idi Amin murdered some 300,000 Ugandans during his rule, expelled the large community of Ugandan-Indians, destroyed the country's economy, and earned himself a reputation as one of the most grotesque stains on Africa's recent history.

While watching the film, I recalled an uncomfortable meeting I'd had one evening, in an opulent house in a suburb of Madison a few years before. I was a medical student at the time, and our host, an Indian surgeon, had invited me and a number of my classmates to his house. After we had eaten, Dr. Gupta ushered us into one of his three lavish living rooms, and went round pouring champagne into our glasses. He and his family, he told us, had been expelled from their homes and lands by Idi Amin. I am successful now, he said, America has made a life possible for me and for my wife and children. My daughter is doing graduate studies in engineering at MIT, and our youngest is at Yale. But, if I may speak frankly, I'm still angry. We lost so much, we were robbed at knifepoint, and when I think about Africans—and I know that we are not supposed to say such things in America—when I think about Africans, I want to spit.

The bitterness was startling. It was an anger that, I couldn't help feeling, was partly directed at me, the only other African in the room. The detail of my background, that I was Nigerian, made no difference, for Dr. Gupta had spoken of Africans, had sidestepped the specific and spoken in the general. But now, as I watched the film, I saw that Idi Amin himself hosted wonderful parties, told genuinely funny jokes, and spoke eloquently about the need for African self-determination. These nuances in his personality, as depicted here, would no doubt have brought a bad taste to the mouth of my host in Madison.

I wished to believe that things were not as bad as they seemed. This was the part of me that wanted to be entertained, that preferred not to confront the horror. But that satisfaction did not come: things ended badly, as they usually do. I wondered, as Coetzee did in *Elizabeth Costello,* what the use was of going into these recesses of the human heart. Why show torture? Was it not enough to be told, in imprecise detail, that bad things happened? We wish to be spared, whether the story was about Idi Amin or Cornelis Van Tienhoven. It is a common wish, and a foolish one: no one is spared. Idi Amin's young sons were named MacKenzie and Campbell—MacKenzie was epileptic—and these two Scots-Ugandans were caught in Idi Amin's nightmare, and Obatala's carelessness.

I came out of the theater at midnight, into warm air. I had V.'s book with me, but after what I had just seen, I knew I would have to put it away for a while. At the almost empty subway station, there was a family of out-of-towners waiting for the train. A girl of thirteen sat on the bench next to me. Her ten-year-old brother came to join her. They were out of earshot of their parents who, save one or two unconcerned glances in our direction, were absorbed in their own conversation. Hey mister, she said, turning to me, wassup? She made signs with her fingers and, with her brother, started laughing. The little boy wore an imitation Chinese peasant's hat. They had been mimicking slanted eyes and exaggerated bows before they came to where I was. They now both turned to me. Are you a gangster, mister? Are you a gangster? They both flashed gang signs, or their idea of gang signs. I looked at them. It was midnight, and I didn't feel like giving public lectures. He's black, said the girl, but he's not dressed like a gangster. I bet he's a gangster, her brother said, I bet he is. Hey mister, are you a gangster? They continued flicking their fingers at me for several minutes. Twenty yards away, their parents talked with each other, oblivious.

I thought about walking home, an hour's walk, but the uptown train arrived. I had a moment of illumination just then, a feeling that my oma (as I am accustomed to calling my maternal grandmother) should see me again, or that I should make the effort to see her, if she was still in this world, if she was in a nursing home somewhere in Brussels. Perhaps seeing me would be some sort of late blessing for her. How I might go about actually locating her, I really had no idea, but the notion seemed suddenly real to me, as did its promise of reunion, as I walked down the platform and entered a distant car.

# THREE

On an afternoon of heavy rain when ginkgo leaves were piled ankle-deep across the sidewalk looking like thousands of little yellow creatures freshly fallen from the sky, I went out walking. I had been spending all the time that wasn't with patients working with a professor, Dr. Martindale, on a paper for publication. The findings of our study were genuinely exciting: we had been able to show a strong correlation between strokes in the elderly and the onset of depression. But our writing of the paper had been complicated by our late realization that another laboratory had recently come to similar conclusions, using a different research protocol. Dr. Martindale was approaching retirement, and the bulk of the rewriting fell to me, as did any new assays that had to be run in the lab. The latter I did a little carelessly, breaking gels twice and having to begin again. I was at it for three arduous weeks. Then I did most of the rewrite over three intense days, and we sent off the paper, and awaited correspondence from the journals. I went out, umbrella in hand, with the idea that I might walk through Central Park, and on to the area just south of it, and as I entered the park, thoughts of my grandmother returned.

My mother and I had become estranged from each other when I was seventeen, just before I left for America. I tend to connect this to my mother's estrangement from her own mother. They might have fallen out for reasons as inchoate as the ones that separated my mother and me. My mother had not returned to Germany since she left in the 1970s. Nevertheless, in recent years I have thought of my oma more often. I usually dwell on the one time she came to visit us in Nigeria from Belgium, to which she had moved sometime after my grandfather's death. The picture my mother had painted of her as a difficult and small-minded person was inaccurate; it was a picture that had nothing to do with my oma, and everything to do with my mother's resentment of her. I was eleven when she came to visit, and I could see that both my parents were barely tolerating this strange old lady (my father sided with my mother). I also knew that part of what I was had come from her, and on this basis a sort of solidarity was established. Once during that visit, toward the end, as I recall, the whole family toured the interior of Yorubaland. Our journey took us no farther than four hours' drive from Lagos. We visited the Deji's Palace in Akure and the Ooni's in Ife, both of them large traditional royal complexes built of mud brick and decorated with massive carved wooden pillars showing aspects of Yoruba cosmology: the world of the living, the world of the dead, the world of the unborn. My mother, deeply interested in the art, explained the iconography to her mother and to me. My father wandered around a little bored.

We drove for hours on muddy, welted roads, through undulating landscape that was sere in parts and thickly forested in others. We stopped at the Ikogosi Warm Springs, and went to the sacred monoliths of Olumo Rock in Abeokuta, in and under which Egba people had taken refuge during the internecine wars of the nineteenth century. At Olumo Rock, Oma and I had stayed at the base while my parents went up with a guide. From where we stood, I could see my parents wending their way up the sheer slope, stopping at caves and outcroppings as the guide pointed out historic and religious features to them, then renewing their climb which, to us looking from below, appeared especially dangerous. That day, I treasured the silence I shared with Oma (her hand on my shoulder, kneading it); my parents were gone an hour, and in that hour we two communed almost wordlessly, simply waiting, sensitive to the wind in the trees nearby, watching the lizards scuttle over the smaller rock formations that pushed through the earth like prehistoric eggs, listening to the thrum of motorcycles on the narrow road some two hundred yards away. When my mother and father came back down, winded, flushed, pleased, they marveled about their experiences. About ours, Oma and I could say nothing, because what it was had been without words.

Afterward, after Oma's visit of a few weeks ended, my parents didn't say much about her. Communication once again ceased between her and my mother, and it was as though she hadn't ever come to Nigeria at all; the quiet, puzzled affection she had toward me faded into the past. As far as I could tell, she had returned to Belgium. And it was in Belgium that I imagined her now, though I could not say for sure if she was still alive. At the time of her visit to Nigeria, I had hoped a normal relationship between her and the rest of my family would begin. But it wasn't meant to be; my guess is that there was a big argument between Oma and my mother just before she left. As things turned out, the only person who could tell me her present whereabouts, who could tell me if she had any present whereabouts, was the one person I couldn't ask.

I ENTERED THE PARK AT SEVENTY-SECOND STREET, AND BEGAN to walk south, on Sheep Meadow. The wind picked up, and water poured down into the sodden ground in fine, incessant needles, ob-

scuring lindens, elms, and crab apples. The intensity of the rain
blurred my sight, a phenomenon I had noticed before only with
snowstorms, when a blizzard erased the most obvious signs of the
times, leaving one unable to guess which century it was. The torrent
had overlaid the park with a primeval feeling, as though a world-
ending flood were coming on, and Manhattan looked just then like
it must have in the 1920s or even, if one was far enough away from
the taller buildings, much further in the past.

The cluster of taxis at Fifth Avenue and Central Park South
broke the illusion. After I had walked another quarter hour, by then
thoroughly drenched, I stood under the eaves of a building on Fifty-
third Street. When I turned around, I saw that I was at the entryway
of the American Folk Art Museum. Never having visited before, I
went in.

The artifacts on display, most from the eighteenth and nineteenth centuries—weather vanes, ornaments, quilts, paintings—
evoked the agrarian life of the new American country as well as the
half-remembered traditions of the old European ones. It was the art
of a country that had an aristocracy but did not have the patronage
of courts: a simple, open-faced, and awkward art. At the landing of
the first flight of stairs, I saw an oil portrait of a young girl in a
starchy red dress holding a white cat. A dog peeked out from under
her chair. The details were saccharine, but they could not obscure
the force and beauty of the painting.

The artists featured at the museum were, in almost every case,
working outside the elite tradition. They lacked formal training, but
their work had soul. The sense of having wandered into the past was
complete once I reached the third floor of the museum. The gallery
had a row of slender white columns running through its middle, and
the floors were polished cherrywood. These two elements echoed
the colonial architecture of the New England and Middle Colonies.

That floor, as well as the one just below it, was given over to a special exhibition of the paintings of John Brewster. Brewster, the son

of a New England doctor of the same name, had modest facility, but the scale of the exhibition made it clear that he had been much in demand as an artist. The gallery was quiet and calm and, save for the guard who stood in a corner, I was the only person there. This heightened the feeling of quietness I got from almost all the portraits. The stillness of the people depicted was certainly part of it, as was the sober color palette of each panel, but there was something more, something harder to define: an air of hermeticism. Each of the portraits was a sealed-away world, visible from without, but impossible to enter. This was truest of Brewster's many portraits of children, all of them self-possessed in their infantile bodies, and often with whimsical elements in their outfits, but with the faces, without exception, serious, more serious even than those of the adults, a gravity all out of keeping with their tender ages. Each child stood in a doll-like pose, and was brought to life by an incisive gaze. The effect was unsettling. The key, as I found out, was that John Brewster was profoundly deaf, and the same was true of many of the children he portrayed. Some of them were pupils at the Connecticut Asylum for the Education and Instruction of Deaf and Dumb Persons, which had been founded in 1817 as the country's first school for the deaf. Brewster was enrolled for three years there as an adult student, and it was while he was there that what later became known as American Sign Language was developed.

As I contemplated the silent world before me, I thought of the many romantic ideas attached to blindness. Ideas of unusual sensitivity and genius were evoked by the names of Milton, Blind Lemon Jefferson, Borges, Ray Charles; to lose physical sight, it is thought, is to gain second sight. One door closes and another, greater one, opens. Homer's blindness, many believe, is a kind of spiritual channel, a shortcut to the gifts of memory and of prophecy. When I was a child in Lagos, there was a blind, wandering bard, a man who was held in the greatest awe for his spiritual gifts. When he sang his songs, he left each person with the feeling that, in hearing him, they had somehow touched the numinous, or been touched by it. Once, in a crowded market at Ojuelegba, sometime in the early eighties, I saw him. It was from quite a distance, but I remember (or imagine that I remember) his large yellow eyes, calcified to a gray color at the pupils, his frightening mien, and the big, dirty mantle he wore. He sang in a plaintive and high-pitched voice, in deep, proverbial Yoruba that was impossible for me to follow. Afterward, I imagined that I had seen something like an aura around him, a spiritual apartness that moved all his hearers to reach into their purses and put something in the bowl his assistant boy carried.

Such is the narrative around blindness. Not so with deafness, which, as in the case of one of my great-uncles, was often seen as merely unfortunate. Many deaf people, it occurred to me just then, were treated as if they were mentally retarded; even the expression "deaf and dumb," far from being a simple description of a physiological condition, had a pejorative sense.

Standing before Brewster's portraits, my mind quiet, I saw the paintings as records of a silent transaction between artist and subject. A laden brush, in depositing paint on the panel or canvas, hardly registers a sound, and how great is the peace palpable in those great artists of stillness: Vermeer, Chardin, Hammershøi. The silence was even more profound, I thought, as I stood alone in that gallery, when the private world of the artist was total in its quietness. Unlike those other painters, Brewster hadn't resorted to indirect gazes or chiaroscuro to communicate the silence of his world. The faces were well lit and frontal, and yet they were quiet.

I stood at the window on the third floor and looked outside. The air had shifted from gray to dark blue, and afternoon had become late afternoon. One image drew me back in, a painting of a child holding a bird on a blue thread. The palette, as was usual for Brewster, was dominated by muted colors; the two exceptions were the electric blue of the thread, which coursed across the face of the painting like a bolt of electricity, and the child's black shoes, which were deeper and blacker than almost anything else in the gallery. The bird represented the child's soul, as it had in Goya's portrait of the ill-fated three-year-old Manuel Osorio Manrique de Zúñiga. The child in the Brewster painting looked out with a serene and ethereal expression from the year 1805. He, unlike many of the others painted by Brewster, had his hearing intact. Was this portrait a talisman against death? One child in three at the time died before the age of twenty. Was it a magical wish that the child would hold on to life, as he held on to the string? Francis O. Watts, the subject of the painting, did live. He entered Harvard at fifteen and became a lawyer, married Caroline Goddard, who was from his hometown of Kennebunkport, Maine, and went on to become president of the Young Men's Christian Association. He eventually died in 1860, fifty-five years after the portrait was made. But, for the moment of the painting, and, therefore, for all time, he is a little boy holding a bird by a blue string, clad in a white chemise with a carefully observed lace frill.

Brewster, born some ten years before the Declaration of Independence, lived his life as an itinerant artist, working all the way from Maine to his native Connecticut and to Eastern New York. He was almost ninety when he died. The elite Federalist milieu of his background had given him access to wealthy, serious-minded patrons (his own ancestors had been on the *Mayflower* in 1620), but his deafness made him an outsider, and his images were imbued with what that long silence had taught him: concentration, the suspension of time, an unobtrusive wit. In a painting titled *One Shoe Off,* which held me transfixed the moment I came before it, the neatly tied bow of a shoe on a little girl's right foot echoed the asterisks of the floor pattern. The other shoe was in her hand, and red pentimenti were visible around the heel and the toes of the now unshod left foot. The child, as secure within her own being as were all Brewster's children, had an expression that dared the observer to be amused.

I lost all track of time before these images, fell deep into their world, as if all the time between them and me had somehow van-ished, so that when the guard came up to me to say the museum was closing, I forgot how to speak and simply looked at him. When I eventually walked down the stairs and out of the museum, it was with the feeling of someone who had returned to the earth from a great distance.

The traffic on Sixth Avenue, with its rush-hour gladiators testing each other's limits, contrasted violently with where I had just been. The rain had begun again, now like a great torrent of mirrors sweep-ing down the sheer sides of the glass buildings; it took me some time to find a cab. When I finally hailed one, a woman suddenly stepped in front of me and said she was in a hurry and would I mind letting her take it? Yes, I said, almost shouting (the sound of my own voice surprised me), I would mind. I had been standing in the rain for ten minutes and wasn't inclined to chivalry. I got in the car and immedi-ately the driver said, Where? I must have looked lost. I tried to re-member my home address. My folded umbrella pooled its water on the mat, and I thought of Brewster's portrait of the deaf teenager Sarah Prince at the pianoforte, an instrument that neither artist nor sitter would have heard: the quietest piano in the world. I imagined her running her hand along the keys but refusing to press down on them. When my address filtered its way back to me, I gave it to the cabdriver and said to him: So, how are you doing, my brother? The driver stiffened and looked at me in the mirror.

Not good, not good at all, you know, the way you came into my car without saying hello, that was bad. Hey, I'm African just like you, why you do this? He kept me in his sights in the mirror. I was con-fused. I said, I'm so sorry about it, my mind was elsewhere, don't be offended, ehn, my brother, how are you doing? He said nothing, and faced the road. I wasn't sorry at all. I was in no mood for people who tried to lay claims on me. The cab was silent, and as we drove north along the Hudson on the West Side, the river and the sky were a sin-gle darkly misted sheet and the horizon had vanished. We came off the highway, and were stuck in traffic at Broadway and Ninety-seventh Street. The driver switched on a talk-radio show: people arguing loudly about things I didn't care about. Anger had welled up within me, unhinging me, the anger of a shattered repose. The traffic finally eased, but the radio continued to blare inanities. The driver took me to the wrong address, several blocks from my apartment. I asked him to correct the error, but he idled the car, switched off the meter, and said, No, that's it. I paid him, adding the standard tip, and walked home in the rain.

# FOUR

The following day, returning to Sheep Meadow, on a circuitous route to a poetry reading at the Ninety-second Street Y, I noticed the masses of leaves dying off in bright colors, and heard the white-throated sparrows within them calling out and listening. It had rained earlier, and the fragmented, light-filled clouds worked off each other; maples and elms stood with their boughs still. Above a boxwood hedge, the swarm of hovering bees reminded me of certain Yoruba epithets for Olodumare, the supreme deity: he who turns blood into children, who sits in the sky like a cloud of bees.

The rain had kept many people from their usual after-work sports, and the park was almost empty. In a cove formed by two large rocks, I went and sat, as though led by an invisible hand, on a pile of gravel. I stretched out and laid my head against one of the rocks, placing my cheek on its damp, rough surface. I must have cut an absurd figure to someone looking on from a distance. The bees over the boxwood lifted as a single cloud and vanished into a tree. After a few minutes, my breath returned to normal and the bellowing in my ribs ceased. I got up slowly, and attempted to clean my clothes, brushing bits of grass and dirt away from my trousers and sweater, rubbing earth stains out of my palms. The sky was now at its last light, and a trickle of blue, seen through the buildings to the west, was all that leaked through.

I sensed a shift in the city's distant commotion; day's end: people heading home or beginning the night shift, preparations for dinner in thousands of restaurant kitchens, and the soft yellow lights that were now glimmering from apartment windows. I hurried out of the park, across Fifth Avenue, Madison, Park, then north on Lexington, to the lecture hall where, when once we were settled in our seats, the poet was introduced. He was Polish, dressed in brown and gray clothes, and though he was relatively young, his hair was a brilliant white halo. He approached the lectern to applause, and said: I don't want to talk about poetry tonight. I want to talk about persecution, if you will permit a poet this license. What can we understand about the roots of persecution, particularly when the target of this perse-cution is a tribe or race or cultural group? I will begin with a story. His English was fluent, but the thick accent, and the elongated vow-els and thickly rolled r's, gave it a halting quality, as though he were translating each line in his mind before speaking. He looked up at the full room, looking out at everyone and at no one in particular, and the lights bounced off his glasses, making it appear as though he had a large white patch over each eye.

LATER THAT WEEK, AT THE END OF A DIFFICULT DAY AT THE IN-patient unit, a day on which I was oversensitive to the hospital's white lights and felt more irritated than usual with the paperwork and small talk, a reprise of the heavy mood, now more sustained, set-tled on me. Psychiatry training programs are reputed to be less bru-tal than some other residency programs—and I had found it so—but the work has its own peculiar challenges. At times, psychiatrists feel the absence of the neat solutions surgeons or pathologists enjoy, and it can be wearying to always have to find the mental preparation, the emotional focus, that is necessary for sitting with patients. The only thing, when I thought it all through, that enlivened the long hours I spent on call or in the office was the trust those patients had in me, their helplessness, their hope that I could help them get better.

In any case, unlike when I had first begun work in the hospital, I no longer spent much time thinking about patients, usually not until the next appointment, and often, when I was on rounds, I needed the chart to recall even the basics of a particular case. That I thought of M. away from the medical campus was, in that sense, an exception; he was, like V., the rare patient whose problems were not relegated to the back of my mind when I stepped out onto the street. M. was thirty-two, recently divorced, and delusional. On bad weeks, the medication seemed to hardly help at all.

A hint of winter was in the air as I began to cross Broadway and was held for a moment in the yellow eyes of the cars hunched in serried ranks at the red light. It was just past five o'clock and night was falling fast. The buildings of the medical complex stood shoulder to shoulder against the charcoal-colored sky and, all around me, people wore padded jackets and knitted hats. I entered the subway at 168th Street and caught a packed southbound 1 train. So absorbed was I in rehearsing that afternoon's consultation with M. that, when the train reached 116th Street, I simply watched the doors open, stay open, and close. The car moved on past my stop, and momentarily I tried to figure out what had happened. I hadn't been asleep. My staying on, I finally decided, was intentional, if not conscious. This was confirmed at the next stop, when again I failed to exit and instead sat there, with the feeling that I was watching myself, waiting to see what would happen next. Everyone in the car seemed to be wearing black or dark gray. One woman, unusually tall, more than six feet, wore a black jacket over a long, black, pleated skirt and knee-length black boots, and the play of depth in these layers of her clothing brought to my memory the virtuoso black-on-black passages in certain paintings by Velázquez. Her pale, pinched face was overwhelmed, nearly, by the black of the clothes. No one on the train spoke and no one, it seemed, knew anyone else. It was as though we were all listening closely to the rattle of the train on the tracks. The lights were dim. I knew then that I was no longer heading directly home.

At Ninety-sixth Street, I switched to the 2 express, which happened to arrive on the platform just at that moment. This carriage was brightly lit. The man sitting across from me wore a pumpkin-colored jacket, and next to him was a woman in a sky blue ski jacket and striped gloves. A few people in this train talked to each other, neither demonstrative nor loud in their manner, but enough to highlight in my mind how somber the other train had been. The brightness, perhaps, gave people permission to open up. To my right sat a man whose full attention was on Octavia Butler's *Kindred*, and to his right, a russet-haired man leaned forward in his seat and read *The Wall Street Journal*. His natural expression was delirious, which gave him the aspect of a gargoyle, but when he straightened up, he had a handsome profile. At Forty-second Street, a man in a pin-striped suit entered holding a volume with the title *You've GOT to Read This Book!* The book was open in his hand, but as he came in and stood by the seats, he kept his eyes fixed on a spot on the floor. He did so for a long time. He kept the book open in front of him, but read nothing out of it. He eventually closed it on a finger when he got off, at Fulton. At Wall Street, more people, all of them probably workers in the financial world, got on the train, but no one got off. Just as the doors were closing at this station, I stood up and slipped out of the car. The doors closed behind me and, this assortment of inwardly focused city types still swirling in my mind, I found myself all alone on the platform.

I took the escalator up, and as I came out onto the mezzanine level, I saw the ceiling—high, white, and consisting of a series of interconnected vaults—slowly reveal itself as though it were a retractable dome in the act of closing. It was a station I had never been in before, and I was surprised that it was so elaborate because I had expected that all the stations in lower Manhattan would be mean and perfunctory, that they would consist only of tiled tunnels and narrow exits. I suspected for a moment that the grand hall now confronting me at Wall Street was a trick of the eye. The hall had two rows of columns running along its length, and there were sets of glass doors on either end. The glass, the dominance of white in the color scheme, as well as the assortment of large potted palms under the columns, made the room feel like an atrium or greenhouse, but the tripartite division of the space, with the center aisle broader than the two to either side of it, was more reminiscent of a cathedral. The vaults strengthened this impression, and what came to mind was the florid Gothic style of England, as exemplified in buildings like Bath Abbey or the cathedral in Winchester, in which the piers and their colonnades spray up into the vaults. Not that the station replicated the stone tracery of such churches. It evoked the effect, rather, by means of its finely checkered or woven surface, a gigantic assemblage of white plastic.

My original impression of the grandeur of the space, though not of its size, quickly changed as I walked through the hall. The columns could have been wrought from recycled plastic chairs, and the ceiling seemed to have been carefully constructed out of white Lego blocks. This feeling of being in a large-scale model was only increased by the lonely palm trees in their pots, and by the few groups of people I now saw seated under the nave aisle to the right. Little round tables had been set up on this side of the hall, and men sat at them playing backgammon. The hall was sparse and, because it was enclosed, full of the echoes of the few voices present. The scene, I imagined, would be different in the middle of a workday. There were five pairs of players now, under the nave aisle to the right in this evening scene, all of them black. On the other side of the hall, under the other long nave aisle, there was another pair of men, both white, playing chess. I walked among the backgammon players, most of whom seemed to be middle-aged, and their languid, focused faces and the slowness of their movements did nothing to correct my impression of being among life-size mannequins. When I moved back into the center of the nave, which was almost free of human presence, a solitary man hurrying across to the subway escalators dropped his briefcase with a loud clatter. He got on his knees, and began gathering pieces. His oversize, mouse-colored trench coat fell like a Victorian dress around him.

I walked out by the doors leading to Wall Street proper. Outside, people moved around, talking on their phones, presumably headed home, but I heard no traffic noise. The reason became clear right away when I saw the blockades that had been set up on both ends of the street, either for security or because of ongoing construction. Wall Street, from where I stood on the corner of William Street all the way down to Broadway, a distance of several blocks, was shut off from vehicular traffic, and had been transformed into a pedestrian zone; what one heard were human voices and the click of heels on pavement. I walked toward the west. People bought food from a falafel vendor whose van was parked on the corner, or walked alone, in pairs, in threes. I saw black women in charcoal gray skirt suits, and young, clean-shaven Indian-American men. Just past Federal Hall, I walked by the glass frontage of New York Sports Club. Right up against the glass in its brightly lit interior was a single row of exercise bicycles, all of them occupied by men and women in Lycra who pedaled in the silence and looked out at commuters in the dusk. Near the corner of Nassau, a man in a scarf and fedora hat stood with an easel before him and painted the Stock Exchange in grisaille on a large canvas. A stack of completed paintings, also grisaille, of the same building seen from different angles, lay at his feet. I watched

him work for a moment, as he loaded his brush, and with careful ges-
tures applied white highlights to the acanthus of the six massive
Corinthian columns of the Stock Exchange. The building itself—
which, following his gaze, I now scrutinized more closely—was illuminated from below with a row of yellow lamps, and with this
footlighting appeared to levitate.

I went on, past Broad Street and New Street, where I noticed another sports club, this one called Equinox, from which another row
of exercisers faced the street, until I came to Broadway, where Wall
Street ended and at which junction stood the east façade of Trinity
Church. The reappearance of traffic on Broadway startled me for a
moment. I crossed Broadway and went up to the church entrance,
with the unpremeditated idea that I might go inside and pray for M.
He'd been sick for a while but, since his divorce came through earlier
in the year, he'd taken a steep turn for the worse. He was by now
completely in the grip of the delirium, and when he spoke it was with
such distress that his heavily accented sentences seemed to be pursu-
ing each other out of the troubled caverns of his mind.

I don't blame her, he'd said to me earlier that day, any woman
would do the same, I screwed up, I screwed up. I should have been
more careful. I don't find it amusing now, but I can imagine that it
seems that way to other people, I can imagine that my suffering
amuses people. I do so much for them, but they find my suffering
amusing. I have to be responsible, though, more discipline, more and
more discipline, and if I tried that I would still be married. Not that
I blame her, or anyone else, they can do what they want, but I have
to be responsible for the world, and none of them knows what that
feels like. If I don't organize things just right, you see, everything will
be destroyed. You understand? I'm not saying I'm God, but I know
what it feels like to carry the world. I feel like the little boy with his
finger in the dike, like I am doing a small thing, but it takes a lot of
concentration. Everything depends on this, I can't even tell you, and
I wish I didn't have this burden, this burden that is so much like

God's own burden, but given to someone, Doctor, do you see the problem, who does not have the powers of God.

The gate at the front of the church was locked. I walked along the railing, first north then, when I couldn't find an entrance there, south. There was a large graveyard that encompassed both sides of the church, white headstones, black ones, and a few monuments, among which Alexander Hamilton's was prominent: THE PATRIOT OF INCORRUPTIBLE INTEGRITY, THE SOLDIER OF APPROVED VALOR, THE STATESMAN OF CONSUMMATE WISDOM, WHOSE TALENTS AND VIRTUES WILL BE ADMIRED. It gave the date—July 12, 1804—as well as his age, forty-seven. Hamilton, actually forty-nine when he died of the single gunshot wound he received in the duel with Burr, was not the only famous person interred in the Trinity churchyard. Among the stones were also those commemorating John Jacob Astor, Robert Fulton, and the abolitionist George Templeton Strong, whose memoirs of late-nineteenth-century life in the city I had once seen on my friend's shelves. And then there were many women from those few centuries since the Europeans had come up the Hudson and settled on this island, women named Eliza, Elizabeth, Elisabeth. Some of them had died old, many others had died young, often during childbirth or, younger still, of childhood illnesses. There was a large number of children's graves.

Going around Rector Street, I came onto Trinity Place, where an ancient wall hemmed the church in and the air was cold and smelled of the sea. Trinity Church was chartered in the waning years of the seventeenth century; seafarers in general and whalers in particular had set out on their outbound journeys with the blessings of its congregation. It was to the same church that they returned, if they had been blessed with a safe and prosperous voyage, to give thanks for journeying mercies. One of the many privileges accorded Trinity in those years was full rights over any shipwrecks or beached whales on the isle of Manhattan. The church was near the water. Water loomed close by it in every direction but north. I walked around, looking for an entrance, thinking of these nearby waters. Later, I would find the story recounted by the Dutch settler Antony de Hooges in his memorandum book:

> On the 29th of March in the year 1647 a certain fish appeared before us here in the colony, which we estimated to be of a considerable size. He came from below and swam past us a certain distance up to the sand bars and came back towards evening, going down past us again. He was snow-white, without fins, round of body, and blew water up out of his head, just like whales or tunas. It seemed very strange to us because there are many sand bars between us and Manhattan, and also because it was snow-white, such as no one among us has ever seen; especially, I say, because it covered a distance of twenty miles of fresh water in contrast to salt water, which is its element. Only God knows what it means. But it is certain, that I and most all of the inhabitants watched it with great amazement. On the same evening that this fish appeared before us, we had the first thunder and lightening of the year.

Fort Orange, from which de Hooges wrote his report, was the settlement that later became Albany, after the British took over the Dutch possessions in this part of the New World. De Hooges wrote of another sighting of a great sea creature in April of the same year. Another writer, the traveler Adriaen van der Donk, reported two sightings, as well as a beached whale, up the Hudson in the Troy area, also in 1647. The latter was plundered for its oil, van der Donk wrote, and its carcass was left to stink up the beach. For the Dutch, though, the sighting of a whale in inland waters, or of its beached hulk on land, was a powerful portent, and de Hooges's link between the presence of the whales and dramatic weather patterns was typical. His sighting was even more ominous than usual, as the animal he described seemed to have been an albino.

There could hardly have been any seventeenth-century Dutch resident of New Amsterdam and the upriver trading posts who would have been unaware of the numerous whale beachings back home in the Netherlands. In 1598, the fifty-four-foot sperm whale that beached itself in the sandy shallows of Berckhey, near The Hague, had taken four days to die and, in that time and in the weeks afterward, had entered into the legend of a nation at the very beginning of its modern history. The whale of Berckhey was memorialized in engravings, taken as an object of commercial value and, when that was exhausted, scientific curiosity. It was, above all, interpreted as a message from the deep. It was not at all difficult for the people of the day to see a link between this dying monster and the atrocities committed by the hated Spanish troops in the principality of Cleves in August of the same year. Between the mid–sixteenth century and the end of the seventeenth, at least forty whales were beached on the shores of Flanders and the northern Netherlands. For the Dutch, who were attempting, at the time, not only to define their new republic but also to consolidate their hold on New Amsterdam and other foreign possessions, the spiritual meaning of the whale was ever-present.

About two hundred years later, when a young man from the Fort Orange area came down the Hudson and settled in Manhattan, he decided he would write his magnum opus on an albino Leviathan. The author, a sometime parishioner of Trinity Church, called his book *The Whale*; the subtitle, *Moby-Dick*, was added only after the first publication. This same Trinity Church had now left me out in the brisk marine air and given me no place in which to pray. There were chains on all the gates, and I could find neither a way into the building nor anyone to help me. So, lulled by sea air, I decided to find my way to the edge of the island from there. It would be good, I thought, to stand for a while on the waterline.

————

WHEN I CROSSED THE STREET AND ENTERED THE SMALL ALLEY opposite, it was as though the entire world had fallen away. I was strangely comforted to find myself alone in this way in the heart of the city. The alley, no one's preferred route to any destination, was all brick walls and shut-up doors, across which shadows fell as crisply as in an engraving. Ahead of me was a great black building. The surface of its half-visible tower was matte, a light-absorbing black like that of cloth, and its sharp geometry made it look like a freestanding shadow or cardboard cutout. I walked under some scaffolding in the alley and, from Thames Street, crossed Greenwich, and came to Albany, from which I saw the tower more clearly, although still at some distance. It was completely veiled in a densely woven black net. Where that narrow, quiet street met Washington, I saw to my right, about a block north of where I stood, a great empty space. I immediately thought of the obvious but, equally quickly, put the idea out of my mind.

Shortly afterward, I was on the West Side Highway. I was the only pedestrian at the crossing. The taillights of cars were chased by their red reflections toward the bridges out of the island, and to the right, there was a pedestrian overpass connecting one building, not to another, but to the ground. And again, the empty space that was, I now saw and admitted, the obvious: the ruins of the World Trade Center. The place had become a metonym of its disaster: I remembered a tourist who once asked me how he could get to 9/11: not the site of the events of 9/11 but to 9/11 itself, the date petrified into broken stones. I moved closer. It was walled in with wood and chain link, but otherwise nothing announced its significance. On the other side of the highway was a tranquil, residential street called South End, on the corner of which was a restaurant. It had neon signs outside (I remember the neon, but I forget the restaurant's name) and, when I peered in through the glass doors, I saw that it was mostly empty. The few patrons, it seemed, were all men, and most sat alone. I went inside, and sat at the bar, and ordered a drink from the waitress.

I had just finished my beer and paid for it when a man came to sit beside me. You don't recognize me, he said, raising his eyebrows. I noticed you at the museum, about a week ago, the Folk Art Museum. My face must have remained foggy because he added: I'm a guard there, and that was you I saw, right? I nodded, faint though the memory was. He said, I knew I recognized your face. We shook hands, and he introduced himself as Kenneth. He was dark-skinned, bald, with a broad, smooth forehead, and a carefully trimmed pencil mustache. His upper body was powerful, but his legs were spindly, so that he looked like Nabokov's Pnin come to life. He was in his late thirties, I guessed. We made small talk, but soon he launched into a monologue, flitting from one subject to another in a Caribbean accent. He was from Barbuda, he said, and was surprised that I'd heard of it.

Most of these Americans don't know anyplace, other than what's right in front of their noses, he said. Anyway, I'm waiting for some friends, and isn't this a nice place? Oh, you haven't been here before? I shook my head. He asked where I was from, what I did. He spoke fast, chattily. One of my housemates, once, in Colorado, he said, was a Nigerian. He was called Yemi. Yoruba, I think he was, and I'm really interested in African culture anyway. Are you Yoruba? Kenneth was, by now, starting to wear on me, and I began to wish he would go away. I thought of the cabdriver who had driven me home from the Folk Art Museum—hey, I'm African just like you. Kenneth was making a similar claim.

I used to live in Littleton, but I was at university in Denver, studying for my associate's degree, he said. You know Littleton, right? The massacre happened just after I arrived there. Terrible thing. Same thing happened with New York, I got here in July 2001. Crazy, right? Completely crazy, so I don't know whether to warn the next city I move to! Anyway, the museum position, you know, it's all right, something to do for now, it's nice, but what I really want to do is . . . Kenneth spoke on, rapid, automatic, but his tawny eyes were immobile. Then it struck me that his eyes were asking a question. A sexual question. I explained to him that I had to meet a friend. I apologized for not having a business card with me, and said something about visiting the museum again soon. I left the restaurant and stepped back out onto South End. It wasn't far from there to the water, and as I moved toward the waterline, I felt a little sorry for him, and the desperation in his prattle.

This strangest of islands, I thought, as I looked out to the sea, this island that turned in on itself, and from which water had been banished. The shore was a carapace, permeable only at certain selected points. Where in this riverine city could one fully sense a riverbank? Everything was built up, in concrete and stone, and the millions who lived on the tiny interior had scant sense about what flowed around them. The water was a kind of embarrassing secret, the unloved daughter, neglected, while the parks were doted on, fussed over, overused. I stood on the promenade and looked out across the water into the unresponsive night. All was quiet and lights called from the Jersey shore across. A pair of joggers sailed softly toward me, and past me. Along South End, facing the water, there were rows of townhouses, small shops, and a little, round gazebo choked with vines and bushes. Out, ahead of me, in the Hudson, there was just the faintest echo of the old whaling ships, the whales, and the generations of New Yorkers who had come here to the promenade to watch wealth and sorrow flow into the city or simply to see the light play on the water. Each one of those past moments was present now as a trace. From where I stood, the Statue of Liberty was a fluorescent green fleck against the sky, and beyond her sat Ellis Island, the focus of so many myths; but it had been built too late for those early Africans—who weren't immigrants in any case—and it had been closed too soon to mean anything to the later Africans like Kenneth, or the cabdriver, or me.

Ellis Island was a symbol mostly for European refugees. Blacks, "we blacks," had known rougher ports of entry: this, I could admit to myself now that my mood was less impatient, was what the cabdriver had meant. This was the acknowledgment he wanted, in his brusque fashion, from every "brother" he met. I walked north, along the promenade, listening to the water breathing. Two old men shuffled toward me in shiny tracksuits, deep in conversation with each other. Why did I feel suddenly that they were visiting from the other side of time? I caught their gaze for a moment, but their eyes signaled nothing other than the usual gap between the old and the young. A little walk north, the promenade broadened, the residential row ended, and there I saw the glass atrium of the World Financial Center, with its assortment of massive indoor plants that made it look like a gigantic aquarium. There was a calm inlet just in front of the building, on which several boats, one of which had a sign for the Manhattan Sailing School, bobbed gently. I went down a short flight of wooden steps, and walked onto the pier and alongside the boats, and beyond them into the section where there was water on both sides. The inlet was to my right, the river to my left, and I faced out to the left, settling my eyes on the black water, the scattered lights of Hoboken and Jersey City, and above them black sky. The soft ululations of the water fell into my ears, and out of those murmurs, M.'s plaintive voice.

How could I be so stupid, Turkish-American wife, Turkish mistress. I always told her I had business in Ankara, which I did, but she didn't know about my other business; and this other one, I gave her three hundred dollars every month, it was a good arrangement, I think, or I should say I thought. I thought. I didn't think. One day, she wrote and asked for more—women are crazy, Doctor, even crazier than me—she wanted five hundred. Can you imagine this? Every

month, five hundred, and my wife said, A letter from Turkey, let me
see who writes my husband. That was the end for me. When I came
home she was waiting with the letter in one hand, and a stick in the
other. How can I blame her? I was thinking with my, I don't know,
Doctor. And now, everybody at home knows this. I was thinking
with my balls. I didn't think. Everything good I have made bad, I disappoint God.

His eyes brimmed. He had told the story before, and had wept
before, but each time it was like never before. He experienced the
pain afresh and dramatized it each time. And, as thought leads to
thought, standing there looking at the river, I felt an unexpected
pang of my own, a sudden urgency and sorrow, but the image of the
one I was thinking of flitted past quickly. It had been only a few
weeks, but time had begun to dull even that wound. It was getting
cold, but I stood awhile longer. How easy it would be, I thought, to
slip gently into the water here, and go down to the depths. I knelt,
and trailed my hand in the Hudson. It was frigid. Here we all were,
ignoring that water, paying as little attention as possible to the pair
of black eternities between which our little light intervened. Our
debt, though, to that light: what of it? We owe ourselves our lives.
This, about which we physicians say so much to our patients, about
which so little can reasonably be said, folds back and also asks us
questions. I wiped my hand on my jacket, and breathed on my fingers to warm them up.

Two boys, late teens, up on the promenade with their skateboards,
were the only people within shouting distance. They were absorbed
in their sport. One of them repeatedly made jumps from a low ramp,
taking off and landing with loud clacks, while the other raced alongside him on another skateboard with a video camera, held low, almost at ankle level, and with a beam of light from its lamp. A security
officer drove past in a motorized cart, and warned the boys against
jumps. They stood and listened respectfully, and seemed chastened.
But as soon as he drove off, they resumed their jumps.

Away from the water, in the plaza behind the World Financial Center, was a small semienclosed space consisting of a fountain, plant beds with rushes, and two marble walls, one higher than the other. The walls were inscribed, and on the lower wall was a plaque: DEDICATED TO THE MEMORY OF THOSE MEMBERS OF THE POLICE DEPARTMENT WHO LOST THEIR LIVES IN SERVICE TO THE PEOPLE OF THE CITY OF NEW YORK. On the other wall, there was a list, with dozens of names on it. At the very top was the first entry—PTL. JAMES CAHILL, SEPTEMBER 29, 1854. It went on like that through the years, one entry after the other, rank, name, date of death; there was the expected, disheartening cluster in the fall of 2001, then a few others who died in the years that followed. Below that was a vast, blank face of polished marble, awaiting those among the living who would die in uniform, and the not yet born, who would be born, grow up to be police officers, and be killed while doing that work.

Across the plaza, on the other side of the West Side Highway, the big buildings of the trading district were lined up on an invisible perimeter like animals jostling for space on the edge of a lake, taking care not to pitch forward. The perimeter marked out the massive construction site. I walked up to a second overpass, the one that once connected the World Financial Center to the buildings that stood on the site. Until that moment, I had been a lone walker, but people then began to troop out of the World Financial Center, men and women in dark suits including a group of young Japanese professionals who, tailed by the rapid stream of their conversation, hurried by me. Above them, for the third time that evening, I saw the bright lights of an exercise facility with the rows of bicycles, in this case looking out onto the construction site. What, I wondered, went through the minds of the exercisers as they pedaled and strained and looked out there? When I came up to the overpass, I was able to share their view: a long ramp that extended into the site, and the three or four tractors scattered around inside it that, dwarfed by the size of the pit, looked like toys. Just below street level, I saw the sudden metallic green of a subway train hurtling by, exposed to the elements where it crossed the work site, a livid vein drawn across the neck of 9/11. Beyond the site was the building I had seen earlier in the evening, the one wrapped in black netting, mysterious and severe as an obelisk.

The overpass was full of people. In its rafters were brightly colored advertisements for various tourist sites in lower Manhattan. SHOW YOUR KIDS WHERE THE ALIENS LANDED, the one for Ellis Island read. The Museum of American Finance was promoted with the words RELIVE THE DAY AMERICA'S TICKER STOPPED. The Police Museum, also entering the spirit of distasteful puns, invited people to visit New York's first cell provider. The commuters with me marched along, shoulders up, heads low, all in black and gray. I felt conspicuous, the only person among the crowd who stopped to look out from the overpass at the site. Everyone else went straight ahead, and nothing separated them, nothing separated us, from the people who had worked directly across the street on the day of disaster. When we descended the stairs into Vesey Street, we were hemmed in on both sides by a chain-link fence, penned in, "like animals" stumbling to the slaughter. But why was it permitted to treat even animals that way? Elizabeth Costello's nagging questions showed up in the strangest places.

But atrocity is nothing new, not to humans, not to animals. The difference is that in our time it is uniquely well organized, carried out with pens, train carriages, ledgers, barbed wire, work camps, gas. And this late contribution, the absence of bodies. No bodies were visible, except the falling ones, on the day America's ticker stopped. Marketable stories of all kinds had thickened around the injured coast of our city, but the depiction of the dead bodies was forbidden. It would have been upsetting to have it otherwise. I moved on with the commuters through the pen.

This was not the first erasure on the site. Before the towers had gone up, there had been a bustling network of little streets traversing this part of town. Robinson Street, Laurens Street, College Place: all of them had been obliterated in the 1960s to make way for the World Trade Center buildings, and all were forgotten now. Gone, too, was the old Washington Market, the active piers, the fishwives, the Christian Syrian enclave that was established here in the late 1800s. The Syrians, the Lebanese, and other people from the Levant had been pushed across the river to Brooklyn, where they'd set down roots on Atlantic Avenue and in Brooklyn Heights. And, before that? What Lenape paths lay buried beneath the rubble? The site was a palimpsest, as was all the city, written, erased, rewritten. There had been communities here before Columbus ever set sail, before Verrazano anchored his ships in the narrows, or the black Portuguese slave trader Esteban Gómez sailed up the Hudson; human beings had lived here, built homes, and quarreled with their neighbors long before the Dutch ever saw a business opportunity in the rich furs and timber of the island and its calm bay. Generations rushed through the eye of the needle, and I, one of the still legible crowd, entered the subway. I wanted to find the line that connected me to my own part in these stories. Somewhere close to the water, holding tight to what he knew of life, the boy had, with a sharp clack, again gone aloft.

## FIVE

It was back in summer, on the day we went on a trip out to Queens with an organization from Nadège's church called the Welcomers, that I saw, for the first time, the link between her and another girl I'd once known. That other girl had been hidden in my memory for more than twenty-five years; to suddenly remember her, and instantly tie her to Nadège, was a shock. I must have been circling subconsciously around the idea for several days, but seeing the link solved a problem. I never spoke to Nadège of the other girl, whose name I had forgotten, whose face had blurred in memory, of whom I now retained only the image of a limp. It wasn't a deception: all lovers live on partial knowledge.

The girl's problem was far worse than Nadège's. She had polio, which had withered her left foot into a twisted stump she dragged behind her when she walked. The articulated steel brace she used for support was always on her left arm. Watching her walk across the field at my primary school, I was afraid that the boys would mock her; that was my first instinct, a gallant, protective one. She was in my class, but I remember little now of what we talked about the three or four times we spoke to each other. I liked her ability to be comfortable with herself, and the way that, once she sat down, she was no different from other children, and in fact had a brightness about her that was out of the ordinary. She might have been the best student in class had she stayed, but her parents withdrew her, and she went to another school. I never saw her again after those first two weeks. And only when Nadège came down from the bus in Queens, on that Welcomers excursion, did I see the similarity, the echo that was like John the Baptist's echo of Elijah, two individuals separated in time and vibrating on a singular frequency, only then did I remember that I had imagined a future life with this other girl when we had both been eight or nine years old, the first time I had ever had such a thought, and of course with no idea of what it might entail.

I had seen myself as a grown man, protecting her as one might protect a pet, having many children with her, but I did not think of having her as a girlfriend. I don't think I even had such a concept then. I didn't pity Nadège as I had the other girl. The limp was only a visual cue, hardly noticeable in Nadège's case, and no great impediment to her; perhaps it offended her vanity a little but that was all. Sometimes, she said, when she wore adjusted shoes, it wasn't even noticeable. It was a hip problem, which she'd had surgery to correct in her late teens, by which time it was too late. It should have been done much earlier, but at least the procedure released her from chronic pain.

We were on the Triborough Bridge returning to Harlem as she told me this, with her head on my shoulder. My thoughts were scattered: I was thinking about her, and about the other girl, and about the young man with whom I had had a long conversation earlier that afternoon. I had gone on the Welcomers trip on Nadège's invitation; she had mentioned it to me, and it seemed an interesting way to get to know her better. Her church organized bimonthly visits to a detention facility in Queens in which undocumented immigrants were held. I showed interest, and when she asked me to come along the following Sunday, I agreed. I met her and the rest of the group, a mix of human-rights types and church ladies, in the basement of the cathedral. Their priest, who gave the blessing, wore no shoes, a practice he had picked up during his long years of service in a rural parish in the Orinoco. Nadège said he had done it out of solidarity with the peasants he served, but that he continued to be shoeless in New York to remind himself and others of their plight. I asked her if he was a Marxist, but she didn't know. The shoeless priest did not come with us to Queens. Most of the group, on the day I went, were women, many with that beatific, slightly unfocused expression one finds in do-gooders. We were on a chartered bus driven by the same route one would take from upper Manhattan to La Guardia Airport, and were on the road for an hour, through slow traffic, until we came to South Jamaica.

It was early summer, but the view was grim, a landscape of wire fences, parked cars, and disused construction equipment. When we came to an industrial-looking area about a mile from the airport proper, weeds grew out of the road and furred the open culverts, and the buildings all looked prefabricated, with aluminum siding as if to blend them into the ugly landscape. I must have seen them before, these buildings at the far end of a tarred field, some of the larger ones of which were used as hangars or repair shops, on previous trips to the airport. But had I seen them, I would have just as quickly forgotten them; they seemed designed not to be noticed. And so also with the detention facility itself, a long, gray metal box, a single-story building that had been contracted out to Wackenhut, a private firm, under the jurisdiction of the Department of Homeland Security. We came to a halt in a vast parking lot behind it.

It was then that I saw Nadège's uneven walk. It was, in a sense, the first time I had really seen her: the slanting afternoon light, the vicious landscape of wire fencing and broken concrete, the bus like a resting beast, the way she moved her body in compensation for a malformation. When we came around to the front of the metal building, we saw a large crowd standing in a long line. People carried plastic bags and small boxes, and near the head of the line, a security guard explained loudly to a couple who seemed to speak little or no English that visiting hours had not begun yet, and would not begin for another ten minutes. The guard made a great show of his exasperation, and the couple looked both apologetic and dissatisfied. The Welcomers group joined the line, which appeared to consist of recent immigrants: Africans, Latinos, Eastern Europeans, Asians. These were the people, in other words, who would have cause to visit someone at a detention facility. A middle-aged man shouted into a cellphone in Polish. The wind was cool, and it soon became cold. The line did not move for twenty-five minutes; then it moved and, one at a time, we showed our ID cards, passed through the metal detectors, and were let into the waiting room. Everyone, with the exception of the Welcomers, seemed to be there to see family members. The security officers—oversize, bored, brusque-mannered people, people who made no pretense of enjoying their work—took the visitors, a half dozen at a time, behind secured doors for forty-five-minute visits. Those waiting their turn were mostly silent, staring into space. No one was reading. That purgatorial waiting room had no windows, and was brightly lit with fluorescent tubes, which seemed to suck into them the little remaining air. I imagined the sun setting outside over the concrete wasteland.

Nadège had gone in. She'd been to the facility several times before, and had two inmates whom she saw regularly, one woman and one man. She'd asked for both by name. I went in with the next group, to see the inmates selected for us by the officials. The meeting room was as expected, perfunctory: a narrow rank of bays, split down the middle by Plexiglas, with chairs on both sides, and small perforations at face level. The man who sat in front of me had a broad white smile. He was young, and dressed in an orange jumpsuit, as were all the other inmates. I introduced myself, and he smiled immediately and asked if I was African. He was as good-looking, as striking in appearance as any man I had ever seen. He had delicate cheekbones, a dark, even complexion, and the whites of his eyes were as vivid as his white teeth.

The first thing he asked, perhaps aware that I was with the Welcomers, was if I was a Christian. I hesitated, then told him I supposed I was. Oh, he said, I'm happy about that because I am a Christian too, a believer in Jesus. So, will you please pray for me? I told him I would, and began to ask him how things were at the detention facility. Not so bad, not as bad as it could be, he said. But I am tired of it, I want to be released. I have been here more than two years. Twenty-six months. They have just finished my case, and we made an appeal, but it was rejected. Now they are sending me back, but there is no date, just this waiting and waiting.

He did not speak too sadly, but he was disappointed, that I could see. He was tired of hoping, but he also seemed unable to suppress his generous smile. There was a certain gentleness in his every sentence, and he began to speak, rapidly, about how he had ended up confined in this large metal box in Queens. I encouraged him, asked him to clarify details, gave, as best as I could, a sympathetic ear to a story that, for too long, he had been forced to keep to himself. He was well educated, there was no hesitation in his English, and I let him speak without interrupting. He lowered his voice a bit, leaned toward the glass, and said that America was a name that had never really been far away when he was growing up. In school and at home, he had been taught about the special relationship between Liberia and America, which was like the relationship between an uncle and a favorite nephew. Even the names bore a family resemblance: Liberia,

America: seven letters each, four of which were shared. America had sat solidly in his dreams, had been the absolute focus of his dreams, and when the war began and everything started to crumble, he was sure the Americans would come in and solve the whole thing. But it hadn't been like that; the Americans had been reluctant to help, for their own reasons.

His name was Saidu, he said. His school, near the Old Ducor Hotel, had been shelled, and burned to the ground in 1994. A year later, his sister had died of diabetes, an illness that wouldn't have killed her in peacetime. His father, gone since 1985, remained gone, and his mother, a petty trader at the market, had nothing to trade. Saidu had slipped through the shadows of the war. He was pressed many times into fetching water for the NPFL (the National Patriotic Front of Liberia), or clearing brush, or moving bodies away from the street. He got used to the cries of alarm and the sudden clouds of smoke, he learned to lie low when recruiters came calling for either side. They would accost his mother, and she would tell them he had sickle-cell disease and was in the throes of death.

His mother and her sister were shot in the second war, by Charles Taylor's men. Two days later, the men returned and took him away with them, to the outskirts of Monrovia. He carried a suitcase with him. At first, he thought the men would make him fight, but they gave him a cutlass, and he worked on a rubber farm with forty or fifty others. At the camp, he saw one of his mates, a boy who had been the best soccer player in school: that boy's right hand had been severed at the wrist, and had healed to a stump. Others had died, he had seen corpses. But it was seeing that stump where a hand used to be that did it for him; that was when he knew he had no choice.

That night, he packed his soccer shoes, two spare shirts, and all his money, around six hundred Liberian dollars. At the bottom of his tattered backpack, he placed his mother's birth certificate. The rest of the things in the suitcase he emptied into a ditch. The suitcase itself he threw into the bush. He did not, himself, have a birth certificate, which was why he took his mother's. He escaped the farm, walking the road alone in the darkness, all the way back to Monrovia. He couldn't return home, so he went to the burnt ruin of his school, near the Old Ducor Hotel, and cleared a corner there. He thought that if he went to sleep, maybe he would die. The idea was new to him, and it felt good. It helped him sleep.

I was startled by a sudden knock on the Plexiglas. One of the Wackenhut guards had walked up, behind me, and I had been so absorbed in Saidu's story that I started, and dropped my hat. The guard said, You fellas have thirty minutes. Saidu looked up at him from the other side of the partition, smiled, and said thank you. Then he lowered his voice again, leaned forward, and spoke even more quickly, as though the words now flowed freely from some hitherto blocked aquifer of his memory.

That night he slept in the breeze from an open window, until a hissing sound woke him up. He opened his eyes, but kept his body still, and in the charred darkness he saw, across the long room, all the way at the other end, a small white snake. He tensed, wondering if the snake had seen him, but it continued to move, as though it were looking for something. Then a gust came through the window, and Saidu saw that the "snake" was actually an open exercise book, its pages fluttering in the wind. The memory of that apparition remained, he said, because he often wondered, then and later, if it meant something for his future. Morning came, and he stayed at the school all that day, hiding, and slept there when night fell. That night again, the book moved in the darkness and kept him company; he stayed half-awake and watched its pages rising and falling, and sometimes he saw it as a snake and sometimes as a book. The following day, he saw some ECOMOG soldiers from Nigeria, who gave him boiled rice. He pretended to be retarded, and he hitched a ride with them, traveling in their armored truck as far as Gbarnga, in the north of the country. Then he went on foot to Guinea, a journey of many days, switching between his sandals and his soccer shoes. Both gave him blisters, but in different places. When he got thirsty, he drank water from puddles. He was hungry, but he tried not to think about it. He couldn't remember how he walked the ninety miles to the small town in the Guinean hinterland, or how that brought him, on the back of a farmer's motorcycle, to Bamako.

By now, the idea of getting to America was fixed in his mind. In Bamako, unable to speak Bamana or French, he'd skulked around the motor park, eating scraps at the marketplace, sleeping under the market tables at night, and dreaming sometimes that he was being attacked by hyenas. In one dream, his mate from school came to him, bleeding from his severed hand. In other dreams his mother, aunt, and sister showed up, all of them crowding around the market table, all of them bleeding.

How much time passed? He was unsure. Maybe six months, maybe a little less. He eventually befriended a Malian truck driver, and washed his truck in exchange for food. Then this driver introduced him to another one, a man with light brown eyes, a Mauritanian. The Mauritanian asked him where he wanted to go, and Saidu said America. And the Mauritanian asked him if he was carrying any hashish, and Saidu said no, he had none. The Mauritanian agreed to take him as far as Tangier. When they left, Saidu wore a new shirt the Malian driver had given him. The truck was packed with Senegalese, Nigeriens, and Malians, and they had all paid, except for him. It was extremely hot during the day, and freezing at night, and the water in the jerry cans was carefully rationed. I wondered, naturally, as Saidu told this story, whether I believed him or not, whether it wasn't more likely that he had been a soldier. He had, after all, had months to embellish the details, to perfect his claim of being an innocent refugee.

In Tangier, he said, he had noticed the way the black Africans moved around, under constant police surveillance. A large group of them, mostly men, and mostly young, had a camp near the sea, and he joined them. They wrapped themselves in blankets against the cold wind from the sea. One man next to him said he was from Accra, and told Saidu that journeying through Ceuta was safer. When we enter Ceuta, the man said, we have entered Spain, we will go tomorrow. The following day, they went to a small Moroccan town near Ceuta in a van, a group of about fifteen of them, then they went on foot to the border with Ceuta. The fence was brightly lit and the man from Accra led them down to where the fence met the sea. A man was shot last week, he said, but I don't think we should be fearful, God is with us. There was a boat waiting, operated by a Moroccan ferryman. They held hands in prayer, then loaded up, and the man rowed across the shallows. They completed the ten-minute journey to Ceuta undetected, rolled ashore, and scattered into the rushes. Ceuta, as the Ghanaian had said, was Spain. The new immigrants split up in many directions.

Saidu entered Spain proper after three weeks, through Algeciras, on a ferry, and no papers were required. He found his way across the southern part of the country, begging in town squares, lining up at soup kitchens. Twice he picked pockets in crowded corners, throwing out the ID cards and credit cards, keeping the cash; this, he said, was the only crime he ever committed. He went all the way across southern Spain until he crossed the Portuguese border, and he kept going until he got to Lisbon, which was sad and cold, but also impressive. And it was only after he arrived in Lisbon that the bad dreams stopped. He fell in with Africans there, working first as a butcher's assistant, and then as a barber.

Those were the longest two years of his life. He slept in a crowded living room with ten other Africans. Three of them were girls, and the men took turns with them and paid them, but he didn't touch them, because he had saved almost enough for the passport and his ticket. If he waited another month, it would be one hundred euros cheaper, but he couldn't wait; he had the option of saving money by flying to La Guardia, and he'd asked the ticketing agent if she was sure La Guardia was also in America. She had stared at him, and he shook his head, and bought the JFK ticket anyway, just to be sure. On the passport, which was made for him by a man from Mozambique, he insisted on using his real name, Saidu Caspar Mohammed, but the man had had to invent a birth date, because Saidu didn't know his real one. The passport, a Cape Verdean one, arrived on a Tuesday; by Friday, he was in the air.

The journey ended at JFK Terminal Four. They took him away at customs. On the table between him and the officer that day, Saidu said, was a plastic bag with his possessions, clothes mostly, and his mother's birth certificate. The bag had been tagged. Voices rose from the other side of the partition. The officer then looked at him, looked at the notes his colleague had made, shook his head, and began to write. Then two women came in, smelling of bleach. One of them was a black American. They took him up, and put a rubber bracelet across both his wrists. The bracelet cut his skin, and when he stood up, the black American woman pushed him. Was he afraid? He wasn't afraid, no. He hadn't thought it would take long to sort it all out. He was thirsty, and after being cooped up in the plane, he longed simply to be outside in the air, and to smell America. He wanted food, and a bath; he wanted a chance to work, perhaps as a barber to start with, then something different. He would go to Florida, maybe, because it was a name he had always liked. They steered him forward, as if they were leading a blind man, and as he crossed the partition and saw into the other room where the rising voices had come from, he saw men in uniform, white men and black men, with guns in their holsters.

They brought me here, he said, and that was the end. I have been here ever since. I have only been outside three times, on the days when I went to court. The lawyer they assigned to me said I might have had a chance before 9/11. But it is okay, I am okay. The food here is bad, it has no taste, but there's a lot of it. One thing I miss is the taste of groundnut stew. You know it? The other inmates are all right, they are good people. Then, lowering his voice, The guards are sometimes harsh. Sometimes harsh. You can do nothing about it, you learn how to stay out of trouble. I am one of the youngest, you know. Then, raising his voice slightly, They let us exercise, and there is cable television. Sometimes we watch soccer, sometimes basketball; most of us prefer soccer, Italian league, English league.

The security officer had returned, tapping his wristwatch. The visit was over. I raised my hand to the Plexiglas, and Saidu did the same. I don't want to go back anywhere, he said. I want to stay in this country, I want to be in America and work. I applied for asylum, but it wasn't given. Now they will return me to my port of entry, which is Lisbon. When I got up to leave, he remained seated, and said, Come back and visit me, if I am not deported.

I said that I would, but never did.

I told the story to Nadège on our way back into Manhattan that day. Perhaps she fell in love with the idea of myself that I presented in that story. I was the listener, the compassionate African who paid attention to the details of someone else's life and struggle. I had fallen in love with that idea myself.

Later, when our relationship ended, that old cliché had come crashing through: we had "drifted apart." She had her list of complaints but they seemed petty to me, and there hadn't been anything in them I was able to make sense of or relate to my life. But I did wonder, in the weeks that followed, whether there was something I had missed, some part of the failure for which I might have held myself responsible.

In early December, I met a Haitian man in the underground catacombs of Penn Station. I was in the passage along which a long arcade of shops sit with their faces open to the commuters and train departure gates of the Long Island Rail Road. I had stopped in one of the newsagents and bought a guidebook to Brussels, having begun to wonder to myself whether I should spend my vacation time there. I don't quite know why I paused that afternoon in front of one of the shoeshine shops. I have always had a problem with the shoeshine business, and even on the rare occasions when I wished to have my scuffed shoes cleaned, some egalitarian spirit kept me from doing so; it felt ridiculous to mount the elevated chairs in the shops and have someone kneel before me. It wasn't, as I often said to myself, the kind of relationship I wanted to have with another person.

But, on this occasion, I stopped and looked into the brightly lit interior which, with all its mirrors and tufted seats upholstered in vinyl, reminded me of an empty barbershop. An elderly black man I hadn't noticed stood up, waved, and said, Come in, come in, I'll shine them very well for you. I shook my head quickly, and raised a hand to decline but, not wanting to disappoint him, gave in. I stepped inside and got up on the little stepping stool, and sat in one of the buffoon-ish red thrones, toward the back of the shop. The air was laced with lemon oil and turpentine. His hair was curly and white, as were his sideburns, and he wore a dirty apron, striped blue and white. It wasn't easy to guess his age; he was no longer young, but he was sprightly. A bootblack, not a shoeshiner: the older term seemed right for him. He said, You just relax, I'll make this black as black as night for you. And, with that peculiar sense of metamorphosis one experi-ences on waking up from an afternoon nap to find that the sun has set, I heard for the first time the faint trace of a Caribbean French accent in his clear, quiet baritone. My name is Pierre, he said. Setting my feet into a pair of brass pedestals, and folding up the cuffs of my trousers, he daubed a rag into the tin of polish in his hand, and began to work the dull color into my shoes. Through the soft shoe leather, I could feel his firm fingers push against my feet.

I haven't always been a bootblack, you know. That is a sign of changing times. I started out as a hairdresser, and that is what I was for long years in this city. You wouldn't know it to look at me, but I knew all the fashions of the day, and always styled according to what the ladies required. I came here from Haiti, when things got bad there, when so many people were killed, blacks, whites. The killings were endless, there were bodies in the streets; my cousin, the son of my mother's sister, and his entire family were slaughtered. We had to leave because the future was uncertain. We would have been targeted, that was almost certain, and who knows what else might have happened. As it got worse, Mr. Bérard's wife, who had relatives here, said, Enough is enough, we must leave for New York. So that's how we came here, Mr. Bérard, Mrs. Bérard, my sister Rosalie, me, and there were many others. Rosalie was in the service with me, in the same house.

Pierre paused. Another customer, a balding businessman wearing a too-tight suit, came into the shop and, seemingly out of nowhere, a sullen young man appeared to clean his shoes. The businessman labored for breath. Pierre glanced at his co-worker. He called out, You need to call Rahul about the schedule for next week. I'm off tomorrow, and I can't do it. Then he rubbed my shoes down with a dry cloth and picked up a foot-long brush.

I learned the trade of hairdressing right here. Our house then was on Mott Street, the area of Mott and Hester. A lot of Irish in the area, Italians, too, later on, and blacks, all working in the service trades. The houses were bigger then and many people needed servants. Yes, some people worked in terrible conditions, I know, inhuman conditions. But it was a question of what family you were with. The loss of Mr. Bérard was like the loss of my own brother. He wouldn't put it that way, of course, but he taught me to read and write. He was a cold man, at times, but he also had a heart, and I give thanks to God who saved me from any lasting injustice. We heard reports of how bad things were, how many people had been executed by Boukman and his army, and we knew we were fortunate to have escaped. The terror of Bonaparte and the terror of Boukman: there was no difference to those who suffered.

When Mr. Bérard died, I could have walked away, but I had to remain in my work, because Mrs. Bérard needed me. They were higher, we were lower, but in truth it was a family, as the apostle describes God's family, in which each part plays a role. The head is not greater than the foot. This is the truth. Through the good graces of Mrs. Bérard, I took the trade of hairdressing, as I told you before, and I went into the houses and salons of many notable women in this city, too many to count, and received money for my work. At times, I went up as far as Bronck's River for work, and no one troubled me. In this way, I earned enough to purchase freedom for my sister Rosalie, and she was shortly afterward married, and blessed with a beautiful daughter. We named her Euphemia. After a while, I had enough money even for my own freedom, but I preferred the freedom within that house and that family to the freedom without. Service to Mrs. Bérard was service to God. My meeting during those years with Juliette, my beloved wife of blessed memory, did not change that. I was willing to be patient. I see from your face that it is hard for you, that it is hard for the young, like you, to understand these things. I was forty-one when Mrs. Bérard died, and I mourned her as I had mourned her husband, and only then did I seek the freedom without.

As a free man, I married my Juliette, and God's mercy was enlarged in our lives. She, like me, had come over from Haiti during the fighting; I bought her freedom before I had mine. Our life together here was difficult at times, abundant at other times, and through the intercession of the most Holy Virgin, we served those who had less than we did, in every way we could. The years of yellow fever were the most difficult. It fell on us like plague, and many were those who died in this city. My own cherished sister Rosalie succumbed to it, and we took her daughter, Euphemia, into our home as though she were ours. I am not a physician, and I know nothing of medicines, but we cared for the sick as best as we could in those years. When the worst of it was over, Juliette and I established our school for black children in St. Vincent de Paul down on Canal, down where the Chinese are now. Many of those children were orphans, and through the learning of a trade, the good Lord improved their situation, so that they were not in the debt of any man. He honored his servant in this work, he honored us both, my Juliette and I, and no honor he did us was greater than to enrich us so that we could further his work. The money we gave for the establishment of the cathedral down on Mulberry was his alone, this is the truth, and it all happened by the good graces of the Holy Virgin. He established it, we only helped build it. Nothing in a man's life happens except as ordained from on high.

OUTSIDE, THE TEMPERATURE HAD DROPPED, AT LAST. I TIGHT-ened my scarf and walked two blocks up to Thirty-fourth Street, past the brick-face Carmelite monastery there. No entrance was apparent on the continuous wall. My shoes gleamed, but the polish revealed only that they were old and in need of replacing, as now the lines and wrinkles in the leather were more visible. At the corner, the lights of a diner flickered with large neon words: SUPPORT OUR TROOPS. The first two letters of TROOPS failed to light. Christmas shoppers stalked the streets, huddled under black cloaks rimmed with fur. As I came to Ninth Avenue, there was a silent commotion along a stand of trees just one block to the south, on Thirty-third, where I saw pamphlets opposing the war fluttering in the wind like a flock taking sudden flight. I had the impression of a crowd dispersing, the height of their activity just past. A police barrier lay on its side.

That afternoon, during which I flitted in and out of myself, when time became elastic and voices cut out of the past into the present, the heart of the city was gripped by what seemed to be a commotion from an earlier time. I feared being caught up in what, it seemed to me, were draft riots. The people I saw were all men, hurrying along under leafless trees, sidestepping the fallen police barrier near me, and others, farther away. There was some kind of scuffle some two hundred yards down the street, again strangely noiseless, and a huddled knot of men opened up to reveal two brawlers being separated and pulled away from their fight. What I saw next gave me a fright: in the farther distance, beyond the listless crowd, the body of a lynched man dangling from a tree. The figure was slender, dressed from head to toe in black, reflecting no light. It soon resolved itself, however, into a less ominous thing: dark canvas sheeting on a construction scaffold, twirling in the wind.

## SIX

My attending NMS, the Nigerian Military School in Zaria, was my father's idea. It was a distinguished institution, its admissions policy was not preferential toward the children of soldiers, and it was famed for producing disciplined teenagers. Discipline: the word had the force of a mantra among Nigerian parents, and my father, who had no military background himself, who indeed had a strong distaste for formalized violence, was taken in by it. The idea was that, in six years, a wayward ten-year-old would be made into a man, a man with all the coolness and strength the word *soldier* implied.

I had no objection to going. King's College was more prestigious academically, but it would have been too close to home, and that would have suited neither me nor my parents and, in any case, going as far north as Zaria promised its own freedoms. It must have been in July 1986 that my parents drove me up for the one-week interview. I had never been in Northern Nigeria before, and its broad, desertified territory, with small trees and parched shrubs, might as well have been another continent, so different was it from the chaos of Lagos. But it was also part of one single country, across which the same red dust blew, all the way from Yorubaland up into the Hausa Caliphate.

Our cohort for interview week consisted of 150 boys. They came from all over the country, and almost none had been away from home before. Walking in the dry grass of the school's compound one day with two other boys, I saw a black mamba. The snake looked at us for a moment, then swiftly vanished into the undergrowth. One of my companions was so immediately deranged by fear that he'd begun to weep. He swore he would never return and ended up going to a day school in Ibadan, where his family lived. It was for the best; he would never have survived Zaria, where poisonous snakes were the least of our worries.

I was admitted, and I sent in my registration details. In September, my parents drove me up again. On this second drive, sitting in the backseat, I recall wrestling with myself about my unexamined loyalty to my father, and my growing antipathy toward my mother. They had made a kind of peace with each other over some rift that had been hidden from me, but I nursed the hurt on my father's behalf. My mother, during their conflict, had become cold, frighteningly so, not just to my father but to almost everyone in her environment. Then she got over it, and moved on. She became, once again, interested in the Nigeria around her, the country she loved but to which she could never belong. When my father passed away, a couple of years later, the vague sense of pique I'd developed during their fight became something harder, though I never, as far as I can now remember, actually blamed my mother for his death.

NMS was a turning point: the new schedule, the deprivations, the making and breaking of school yard friendships and, above all, the endless lessons in where one stood in the hierarchy. We were all boys, but some boys were men; they had natural authority, were athletic, or intelligent, or from rich families. No one thing was enough, but it became clear that we were not all equal. It was a strange new life.

In February of my third year, my father was diagnosed with tuberculosis, and by April he was dead. Our relatives, my father's relatives in particular, were hysterical, too present, too eager to help and demonstrate their grief, but my mother and I countered them with stoicism. This must have baffled people. But they did not know that our stoicism was disunited, my mother and I saying little to each other, our glances full of dark rooms. Only once did I interrupt that silence. I told my mother that I wanted to see my father, but not the body in the morgue. I was asking to have him restored to me and to life, pretending to an innocence that, at fourteen, I no longer had. Julius, she said, what is the meaning of this? It seemed to her a cruelty, this obvious pretense, and her heart was doubly broken.

The name Julius linked me to another place and was, with my passport and my skin color, one of the intensifiers of my sense of being different, of being set apart, in Nigeria. I had a Yoruba middle name, Olatubosun, which I never used. That name surprised me a little each time I saw it on my passport or birth certificate, like something that belonged to someone else but had been long held in my keeping. Being Julius in everyday life thus confirmed me in my not being fully Nigerian. I don't know what my father had hoped for in naming his son after his wife; she must have disliked the idea, as she disliked anything that came from sentimentality. Her own name must have been taken from somewhere in her family line, too, a grandmother, perhaps, or some distant aunt, a forgotten Julianna, an unknown Julia or Julietta. She had in her early twenties extricated herself from Germany and run off to the United States; Julianna Müller had become Julianne Miller.

Her bright yellow hair had already, by that April of my father's death, begun to show traces of gray. She'd taken to wearing a scarf, which was usually pulled back, so that her shiny forehead and the first inch or so of her hair were visible. She was wearing the scarf the afternoon she decided to take me with her into her memories. None of our many helpers was around that day, none of the aunts and friends who were making food for us and taking care of the house. We were in the living room together, the two of us. I had been reading a book, and she'd come in and sat down and begun to talk, in an abstracted but unhurried way, about Germany. Her voice, I remember, had had the tone of someone continuing a story, as though we had been interrupted and she were simply picking up a dropped thread. When she said "Julianna" and "Julia," with no concession to English pronunciations, she suddenly seemed even stranger to me. I felt, at that moment, the anger leaving my body, and I saw this woman with her graying hair and gray-blue eyes, and a faraway voice which, because it could not talk about the death that had just shattered us, had begun to describe long-ago things.

I had nothing to put in the place of my fading anger. I had no feeling for the stories she was telling or the longing behind them. I struggled to concentrate. Mother spoke about Magdeburg, about her girlhood there, things I had had only the shadowiest idea about, things that she now moved hesitantly into lighter shadow. Because I wasn't attentive, many of the details eluded me. Was I distracted because I was embarrassed? Or was it simple surprise at this sudden willingness of hers to lay the past bare? As she spoke, she would smile slightly at one memory, frown slightly at another. There was a mention of harvesting blueberries, another of an upright piano that refused to stay tuned. But, the idylls done with, it became a story of suffering: the suffering of her childhood years, when there had been little money and no father. Her father wasn't to return to home from his elongated war until the early fifties, when the Soviets finally released him, a broken and withdrawn man. He lived less than a decade after that. But Mother's story was about a deeper hurt and, as she told it, she grew in confidence, addressing not the teenage child before her but, as it seems to me now, an imaginary confessor.

She had been born in Berlin, only a few days after the Russians had taken over the city, in early May 1945. She had no memory, of course, of the months that followed. She couldn't have known the absolute destitution, the begging and wandering with her mother through the rubble of Brandenburg and Saxony. But she had retained the memory of having been aware of this hard beginning: not the memory of the suffering itself but the memory of knowing that it was what she had been born into. The poverty of life in Magdeburg, when they had finally returned there, had been intensified by the horrors each relative, neighbor, and friend had endured during the war. The rule was to refrain from speaking: nothing of the bombings, nothing of the murders and countless betrayals, nothing of those who had enthusiastically participated in all of it. It was only years later, when I became interested in these things for my own sake, that I surmised that my oma, heavily pregnant, had likely been one of the countless women raped by the men of the Red Army that year in Berlin, that so extensive and thorough was that particular atrocity, she could hardly have escaped it.

It was unimaginable that this was something she and my mother had ever discussed, but Mother herself would have known, or guessed it. She'd been born into an unspeakably bitter world, a world without sanctity. It was natural, decades later, losing a husband, for her to displace the grief of widowhood onto that primal grief, and make of the two pains a continuity. I listened with only half an ear, embarrassed by the trembling and the emotion. I couldn't see why she was telling me about her girlhood, about pianos and blueberries. Years later, long after we became estranged, I tried to imagine the details of that life. It was an entire vanished world of people, experiences, sensations, desires, a world that, in some odd way, I was the unaware continuation of.

That day at home was the last time, as far as I remember, that my mother and I had had anything like an intimate conversation. The afternoon was time taken out of time. After it, silence enfolded us once more, an easier silence, which allowed us to each experience our particular grief. But it became a bad silence again, and with the passing months turned into the rift that wouldn't heal.

AFTER MY FATHER'S BURIAL, I WAS KEEN TO RETURN TO SCHOOL. I did not play the helpless orphan, had no time for it. A surprising number of my classmates had been through the same thing, losing parents to illness or accidents. One good friend had lost his dad in the executions that followed the failed military coup of 1976. He never spoke about it, but he wore it as a sort of badge of honor. What I wanted for myself that year was some sense of belonging, and loss paradoxically helped enrich that sense. I threw myself into the military training, the classes, the physical workouts, the rhythms of prep and manual labor (cutting grass with cutlasses, doing duties on the school's maize farms). Not that I liked labor for its own sake—far from it—but I found something true in the work, found something of myself in it. Then that seriousness, in which I was accruing some sort of manly virtue, was interrupted by an incident that seemed needlessly tragic at the time, but that became comic from the point of view of passing years.

It had begun at the mess hall after lunch one day, after we had been dismissed for siesta. As usual, I had gone back to the dormitory. Ahead were the two hours of mid-afternoon tranquillity to which I had become accustomed. During my first year, I had passed them restlessly, not understanding why anyone would choose to sleep in the afternoon, but by year three they had become welcome still points intervening in the intensity of the school days. We slept on our bunks, without mosquito nets. Juniors who chatted or refused to sleep were disciplined as necessary, and a boy who thought siesta time was ideal for masturbation was quickly put in his place with a thwack of the house prefect's stick. Everyone learned to sleep when sleep was ordered. But that afternoon, a commotion forced me out of bed well before the two hours were over. I heard a voice shouting my family name, and I jumped out of my bunk. The person shouting my name was Musibau, a second-class warrant officer. He was our music teacher, and he lived in private quarters among the dorms.

He grabbed me by the collar, and dragged me to the middle of the wide hall. He was crazed by some anger that I scrambled to identify. Nothing came to mind; as far as I could recall, it had been an ordinary week. A crowd had gathered. Musibau was slight of figure; most of the senior boys were bigger than he was and, at fourteen, I matched him for height and build. He was famous for his rage, and we called him Hitler behind his back. Why had he ended up teaching music to children? He must have once been attached to the Nigerian Army Band Corps. Ell King, he would say, it is a leader by France Shuba. His classes never involved any listening to music, or the use of instruments, and our musical education was composed of memorized facts: Handel's birth date, Bach's birth date, the titles of Schubert lieder, the notes of the chromatic scale. Beyond a vague sense of the correct answers to put down on exams, none of us had any idea what a chromatic scale actually was or what it sounded like.

Bloody civilian, he said. You stole my paper, you lying maggot. There were low whistles around the room as Musibau's open palm resounded off the back of my head. I stood in mute confusion. Several dozen eyes watched my every move, and the terror of the situation dawned on me. But when Musibau said, in his affronted voice, that he had heard, that he had been *informed*, that I was the one who had stolen his newspaper from the mess hall, the tightness in my chest vanished. It was a case of mistaken identity. All would turn out for the best.

Just then, our house prefect arrived, fresh from a raid of my possessions, holding the newspaper aloft. He had found it next to my bag, under my bunk. It wasn't a plant: I had placed it there. I had glanced at it, found nothing of interest in it, and dropped it under my bed. Under the glare of an interrogation, with my collar violently chafing my neck, in Musibau's grip, and a sudden sense of isolation, I connected, for the first time, this alleged theft with my own actions. When lunch had ended that afternoon, I had seen a discarded copy of the *Daily Concord* on a bench, and brought it back to the house with me. There was the error. My conscience clouded, and I began to beg and to explain, until another slap silenced me.

Musibau frog-marched me to each of the neighboring houses, and in each the house prefect roused his charges, and Musibau, his clawlike hand again welded to my collar, began his recitation: thief, maggot, newspaper, bloody civilian. The senior boys joked and sniggered. The juniors were more solemn but equally seized by the spectacle. This is what happens to rich little thieves, Musibau said, his anger settling into a pattern, these are the rich little maggots who swallow our country whole, see with your eyes how they are. We went around to each of the six houses, my hands clasped behind me, my legs on the edge of collapse, and eventually every boy in school was introduced to me, the little thief. But they would have seen, too, Musibau's bitterness; a lieutenant headed the arts department, a colonel ran the school, a council of generals ruled the country. In this hierarchy, Musibau was both secure and utterly lost. He was no longer young; he would probably die a second-class warrant officer. He looked at me, a half-Nigerian, a foreigner, and what he saw was swimming lessons, summer trips to London, domestic staff; and thus, his anger. But his imagination misled him.

My ordeal that afternoon ended, and I went back to my dormitory. I changed into a clean uniform, shined my boots, straightened my beret, and got ready for evening prep. The following morning, while I was in technical drawing class, Musibau reappeared. He had a quick word with my teacher, then invited me to the front of the class. He stood without a word for a moment, facing the boys. Then he rehearsed his litany, refined now to a minimalist statement of indictment: This boy is a thief. He stole a newspaper, a newspaper that rightfully belonged to a member of staff. He is a disgrace to the Federal Republic of Nigeria, and to the armed forces of the Federal Republic of Nigeria, and to the Nigerian Military School. He did not think of the consequences, and will now be punished.

Musibau motioned to me to undo the metal side fastener on my shorts. I bared my buttocks and bent over, using the blackboard for support. He caned me. It took effort, and he sweated from the exertion, methodically bringing the cane down on me. I flinched but held back tears as the welts rose in quick, sharp lines. I had assumed he would stop at six, but he only paused at six, and then continued, all the way to twelve. My classmates were silent. I was a popular boy, and they were genuinely sorry for me. I pulled my shorts back on. Sitting was difficult; my entire body burned. The technical drawing teacher continued his lecture without comment.

When that semester ended and I went home, I could say nothing about any of this to my mother. If I hadn't forced myself back into the normal life of the school, I might have sunk. I learned not to be angry when the senior boys called me Daily Concord. The junior boys didn't say anything to my face. I won some dignities back and, in fact, my performance under the cane became a little legend of its own. In some iterations, it was twenty-four strokes across the back; in others, blood had flowed freely, and I had told Musibau to go hang himself. I gained a reputation for fearlessness and, coincidentally or not, I also began to do well academically. By the fourth year, I was popular with the girls at some other schools in the town, and had developed a somewhat callous self-confidence. In my final year at NMS, I was named health prefect. Some of my mates said that, had it not been for the incident with Musibau, I might even have made head boy.

The end of my time at the school coincided with the end of my time in Nigeria. My mother knew I was taking the SAT, but she didn't know about my applications to colleges in America; my purchase of a post office box helped perfect the concealment. I used up my few savings on college application fees. I had no luck with Brooklyn College, Haverford, or Bard (names I had plucked out of a tattered volume at the library of the United States Information Service in Lagos). I got into Macalester, but was offered no money; but Maxwell accepted me, and gave me a full scholarship. My course had been charted. With borrowed money from my uncles, I bought a ticket to New York to begin life in the new country, fully on my own terms.

# SEVEN

Winter deepened without becoming appreciably colder. I had decided definitively to use up all my vacation time, which came to a little over three weeks, on a trip to Brussels. The days I had accumulated were too many to make a hotel, or even a hostel, a reasonable option, and so I went online, and found a short-term flat rental in a central district of the city. The apartment, as pictured, was rudimentary to the point of being spartan; it was, as such, ideal for my purposes. I exchanged a few emails with a woman named Mayken, and once the matter of housing was settled, I bought a ticket for departure the following weekend.

On the flight, I was seated next to an elderly lady. She was older than my mother, but perhaps not old enough to be my grandmother. We had taken our seats in silence, and her voice, when it first reached me, did so out of darkness. My eyes were closed: I was relieved to have ended the long day of preparing for the journey, having worked overnight the previous night. I was in a fatigued blur all through the process of packing my bags, taking the subway to Kennedy Airport, confronting the disorder of holiday crowds, and controlling my anger at the inept boarding agents at Terminal Three. Finally, settling into my seat on the plane, I leaned back for a nap even before the other passengers had stowed their luggage or taken their seats.

Normally, I would have been curious about the person in the seat next to mine, a curiosity that was almost always disappointed. I would soon afterward find myself eager to get the small talk done with and, the absence of mutual interests firmly established, to return to the book I was reading. On this occasion, though, I was already asleep when my flight partner arrived. I had a sleeping mask on, and it was only when we were aloft, and I heard the jangle of the approaching refreshment cart, that I revived and took the mask off. I didn't open my eyes right away; I was trying to decide whether to interrupt my sleep for airline food, and was poised on the indecision. That was when I heard her voice, the measured voice of an elderly woman. I envy people like you, she said. I wish I was the kind of person who had the ability to fall asleep in any situation.

What I saw when I opened my eyes was a person with a head of gray hair, hair so thin it was as though the very substance of it, and not merely the color, were fading away. The face underneath this fragile crown was narrow and wrinkled, and the skin was covered in fine liver spots. But there was a firmness around the mouth and jaw, a prominence in the forehead, and a sharpness in the eyes. Undoubtedly, for most of her life, she had been a great beauty. The first thing she did, as I put my sleeping mask away, was wink, which took me aback, but to which I responded with a smile. She was dressed simply, in a tan-colored wool sweater, plaid pants, and brown leather boating shoes. She wore a double string of tiny pearls, and had on pearl earrings. The book on her lap, bookmarked with her index finger, was *The Year of Magical Thinking*. I hadn't read the book, but I knew it was Joan Didion's memoir of coming to terms with the sudden loss of her husband. Dr. Maillotte (she didn't actually tell me her name until an hour or so later) wore a wedding ring.

I usually have great difficulty sleeping in noisy environments, I said, so it's fair to say I envy such people, too. She brightened and said, Well, sometimes it's an absolute necessity. By the way, do you prefer English or French? I recalled that the announcements on the intercom were already in three languages, as we flew over Long Island; I told her my French was poor. She asked where I was from. Oh, Nigeria, she said, Nigeria, Nigeria. Well, I know a great many Nigerians, and I really should tell you this, many of them are arrogant. I was struck by her manner of talking, the unapologetic directness of it, the risk of alienating the person she was talking to. She was at an age, I supposed, at which she had long ceased to care what other people thought. This directness could certainly be taken in the wrong way if it came from a younger person, but there was no such risk in this case.

Ghanaians, on the other hand, Dr. Maillotte went on, are much calmer, easier to work with. They don't have such a big concept of their place in the world. Well, I suppose it's true, I said, we are a bit aggressive, but I think the reason is that we like to get ahead, make our presence felt. We think of ourselves as the Japanese of Africa, without the technological brilliance. She laughed. She put her book away, and when the dinner cart came by, we both selected the fish option on the menu—microwaved salmon, potatoes, dry bread—and ate in silence. Then I asked what she did. I'm a surgeon, she said, retired now, but I did gastrointestinal surgery in Philadelphia for the last forty-five years. I told her about my residency, and she mentioned the name of a psychiatrist. Well, he used to be there, maybe he's gone now. This is all so long ago, anyway. Did you have any rotations at Harlem Hospital? I shook my head and told her I'd gone to medical school outside the state. I only mention it because I consulted there a few times recently, she said, I'm retired, but I wanted to participate in a voluntary thing, so I've been in Harlem. I was a little unfair earlier, she added, I should say the Nigerian residents are excellent. Oh, don't worry about it, I said, I've heard much worse. But tell me, there aren't many American residents at Harlem Hospital, are there? Oh, they have a few, but yes, a lot of Africans, Indians, Filipinos, and really, it's a good environment. Some of these foreign graduates are a lot better trained than people who went through the American system; for one thing, they tend to have outstanding diagnostic skills.

Her diction was precise, and the accent only vaguely European. She told me that she had done her training in Louvain. But you must be a Catholic to be a professor there, she said with a chuckle. Not so easy for an atheist like me: I've always been one, I'll always be one. Anyway, it's better than Université Libre de Bruxelles, where no one can achieve anything professionally without being a Mason. I'm serious: it was founded by Masons, and it's still a kind of Masonic mafia. But I like Brussels, it is still home, after all these years. It has its advantages. For one thing, it's color-blind in a way the U.S. is not. I have been spending three months each year there since I retired. I have an apartment, yes, but I prefer to stay with my friends. They have a big house, it's in the southern part of the city, in Uccle. Where will you be staying? Ah, right, well it's not far from there, you just go south from Parc Léopold, and that's the neighborhood. If you had a map, I would show you.

Then, as if the talk of Brussels had gently pushed a door in her memory ajar, she said: Belgium was stupid during the war. The Second World War, I mean, not the First, I was born much too late for the First. That was my father's war. But I was just about to enter my teens during the Second World War, and these damned Germans, I remember them coming into the city. The blame really is on Leopold III; he made the wrong alliances or, I should say, he refused to make alliances, he thought it would be easy to defend the country. He was an old fool. There was a canal from Antwerp to Maastricht, you see, and a line of concrete fortifications, and this was supposed to be the perfect defense, this line. The idea was that the water would be too difficult to bring a large army across. Of course, the Germans had planes and paratroopers! All it took was eighteen days, and the Nazis marched in, and stayed, like parasites. The day they finally left, the day the war ended for Belgium, was the happiest day of my life. I was fifteen, and I remember that day perfectly, I will never forget that day as long as I live, and I'll never be happier than I was that day. And here she paused, extended her hand, and said, I suppose I should introduce myself. Annette Maillotte.

Then she went on, falling deeper, it seemed, into her memory, telling me about her days as a young girl, how difficult things had been during the war, how Leopold III had bargained with Hitler for better rations, the devastation of the countryside afterward, when straggling figures covered the landscape and went from house to house begging for food and shelter, her decision to go into medicine, then her subsequent training in surgery, which was unusual for women at the time. Somehow, as she spoke, I could still see in her that resolute girl.

You must have been determined, I said. Well, no, no, you don't think of it like that, she said, you just find what you must do, and you do it. There's really no opportunity to stop and praise yourself, so I won't say determined. I nodded. Listening to her, I felt as if the objective fact of her age—if she was fifteen when the war ended, it meant she had been born in 1929—stood in an indirect relationship with the fact of her mental and physical vitality. At that moment, the flight attendants came to take our trays away, and Dr. Maillotte took up her book again. I lowered the light above my seat and, closing my eyes, imagined the frigid nighttime Atlantic racing by below us.

Although I was tired, I managed to sleep only fitfully, and woke again after a few hours, with a sore neck. Dr. Maillotte must have slept as well, but by the time I woke, she was again reading. I asked her how the book was. Yes, it's good, she said, nodding, and went back to reading. I signaled that I had to go to the bathroom and apologized for disturbing her. She stood up in the aisle, and was still standing when I came back. I have to keep the circulation moving, she said, especially important when you're as old as I am. When we sat down again, she said: Do you know Heliopolis? It's in Egypt, just outside Cairo. Helio-Polis, it means city of the sun, sun city. Well, I told you I was going to stay with a friend of mine in Brussels. His name is Grégoire Empain, and we've been friends since we were young, maybe when we were both twenty, and it was his grandfather who built Heliopolis.

If you ever get a chance to go there, you should. It's a fantastical place, and Édouard Empain, or Baron Empain as they call him, was the engineer who designed and built it. That was in 1907. It was a real luxury capital, broad avenues, big gardens. There's a building there called Qasr Al-Baron, the Baron's Palace, that was modeled on Angkor Wat in Cambodia and also on a Hindu temple, a specific one, but I don't recall the name. And you know, this is now the most important suburb of Cairo; in fact it's within the city boundaries now. The president of Egypt lives there today. But the Empains are in a tussle with the Egyptian government, because part of Heliopolis belongs to them, and they are trying to claim it, or at least get compensated for it. The family is still wealthy, anyway, one of the wealthiest in Belgium. Baron Empain was a great industrialist—not just Heliopolis, he built the Paris Métro as well, when the Belgians wouldn't let him build one in Brussels—and his son was an industrialist also. The grandson Grégoire is modest, he doesn't like to be in the limelight. But Grégoire has a brother, Jean, and he's a different story.

I used to be crazy about skiing, and my husband, too, all my children—and we went to Mont Blanc with Grégoire, Jean, their sisters, and we skiied at Chamonix, at Megève. Not Negev, like in Israel, but Megève, close to Mont Blanc in the Swiss Alps. And the Empains had this large chalet there, and all sorts of people showed up, you know, Jean-Claude Aaron, Edmond de Rothschild of the

French Rothschilds. And this always amuses me to think of it, but once the queen of Sweden came, and the poor thing, she came with her husband and, you know, I don't think she had any idea the man was a complete faggot. It was obvious to everyone, but she was oblivious, and they just carried on. Anyway, we went, but it wasn't because these people were there, it was just good skiing. And I needed to get away from America from time to time, this terrible, hypocritical country, this sanctimonious country. I really can't stand it sometimes. Do you know what I mean?

But let me tell you about Grégoire's brother, Jean. He is not as quiet as Grégoire, quite the opposite: he likes to do deals, to jet-set. He's the one who inherited the title. He's Baron Empain now, and sports cars, royal families, billionaire friends, that's his kind of thing. But poor fellow, you know, he was in all the papers in the late seventies. I think it was in 1978 that he was kidnapped, you see, and held for two months. Grégoire, the whole family, they were of course frantic. The kidnappers were French, and demanded something like eight or nine million dollars, a ridiculous amount of money, but not impossible for the Empains. The family was willing to pay. But there had been a lot of kidnappings at the time, all through the seventies, and the French government had a strict policy of no negotiations, no payments. So these kidnappers, I think one of them was called Duchâteau—it is funny that I remember that, but you have to understand, we were following this story so intensely day after day in the newspapers—what Duchâteau and his mates said was: Money brings liberty. I mean, it's ridiculous, they sound like philosophers, but they really meant it, and when the money was not forthcoming, they sliced off Jean's little finger and put it in an envelope and mailed it to his wife. They cut it off with a kitchen knife, without anesthetic, and threatened to amputate additional fingers for each day of delay with the payment. But the negotiators refused, and somehow, the kidnappers didn't follow through on their threat. Eventually, the po-

lice were able to ambush them, and they killed one of them, and captured the other two, and Jean was released.

I tell you, that was two months of hell for the family. And
Duchâteau, the kidnapper, had written somewhere: These are tiny
little slips of paper, but they mean everything, money brings liberty.
If you see Jean now, there's a little knob where that finger used to be.
But the worst, if you ask him, was not that amputation, it was the
cold. I think he was terribly cold for the two months; they made him
sleep in a tent in an unheated room. And light deprivation, so he
wouldn't recognize his captors. Cold and dark. For these tiny little
slips of paper, right?

It was morning. We were flying with a bank of clouds above us
and a bank of clouds below, and Europe was close. I asked Dr. Maillotte to tell me more about her children. They are all doctors, she
said, all three of them, like my husband and me. I think it's what they
wanted, but who knows? My eldest, well, he was thirty-six last year
when he died. He had just finished his residency in radiology. Cancer of the liver, and a quick decline. It's an impossible thing to go
through, watching a son die. He was married, and had a three-year-
old daughter. It was impossible; it still is. The other two: one is in
California, one is in New York. They are the younger ones. And my
husband is with me in Philadelphia, well, we're just outside Philadelphia, and he's a cardiologist, and he just retired, too.

A silence fell on us. And you, she said, tell me, why Brussels? It's a
strange place for a vacation in winter! I smiled. Cozumel was the
other possibility, I said, but I don't know how to dive. Well, she said,
here's the number at Grégoire's. Friendly people, you know, they
don't put on airs. I'll be there for six, maybe eight, weeks. You should
come around and have dinner with us. I thanked her for the invitation and told her I would consider it. And, as I looked at the number she had written down for me, I thought about the Paris Métro,
that expression of optimism and progress, and about the ancient city

in Egypt that had also been known as Heliopolis, before Baron Empain built his version, and of underground travel, we millions moving around underneath cities, inhabitants of an age in which, for the first time, traveling great distances beneath the earth had become normal for humans. I thought, too, about the numberless dead, in forgotten cities, necropoli, catacombs. The pilot announced the final approach for landing, in English, French, and Flemish, and as we broke through the lower bank of clouds, I saw the city spread across the low landscape.

# EIGHT

ayken, the woman who owned the Brussels apartment, had offered to pick me up from the airport for an additional fee of fifteen euros. The other options, she had told me on the phone, were to take a taxi for thirty-five euros, or to take public transportation and risk being robbed. And so, when I arrived on the overnight flight, she was waiting in the arrivals lounge with a sign that had my name on it. Her bleached hair sat on her head like yellow cotton candy, and looked likely to lift and sail away if caught in the wind. I bid goodbye to Dr. Maillotte, and walked over, waving until Mayken spotted me. She was in her fifties, friendly, but with a sharp business manner that, as we later went over the short-term lease papers—pages and pages of picayune legal detail—became, with her bouffant hair, the only visible part of her personality.

The original idea of Brussels, she said, as we drove out of the airport, was that it should be equally Flemish and Walloon. Of course, it's not that way anymore, she went on, now it is ninety-five percent

Walloon and other French speakers, one percent Flemish, and four percent Arab and African. She laughed, but quickly added: These are real numbers. And the French are lazy, she said, they hate working and are envious of the Flemish. I'll tell you this in case you don't hear it from anyone else.

I looked outside the window, and in my mind's eye, I began to rove into the landscape, recalling my overnight conversation with Dr. Maillotte. I saw her at fifteen, in September 1944, sitting on a rampart in the Brussels sun, delirious with happiness at the invaders' retreat. I saw Junichiro Saito on the same day, aged thirty-one or thirty-two, unhappy, in internment, in an arid room in a fenced compound in Idaho, far away from his books. Out there on that day, also, were all four of my own grandparents: the Nigerians, the Germans. Three were by now gone, for sure. But what of the fourth, my oma? I saw them all, even the ones I had never seen in real life, saw all of them in the middle of that day in September sixty-two years ago, with their eyes open as if shut, mercifully seeing nothing of the brutal half century ahead and, better yet, hardly anything at all of all that was happening in their world, the corpse-filled cities, camps, beaches, and fields, the unspeakable worldwide disorder of that very moment.

Mayken's English was slightly inflected with wavering Dutch vowels. I looked out on both sides of the speeding car, and the Brussels of my experience came back to me. It was my third visit to the city, but the previous ones had been brief, the first having been more than twenty years before, during a two-day layover on the way to the United States from Nigeria when I was seven. At the time, my mother had said nothing about her mother, though my oma had moved there by then. The details of that journey were buried in my memory until I saw the Novotel Hotel near the airport, where the airline had put us up. How ideal it had all seemed back then: the black Mercedes-Benzes that were used as taxicabs at the airport, the strange food at the hotel buffet. It was a glimpse of impressive sophistication and wealth, that first experience of Europe. Outside the hotel, I had noticed the order and grayness, the modesty and regularity of the houses, and the cool formality of the people, against which American life, my first real contact with which came a few weeks later, had seemed lurid.

It is easy to have the wrong idea about Brussels. One thinks of it as a technocrats' city, and because it was so central to the formation of the European Union, the assumption is that it is a new city, built, or at least expanded, expressly for that purpose. Brussels is old—a peculiar European oldness, which is manifested in stone—and that antiquity is present in most of its streets and neighborhoods. The houses, bridges, and cathedrals of Brussels had been spared the horrors visited on the low farmland and forests of Belgium, which had borne the brunt of the countless wars fought on the territory. Slaughter and destruction, ferocious to a degree rarely experienced in history, had taken place on the Somme, in Ypres, and before that, out at Waterloo.

Those were the theaters, so conveniently set at the intersection of Holland, Germany, England, and France, in which Europe's fatal tussles had played out. But there had been no firebombing of Bruges, or Ghent, or Brussels. Surrender, of course, played a role in this form of survival, as did negotiation with invading powers. Had Brussels's rulers not opted to declare it an open city and thereby exempt it from bombardment during the Second World War, it might have been reduced to rubble. It might have been another Dresden. As it was, it had remained a vision of the medieval and baroque periods, a vista interrupted only by the architectural monstrosities erected all over town by Leopold II in the late nineteenth century.

During my visit, the mild winter weather and the old stones lay a melancholy siege on the city. It was, in some ways, like a city in waiting, or one under glass, with somber trams and buses. There were many people, many more than I had seen in other European cities, who gave the impression of having just arrived from a sun-suffused elsewhere. I saw old women with dotted black patterns around their eyes, their heads swaddled in black cloth, and young women, too, likewise veiled. Islam, in its conservative form, was on constant view, though it was not clear to me why this should be so: Belgium had not had a strong colonial relationship with any country in North Africa. But this was the European reality now, in which borders were flexible. There was a palpable psychological pressure in the city.

I'm sure Mayken's "four percent Arab and African" was intended to be snide, but from what I saw, it might have been a modest estimate. Even in the city center, or especially there, large numbers of people seemed to be from some part of Africa, either from the Congo or from the Maghreb. On some trams, as I was to quickly discover, whites were a tiny minority. But that was not the case with the morose crowd I met on the metro some days after my arrival. They had been to a rally at the Atomium to protest racism and violence in general, but in particular a murder that had happened much earlier, in April of that year. A seventeen-year-old, after refusing to give up his MP3 player, had been stabbed by two other youths at the Gare Centrale; this had happened on a crowded platform, during rush hour, with dozens of people around; the fact that no one had done anything to help the boy had become a point of discussion in the days following the murder. The murdered boy was Flemish; the murderers, reports said, were Arab. Fearful of racial backlash, the prime minister had appealed for calm, and in his homily that Sunday, the bishop of the city had bemoaned a society so indifferent that everyone around had refused to help a dying boy. Where were you at 4:30 P.M. that day? he had said to the crowded congregation at the Cathédrale des Saints Michel et Gudule.

The bishop's hand-wringing had gotten a swift and impassioned response from the Vlaams Belang (the Flemish right-wing party) and its sympathizers. Well-known columnists took a wounded tone and complained of reverse racism. The victims were being blamed, they said; the problem was not with uncaring passersby but with the foreigners who committed crimes. It was easier to get flagged for violating biking rules than for actually stealing a bike, because the police were afraid of being seen as racist. One journalist wrote on his blog that Belgian society was fed up with "murdering, thieving, raping Vikings from North Africa." This was quoted approvingly in certain mainstream sources. Efforts by the Muslim community in Brussels to heal the wound, such as their distribution of home-baked bread at the public memorial service for the murdered boy, drew a furious response from right-wingers. Later, during the elections, the politicians of the Vlaams Belang recorded gains once again, consolidating their position as possibly the biggest party in the country. Only the coalitions of the other groups kept them out of power. But the murderers in the Gare Centrale case, it turned out, weren't Arab or African at all: they were Polish citizens. There was some debate about whether they were Roma, gypsies. One of them, a sixteen-year-old, was arrested in Poland; his seventeen-year-old partner was arrested in Belgium and extradited to Poland, and with his departure, some of the tensions around the case dissipated.

But there were other ugly incidents. I was there at the very end of 2006, a year in which several hate crimes had ratcheted up the tension experienced by nonwhites living in the country. In Bruges, five skinheads put a black Frenchman into a coma. In Antwerp, in May, an eighteen-year-old shaved his head and, after fulminating about *makakken,* headed for the city center with a Winchester rifle, and started shooting. He seriously injured a Turkish girl and killed a nanny from Mali, as well as the Flemish infant in her care. Later on, he expressed a specific regret: for having accidentally shot the white child. In Brussels, a black man was left paralyzed and blind after an attack at a petrol station. The paradoxical result of these crimes was that even politically centrist parties like the Christian Democrats began to lean rightward, adopting the language of the Vlaams Belang in order to cater to voter discontent about immigration. The country was in the grip of uncertainties—the sense of anomie was apparent even to a visitor.

I went to the Parc du Cinquantenaire. It was covered in fog, but this made the scale of the monuments seem even bigger. The already gigantic arcades shot up vertiginously and lost their heads in faint white veils, and the rows of trees before and beyond them, rigid as sentries, stretched into eternity. The park, built by a heartless king, was also of inhuman scale. A handful of tourists, so dwarfed by the monuments that, from a distance, they looked like toys, roamed around silently, taking photographs. When they came closer, I heard them speaking Chinese.

It was half past four, night fast falling, and the air was misty and cold; the area just southeast of the park looked out into Etterbeek and the Mérode metro station, a complex assortment of roads, tram tracks, and signs, but few people were about on Christmas Eve. In the park, right in front of the Musées Royaux d'Art et d'Histoire, which I had initially taken for the better known Musées Royaux des Beaux-Arts, a broad-headed horse stood by a carriage marked POLITIE, but there were no police officers in sight, and the museum was closed. Under the arcade was a bronze plaque displaying in relief the portraits of the first five Belgian kings: Leopold I, Leopold II, Albert I, Leopold III, and Baudouin, and beneath it an inscription that read: HOMMAGE A LA DYNASTIE LA BELGIQUE ET LE CONGO, RECONNAISSANTS, MDCCCXXXI. Not triumph, then, but gratitude; or gratitude for triumphs achieved. I stood under the arcade and watched the Chinese family enter their car. They drove away, leaving just me and the patient horse. We were the two living animals in that place, and with every breath cold fog entered our lungs. I was there, it seemed to me, to no purpose, unless being together in the same country, as I and my oma now were (if, that is, she were still alive), was, by itself, a comfort.

IN THOSE FIRST FEW DAYS IN BRUSSELS, I MADE SOME DESUL-
tory efforts to find her. I had little idea of where to begin. The list-
ings gave no help: there was no Magdalena Müller in the phone book
in the apartment, or in another one I consulted in a phone booth. I
briefly considered visiting nursing homes; and I felt, suddenly, an ir-
rational shame at speaking French badly and Flemish not at all. A
five-minute walk from my Brussels apartment was an Internet and
telephone shop, located on the ground floor of a narrow building. I
visited it in the hope of doing some online searches.

The shop contained a row of glass-fronted wooden booths for
phone calls and a half dozen computers. The man behind the
counter must have been in his early thirties. He was clean-shaven,
with a lean, pleasant face and lank black hair. He pointed me to a
computer terminal near the back. I found the Belgian white pages
quickly. The site came up, to my surprise, in English, and I quickly
entered the search terms: Magdalena Müller. The results listed many
people named Magdalena M., many others listed as M. Müller, and
two hits with Magdalena Müller, but both with hyphenated last
names.

I shut the site down and went back up to the counter. I commu-
nicated with the man in broken French, paying for the service, which
had come to fifty centimes for the twenty-five minutes of Internet
use.

I WENT INTO THE SHOP THE FOLLOWING DAY, TO CHECK EMAIL,
and paid when I was done. But this time, as I left, I surprised him
by asking for his name, in English. Farouq, he said. I introduced myself, shaking his hand, and added: How are you doing, my brother?
Good, he said, with a quick, puzzled smile. As I stepped out onto the

street, I wondered how this aggressive familiarity had struck him. I wondered, also, why I had said it. A false note, I decided. But soon after I changed my mind. I would be going into the shop for a few weeks, and it was best to make friends; and that interaction, as it turned out, set the tone the following day.

The shop was busy. Farouq, reading a book at the counter, paused to attend to the people coming in or leaving. Customers sat at all the computer terminals, and I could hear the conversations taking place in the wooden booths. I called my father's sister, my aunt Tinu, in Lagos, and friends in Ohio. I also called the hospital in New York to approve and renew some prescriptions. V.'s was among them: she'd been on Paxil and Wellbutrin, but neither was working, and I had recently started her on tricyclics. I gave the necessary permissions to the head nurse, who told me that V. had wanted to know how I could be reached. I can't be reached, I said, have her call Dr. Kim, the resident covering for me. Then, feeling the vigor of ticking things off my list, I also called Human Resources to check up on some paperwork having to do with my vacation time; I was told the department had closed early and wouldn't be open again until the third of January. I came out of the booth annoyed at this and waited until Farouq was done attending to another customer. He looked at his computer log and then at me and said, United States? Yes, that's right, I said, and you, where are you from? Morocco, he said. Rabat? Casablanca? No, Tétouan. It's a town in the north. That's it in the picture behind me.

He pointed at an old color photograph in a metal frame of a broad cluster of white buildings and, behind them, massive green mountains. I said, I just finished a novel by a Moroccan writer, Tahar Ben Jelloun. Yes, I know him, Farouq said, he has a big reputation. He was about to say more, but just then, another customer came up to pay for his computer use and, as he did the reckoning, collecting payment and giving out change, I caught, belatedly, the note of disapproval in his "big reputation." I saw that the book Farouq had been reading was in English. He noticed my curiosity and turned it around. It was a secondary text on Walter Benjamin's *On the Concept of History*. It's difficult reading, he said, requires a lot of concentration. Not much of that here, I said. Another customer came up, and again Farouq flipped seamlessly into French, and back again into English. He said: It's about how this man, Walter Benjamin, conceives of history in a way that is opposed to Marx though, for many people, he is a Marxist philosopher. But Tahar Ben Jelloun, as I was saying, he writes out of a certain idea of Morocco. It isn't the life of people that Ben Jelloun writes about but stories that have an oriental element in them. His writing is mythmaking. It isn't connected to people's real lives.

I nodded as he spoke, and I tried to align the drab Brussels neighborhood, the hum of petty business, the boxes of gaudily wrapped sweets and chewing gum on the wall shelf with the smiling, serious-faced thinker sitting in front of me. What had I expected? Not this. A man who works in a shop, yes, a man who works in a shop that's open on Christmas Day, sure. But not this: the crisp, self-certain intellectual language. I greatly admired Tahar Ben Jelloun for his flexible and tough-minded storytelling, but I did not contradict Farouq's statement. I was too surprised for that and only offered, weakly, the idea that perhaps Ben Jelloun did capture the rhythm of everyday life in his novel *Corruption*. The book was about a government functionary and his inner struggle with bribe taking: What could be closer to everyday life than that? Farouq's English came out in a succession of lucid sentences as he put my protest down. I couldn't follow his argument. He wasn't saying that Ben Jelloun pandered to Western publishers, exactly, but he was suggesting that the social function of his fiction was suspect. But when I seized on that idea, he shook it off, too, and only said: There are other writers whose work is connected with everyday life and with the history of the people. And this doesn't mean they have any connection to nationalist ideals. Sometimes, they even suffer more at the hands of nationalists.

So I asked him to recommend something different to me, some-thing more in keeping with his idea of authentic fiction. Farouq solemnly took a scrap of paper from the desk and wrote out, in a slow and jagged cursive: "Mohamed Choukri—*For Bread Alone*—translated by Paul Bowles." He studied the scrap for a moment, then said: Choukri is a rival to Tahar Ben Jelloun. They have had disagree-ments. You see, people like Ben Jelloun have the life of a writer in exile, and this gives them a certain—here Farouq paused, struggling to find the right word—it gives them a certain *poeticity*, can I say this, in the eyes of the West. To be a writer in exile is a great thing. But what is exile now, when everyone goes and comes freely? Choukri stayed in Morocco, he lived with his people. What I like best about him is that he was an autodidact, if it is correct to use this word. He was raised on the street and he taught himself to write classical Ara-bic, but he never left the street.

Farouq spoke without the faintest air of agitation. I didn't quite grasp all the distinctions he was making, but I was impressed with the subtlety in them. He had the passion of youth, but his clarity was unfussy and seemed to belong (this was the image that came to me) to someone who had undertaken long journeys. This calmness of his put me off balance. Finally, I said: It is always a difficult thing, isn't it? I mean resisting the orientalizing impulse. For those who don't, who will publish them? Which Western publisher wants a Moroccan or Indian writer who isn't into oriental fantasy, or who doesn't satisfy the longing for fantasy? That's what Morocco and India are there for, after all, to be oriental.

This is why Said means so much to me, he said. You see, Said was young when he heard that statement made by Golda Meir, that there are no Palestinian people, and when he heard this, he became in-volved in the Palestinian question. He knew then that difference is never accepted. You are different, okay, but that difference is never seen as containing its own value. Difference as orientalist entertain-ment is allowed, but difference with its own intrinsic value, no. You can wait forever, and no one will give you that value. Let me tell you something that happened to me in class.

Farouq opened the register. I wished the customers would stop interrupting us. For a moment, too, I thought I should correct his slightly inaccurate quotation of Meir. But I was unsure of my ground, and he continued as though there had been no interruption at all. A question was asked, he said, during a discussion of political philosophy. We were supposed to choose between Malcolm X and Martin Luther King, and I was the only person who chose Malcolm X. Everyone in class was in disagreement with me, and they said, Oh, you chose him because he is a Muslim and you are a Muslim. Yes, fine, I am a Muslim, but that is not why. I chose him because I agree with him, philosophically, and I disagree with Martin Luther King. Malcolm X recognized that difference contains its own value, and that the struggle must be to advance that value. Martin Luther King is admired by everyone, he wants everyone to join together, but this idea that you should let them hit you on the other side of your face, this makes no sense to me.

It's a Christian idea, I said. He was a churchman, you see, his principles came from the Christian concept. That is it exactly, Farouq said. This is not an idea I can accept. There's always the expectation that the victimized Other is the one that covers the distance, that has the noble ideas; I disagree with this expectation. It's an expectation that works sometimes, I said, but only if your enemy is not a psychopath. You need an enemy with a capacity for shame. I wonder sometimes how far Gandhi would have gotten if the British had been more brutal. If they had been willing to kill masses of protesters. Dignified refusal can only take you so far. Ask the Congolese.

Farouq laughed. I looked at my watch, though I really had nowhere to go. The victimized Other: how strange, I thought, that he used an expression like that in a casual conversation. And yet, when he said it, it had a far deeper resonance than it would have in any academic situation. It occurred to me, at the same time, that our conversation had happened without the usual small talk. He was still just a man in a shop. He was a student, too, or had been one, but of what? Here he was, as anonymous as Marx in London. To Mayken and to countless others like her in this city, he would be just another Arab, subject to a quick suspicious glance on the tram. And of me, he knew nothing either, only that I had made phone calls to the United States and to Nigeria, and that I had been into his shop three times in five days. The biographical details had been irrelevant to our encounter. I extended my hand and said, I hope we can continue this conversation soon, peace. I hope so too, he said, peace.

Thinking back to Mayken's assertions, I had been wrong, I decided. What Farouq got on the trams wasn't a quick suspicious glance. It was a simmering, barely contained fear. The classic anti-immigrant view, which saw them as enemies competing for scarce resources, was converging with a renewed fear of Islam. When Jan van Eyck depicted himself in a large red turban in the 1430s, he had testified to the multiculturalism of fifteenth-century Ghent, that the stranger was nothing unusual. Turks, Arabs, Russians: all had been part of the visual vocabulary of the time. But the stranger had remained strange, and had become a foil for new discontents. It occurred to me, too, that I was in a situation not so radically different from Farouq's. My presentation—the dark, unsmiling, solitary stranger—made me a target for the inchoate rage of the defenders of Vlaanderen. I could, in the wrong place, be taken for a rapist or "Viking." But the bearers of the rage could never know how cheap it was. They were insensitive to how common, and how futile, was their violence in the name of a monolithic identity. This ignorance was a trait angry young men, as well as their old, politically powerful rhetorical champions, shared the world over. And so, after that conversation, as a precaution, I cut down on the length of my late-night walks in Etterbeek. I resolved, also, to no longer visit all-white bars or family restaurants in the quieter neighborhoods.

I hoped, on my next visit to the shop, to talk to Farouq about the

Vlaams Belang, and what life had been like in the wake of all the acts of violence. But on the day I next went there, he was in conversation with someone else, an older Moroccan man, who seemed to be in his mid-forties. I nodded to both of them in greeting, and went into one of the phone booths, and placed a call to New York. When I came out they were still talking. The older man rang up my charges, and Farouq said, My friend, my friend, how are you doing? But it suddenly occurred to me that, even if he had been alone, I wouldn't have wanted to talk. He, too, was in the grip of rage and rhetoric. I saw that, attractive though his side of the political spectrum was. A cancerous violence had eaten into every political idea, had taken over the ideas themselves, and for so many, all that mattered was the willingness to do something. Action led to action, free of any moorings, and the way to be someone, the way to catch the attention of the young and recruit them to one's cause, was to be enraged. It seemed as if the only way this lure of violence could be avoided was by having no causes, by being magnificently isolated from all loyalties. But was that not an ethical lapse graver than rage itself?

One euro exactly, the older man said, in English. I paid, and left the shop.

# NINE

The days went by slowly, and my sense of being entirely alone in the city intensified. Most days I stayed indoors, reading, but I read without pleasure. On the occasions when I went out, I wandered aimlessly in the parks and in the museum district. The stones paving the streets were sodden, liquid underfoot, and the sky, dirty for days, was redolent with moisture.

I went to a café in Grand Sablon one afternoon, sometime after the lunch hour. I was one of only two customers, the city being rather quiet in the week between Christmas and New Year's Day. The other person in the café was a middle-aged tourist who, I noticed when I came in, was scrutinizing a map. In the small interior, which was lit by the diffuse light from outside, she looked pallid, and her gray hair caught the light with a dull shine. The café was old, or had been done up to look old, with darkly polished wood lining its walls and several oil paintings in tarnished gold-leaf frames. The paintings were marine scenes, choppy seas on which quartermasters and merchant ships listed perilously. The seas and skies were without a doubt much darker than they were when they had been painted, and the once-white sails had yellowed with age.

The tall girl who brought my coffee had a Parisian rather than Bruxelloise affect. She set the coffee down and, to my surprise, she herself sat for a moment at my table, and asked where I was from. She was about twenty-two or twenty-five, I guessed, with heavy-lidded eyes and a winning smile. I was flattered by the approach, and by her obvious interest in me; she was undoubtedly used to having a strong and immediate effect on men. But, flattered as I was, I was uninterested, and my responses to her were polite and even a little curt, and when she stood up again, with her tray, it was less with displeasure than with puzzlement.

Some fifteen minutes later, I paid the man at the counter. At the same time, the pallid tourist had come up to settle her bill. She spoke halting English with an Eastern European intonation. When we both stepped outside, into the by now heavy rain, and stood under the café's awning, I saw that she was more blond than gray, with heavy circles around her eyes, and a kind smile. I had an umbrella, and she didn't. There was a quiet friendliness in her manner; there was, perhaps, expectation. I turned to her and asked if she was Polish. No, she said. Czech.

By fifty, which is what I estimated her age to be, a woman's appearance often requires effort. For someone the age of the waitress, someone in her twenties, to be even a little good looking was enough. At that age, everything else falls into accord: skin is taut, stature straight, gait sure, hair healthy, voice clear and unwavering. By fifty, there is a struggle. And for these reasons, the afternoon was a surprise—a surprise for the tourist, at the clearly expressed, if largely wordless, interest she began to pick up from me, and surprise for me, too, at her large gray-green eyes, their sad intelligence, their intense and entirely unanticipated sexual allure. The afternoon had taken on the character of a dream, a dream that now extended to her

hand touching my back lightly, for a moment, as I moved the umbrella so that it covered her fully. We stood there for a moment and
watched the rain continue to come down in sheets. Then we walked
together a little way along the little cobblestone streets, up the busy
rue de la Régence, hardly speaking, using the shared umbrella as a
pretext as far as we could take it. But when she suggested a drink at
her hotel, the ambiguous touch on the back had given way to clarity,
and my resolve became correspondingly strong. I would take the
folly, I said to myself, as my heart raced, just as far as she was willing
to go with it. And clarity gave us both courage. I followed her up, my
eyes set on the hemline of her gray skirt, which was guillotined at the
calf.

In the faux Louis XV bedroom, her shyness dissolved. She embraced me, and the embrace became a kiss on the cheek. I kissed her
neck—long, a surprise—and her forehead, topped by that mane of
hers, which had become mostly gray again in interior light, then, finally, her mouth. Her waist was thick, pliant; she went down on her
knees, quickly, and sighed. I pulled her back up, shaking my head.
Then we both went down together, by the side of the Baroque bed,
both pushed up against its satin shams, and I pulled the linen skirt
upward to her waist.

Afterward, she told me her name—Marta? Esther? I forgot it
immediately—and explained, with some difficulty, that she handled
the travel bookings for the Constitutional Court in Brno. She had a
grown daughter who was a ski instructor in Switzerland. She said
nothing about a husband, and I didn't ask. I introduced myself as
Jeff, an accountant from New York; the unimaginative falsehood felt
seedy, but it also had a comedy that I appreciated, and was resigned
to appreciating alone. Then we drew back the sheets on the unrum-
pled bed, and slept. By the time we woke up, two or three hours later,
night had fallen. Wordlessly, I got dressed, but this time the silence
was wreathed with smiles. I kissed her on the neck again, and left.

The lights in the park had come on, and the rain had stopped.

People were out in pairs, in families, heading to performances or to restaurants. I felt light and grateful. Rarely had I seen Brussels looking so generous. A wind rustled the leaves, and I wondered if I would remember her face; it was unlikely that I would. But she had made the whole thing easy for me, my first since Nadège, and something needful that I'd neglected to do. Now it was done, and I couldn't have wished it different. Best of all, I decided, had been her pleasure; we were simply two people far away from home, doing what two people wanted to do. To my lightness and gratitude was added a faint sorrow. It was a few miles back to Etterbeek, and walking there, I returned to my solitude. This cannot happen again, I had wanted to say to her; but I found that it was not quite what I meant to say, and that nothing really needed saying. I returned to the apartment, and the following day I didn't go out. I remained in bed and read Barthes's *Camera Lucida*. Later in the afternoon, Mayken came round, and I gave her money.

The following evening, or the one after that, I found the scrap of paper on which Dr. Maillotte had written her phone number, and this spurred me to go to the phone shop. Farouq wasn't there. The older fellow, solemn, with sallow skin, was working at the desk. He had a brush mustache and bulbous eyes. I nodded to him, and went into a phone booth. A man answered the phone on the other end, but when I spoke in English, he called Dr. Maillotte.

She came to the phone and said, Hello, who is this? Oh, yes, how are you, but I am sorry, tell me how we know each other again. I reminded her. Ah, yes, of course. You are in Belgium for a month, three weeks? When do you leave? Ah, so soon. I see. Well, why don't you call me on Monday, and we can go out for dinner or something, before you leave the country.

When I replaced the handset, and went out to pay, Farouq had arrived and the solemn man was chatting with him. Farouq saw me. My friend, he said, how are you? He insisted that I not pay for the call, which in any case had been brief and local. The colleague went away, and a customer came in. Farouq greeted her, *Ça va? Alhamdulíl-lah*, the woman replied. Farouq turned to me and said, It's very busy, as you can see. Not only for all the people making New Year greetings but also for a lot of people calling home for the Eid. He gestured to the computer monitor behind him, and on it was a log of the calls ongoing in all twelve booths: Colombia, Egypt, Senegal, Brazil, France, Germany. It looked like fiction, that such a small group of people really could be making calls to such a wide spectrum of places. It's been like this for the past two days, Farouq said, and this is one of the things I enjoy about working here. It's a test case of what I believe; people can live together but still keep their own values intact. Seeing this crowd of individuals from different places, it appeals to the human side of me, and the intellectual side of me.

I used to work as a janitor, he said, at an American school in Brussels. It was the foreign campus of a university in the States, and for them I was just the janitor, you see, the man who cleaned the classrooms when their classes were finished. And I was nice, quiet, like a janitor should be; I pretended not to have any ideas of my own. But one day, I was cleaning one of the offices, and the principal of the school, the head of academics, came around, and somehow we got talking, and I just had this idea to really speak as myself, not as a janitor, but as someone with ideas. So I started talking, and I used a bit of my jargon. I was talking about Gilles Deleuze and, of course, he was surprised. But he was open, and I went on, and we discussed Deleuze's concept of waves and dunes, about how it is the spaces between those forms, the necessary spaces, that gives them their definitions as waves or dunes. The principal was completely responsive to this conversation, and in this generous American way, he said, Come to my office sometime and we'll talk more.

When Farouq said this, I imagined the man's tone of voice. It was like an arm around the shoulder, a disarming gesture, a promise of complicity: Come to my office sometime, let us engage with each other. But, Farouq said, continuing his story, when I saw him next, he not only refused to speak to me but actually pretended he had never seen me before. I was just the janitor, mopping the floor, nothing more than a part of the furniture. I greeted him, tried for a moment to remind him of our Deleuze conversation, but he said nothing. There was a line, and I was wasting my time in the attempt to cross it. As Farouq spoke, people went in and out of the booths rapidly, and he greeted each person, the level of familiarity determined, I guessed, by how often they'd come into the shop before. He spoke French, Arabic, English, as was appropriate; with the man who had been calling Colombia, he exchanged a few words of Spanish. His judgment of the right language to use with each person was swift, and his manner so friendly that I wondered why I had had the impression, when I first met him, that he was distant.

I have two projects, Farouq said. There is the practical one, and there's a deeper one. I asked if the practical one was his job at the shop. No, he said, not even that; the practical thing, for the long term, is my studies. I'm studying to be a translator between Arabic, English, and French, and I'm also doing some courses in media translation and subtitles for films, this kind of thing. That's how I will find a job. But my deeper project is about what I said last time, the difference thing. I strongly believe this, that people can live together, and I want to understand how that can happen. It happens here, on this small scale, in this shop, and I want to understand how it can happen on a bigger scale. But as I told you, I'm an autodidact, so I don't know what form this other project will take.

I asked him if he thought he could be a writer, and he said that even that was unclear to him. He would study first, he said, and come to an understanding, and only then decide what form his action would take. I was struck by the purity of the goal, its idealism and old-fashioned radicalism, and the certainty in the way he expressed it, as though it was something he had nurtured for many years; and I trusted it, in spite of myself. But I also thought about his reference to our previous conversation, when he said he had referred to himself as an autodidact. It was a minor thing, of course, but (and I was sure I wasn't misremembering) he had only used the word in reference to Mohamed Choukri, not to himself. This was a small instance, not of unreliability, but of a certain imperfection in Farouq's recall which, because of the absolute sureness of his manner, it was easy to miss. It in any case made me revise my previous impression of his sharpness, even if only modestly. These minor lapses—there were others, and they were irrelevant lapses, actually, not even worthy of the label *mistake*—made me feel less intimidated by him.

My experience at the American school, Farouq said, became combined in my mind with Fukuyama's idea of the end of history. It is impossible, and it is arrogant, to think that the present reality of Western countries is the culminating point of human history. The principal had been talking in all these terms—melting pot, salad bowl, multiculturalism—but I reject all these terms. I believe foremost in difference. Remember what I said about Malcolm X: this is what the Americans don't understand, that the Iraqis can never be happy with foreign rule. Even if Egypt invaded Palestine to save them from Israel, the Palestinians cannot accept this, they would not want Egyptian rule. No one likes foreign domination. Do you know how much Algeria and Morocco hate each other? So you can imagine how bad it is when it is a Western power doing the invasion. I believe that Benjamin can help me understand this better, and I believe that his subtle revisions of Marx can help me understand the historical structure that makes difference possible. But I believe, also, in the divine principle. There are those things that Islam can offer our thinking. Do you know Averroës? Not all Western thought comes from the West alone. Islam is not a religion; it is a way of life that has something to offer to our political system. I say all this not to make myself the representative of Islam. Actually, I am a bad Muslim, you see, but one day I will return to my practice. At the moment I don't practice very well.

He paused, and laughed, assessing my reaction to what he had been saying. I gave no indication of my thoughts. I only nodded, signaling that I was listening. Three or four customers had gathered around the desk and, with a smile, Farouq continued. The thing, though, is that I am a pacifist. I don't believe in violent compulsion. You know, even if someone is right here, with a gun pointed at my family, I cannot kill this person. I mean it, so don't look so surprised. But, my friend, he said, in a tone that indicated he was wrapping things up, let us meet the day after tomorrow. You're a man of philosophy, but you're an American also, and I want to talk to you more about some things. On Saturday, I get off work at six. Why don't you meet me across the street? That Portuguese place, Casa Botelho, right at that corner here—he pointed across the street—let us meet there on Saturday evening.

On Saturday, I went up the steep hill of the Chaussée d'Ixelles all the way to Porte de Namur, and from there I cut across the throng of weekend shoppers to Avenue Louise, and then on to the Royal Palace. Every now and again, looking into the faces of the women huddled at the tram stops, I imagined that one of them might be my oma. It was a possibility that had come to me each time I was out in the city, that I might see her, that I might be tracing paths she had followed for years, that she might indeed be one of the old women with their orthopedic shoes and crinkly shopping bags, wondering from time to time how her only daughter's only son was doing. But I could recognize the nostalgic wish-fulfillment fantasy at work. I had almost nothing to go on, and my search, if my poor effort could be called by that term, became insubstantial and expressed itself only as the faint memory of the day she had visited Olumo Rock with us in Nigeria, and had wordlessly massaged my shoulder. It was in these thoughts that I began to wonder if Brussels hadn't

somehow drawn me to itself for reasons more opaque than I suspected, that the paths I mindlessly followed through the city followed a logic irrelevant to my family history.

The weather had become drizzly again, but as a fine mist, not
rain. I had not taken an umbrella, so I went to the Musées Royaux
des Beaux-Arts, but once I was inside, I found that I was not at all in
the mood to look at paintings. I stepped outside again, into the mist.
From then on, I simply wandered aimlessly, through the Egmont
Park and its morose gallery of bronze statues, then down to Grand
Sablon, with its antiques dealers who hovered with suspicious
glances over their worthless old coins, past the little café I'd visited
before, having a quick glance in to see if my tall waitress was there
(she wasn't), and from there down to Place de la Chapelle. The
cathedral there was like the streaked hull of a sunken ship, and the
few people around it were tiny and drab, like midges. The sky, already gloomy, had quickly begun to darken. There was an Indian
restaurant I had seen in the area once, and I thought I should find it
and eat there. When I had walked by before, I had noticed a menu
board that included Goan fish curry, and I started craving that dish;
but I simply ended up lost, tramping around in an area of derelict
government housing in which not a single wall was free of graffiti.
My wool coat was sodden by this time. Because there was no metro
in the immediate vicinity, I walked back to Porte de Namur and took
a bus from there down to Philippe. I hurried to my apartment and
changed out of the soaked coat, then went out immediately again to
meet Farouq at Casa Botelho.

Three men sat playing cards in a corner of the café. Their dowdy
clothes, the slow deliberation of their movements, and the clutter of
bottles on the table cumulatively created an exact Cézannesque
tableau. It was accurate even down to the detail of one man's thick
mustache, which I could swear I had already seen on a canvas at the
Museum of Modern Art. The room was busy, but as I came in I saw
Farouq at a table farther inside, near the window. He raised a hand,

and smiled. There was a man sitting there with him and, as I approached, they both stood up. Julius, Farouq said, I want you to meet Khalil. He's one of my friends, in fact I can say he's my best friend. Khalil, this is Julius: he is more than a customer. I shook hands with them and we sat. They were already drinking—both of them had bottles of Chimay beer—and were also smoking. Behind Khalil, and just visible in the nicotine haze, was a sign warning that smoking was not permitted in the restaurant. It was a new law; it had come into effect just a few days before, with the new year, and no one, neither management nor customers, seemed to have any interest in enforcing it. The waitress, with whom they both appeared to be familiar, came to take my order. She speaks English, Khalil said in English, but I don't. We laughed, but it was true: that was the most fluent English he would speak to me. I ordered a Chimay.

Khalil, round-faced and talkative, interrogated me in French. He asked about where I was from; I responded in English. He wanted to know what I was doing in Brussels; I gave him a version of the truth about that. This man just got married, Farouq said. I congratulated him, and asked Farouq if he was married. They both laughed, and he shook his head and said, Not yet. Khalil said something to me that sounded like: America is a great country that is not a great country. I asked him to speak a bit more slowly, because my French was only a little bit better than his English. Does America really have a left? he said. Khalil is a Marxist, you see, Farouq said, in a gently mocking tone. Yes, I said, America has a left, an active one. Khalil looked genuinely surprised. The left there, he said, must be further to the right than the right here. Farouq had to translate this for me, because Khalil had spoken too quickly for me to catch. Not exactly, I said, the issues are emphasized differently. There are the Democrats, who share the political power, but there is also a genuine left, who would probably agree with you on many things. What are the important issues there? Khalil asked. What do left and right disagree on? As I began to answer him, as I enumerated the divisive issues, I felt faintly embarrassed at how tawdry they were: abortion, homosexuality, gun control—Khalil looked confused by that last term, and Farouq said *des armes.* Immigration's also an issue, I said, though not in the same way as in Europe. Well, Khalil said, what about Palestine? I think your Democrats and Republicans are united on that issue.

The waitress, whose name was Paulina, finally brought my beer, and we raised our glasses. The beer went down easily, and I felt myself set into a new, pleasant keel by it. I said, it's not so simple. There's a strong leftist support for Palestinian causes in the United States. Many of my friends in New York, for example, think that Israel is doing terrible things in the Occupied Territories. But in practical terms, in terms of our government, well, the support for Israel is pretty solid in both parties. I think it has to do with religion, because the Christians walk in step with Jewish ideas about Jerusalem to a large extent, but it also has to do with the strong Israel lobby. At least that's what the left-leaning magazines and journals say. And then there's also the perception that we share elements of our culture and government with Israel.

This is the strange thing, Farouq said. They say that Israel is democratic, but it's actually a religious state. It functions on a religious idea. He translated this into French for Khalil, who nodded in agreement. They were both chain-smoking. Pack a day? I said. For me, two packs, Khalil said. But wait, this interests me, he added, this obsession with communitarianism in the United States. I asked Farouq what the word meant, whether it was something like identity politics, but he said no, it wasn't that, exactly. Khalil started speaking about communitarianism, about how it gave unfair leverage to minority interests, about how it was logically flawed. White is a race, he said, black is a race, but Spanish is a language. Christianity is a religion, Islam is a religion, but Jewishness is an ethnicity. It makes no sense. Sunni is a religion, Shiite is a religion, Kurd is a tribe, you see? He continued in this vein for a few minutes, and I lost the thread of his argument, but I didn't ask Farouq to translate. I drank my beer.

Khalil was quite exercised by the subject. It was easier to nod once in a while and make a show of following him.

I was getting hungry, and when Paulina came around again I ordered a salad and some grilled ribs. Khalil seemed to have gotten the communitarianism thing off his chest. Let me ask you something, he said, with mischief in his eye. The American blacks—he used the English expression—are they really as they are shown on MTV: the rapping, the hip-hop dance, the women? Because that's all we see here. Is it like this? Well, I said slowly and in English, let me respond this way: Many Americans assume that European Muslims are covered from head to toe if they are women, or that they wear a full beard if they are men, and that they are only interested in protesting perceived insults to Islam. The man on the street—do you understand this expression?—the ordinary American probably does not imagine that Muslims in Europe sit in cafés drinking beer, smoking Marlboros, and discussing political philosophy. In the same way, American blacks are like any other Americans; they are like any other people. They hold the same kinds of jobs, they live in normal houses, they send their children to school. Many of them are poor, that is true, for reasons of history, and many of them do like hip-hop and devote their lives to it, but it's also true that some of them are engineers, university professors, lawyers, and generals. Even the last two secretaries of state have been black.

They are victims of the same portrayals as we are, Farouq said. Khalil agreed with him. The same portrayal, I said, but that's how power is, the one who has the power controls the portrayal. They nodded. My food arrived, and I invited them to join me. They both picked at the fries without protestation, and they ordered more beer.

If we talk of portrayal, Khalil said, Saddam is the least of the dictators in the Middle East. The least. I turned to Farouq to make sure I understood what he was saying. It's true, Farouq said, I also think Saddam was the most moderate. They killed him only because he defied the Americans. But in my opinion he should be admired because he stood up for the right of his country against imperialism. I don't see it that way at all, I said. The man was a butcher, and you know that. He killed thousands. Farouq shook his head and said, How many thousands more have died under the Americans now? Saddam was convicted of killing only 148, Khalil said. The king of Morocco is worse, I can tell you this; Gaddafi in Libya, Mubarak in Egypt, you can go all the way across like that—he made a sweeping motion with his hands—the whole region is full of dictators, and not only dictators, but terrible ones. And they remain in power because they sell the national interests of their countries to the Americans. We hate the king in Morocco, some of us really hate him. This man, when the communists were ascendant in the seventies, he appealed to Islamism; but when the Islamists started gaining political strength, he catered to capitalist and secularist factions. Thousands of people died under his rule, and thousands disappeared. How is this different from Saddam? But one thing I can tell you: I support Hamas. I think they are doing the work of resistance.

And Hezbollah, I said, you support them, too? Yes, he said, Hezbollah, Hamas, same thing. It is resistance, simple. Every Israeli home has weapons. I looked at Farouq. He looked at me levelly and said, It's the same for me. It is resistance. And what about Al-Qaeda? I said. Khalil said, True, it was a terrible day, the twin towers. Terrible. What they did was very bad. But I understand why they did it. This man is an extremist, I said, you hear me, Farouq? Your friend is an extremist. But I was pretending to an outrage greater than I actually felt. In the game, if it was a game, I was meant to be the outraged American, though what I felt was more sorrow and less anger. Anger, and the semiserious use of a word like *extremist,* was easier to handle than sorrow. This is how Americans think Arabs think, I said to them both. It really saddens me. And you, what about you, Farouq? Do you support Al-Qaeda, too?

He was quiet for a moment. He poured his beer, and drank, and for what seemed a few long seconds, we sat in silence. Then he said,

Let me tell you a story from our tradition, a story about King Solomon. King Solomon gave a teaching once about the snake and the bee. The snake, King Solomon said, defends itself by killing. But the bee defends itself by dying. You know how a bee dies after a sting? Like that. It dies to defend. So, each creature has a method that is suitable to its strength. I don't agree with what Al-Qaeda did, they use a method I would not use, so I cannot say the word *support*. But I don't cast judgment on them. As I said before, Julius, and I think you should understand this: in my opinion, the Palestinian question is the central question of our time.

Farouq's face—all of a sudden, it seemed, but I must have been subconsciously working on the problem—resolved itself, and I saw a startling resemblance: he was the very image of Robert De Niro, specifically in De Niro's role as the young Vito Corleone in *The Godfather II*. The straight, thin, black eyebrows, the rubbery expression, the smile that seemed a mask for skepticism or shyness, and the lean handsomeness, too. A famous Italian-American actor thirty years ago and an unknown Moroccan political philosopher in the present, but it was the same face. What a marvel that life repeated itself in these trivial ways, and it was something I noticed only because he hadn't shaved for a day or two, and had a shadow on his jaw and around his mouth. But once I saw it, it was impossible not to be incessantly drawn into the comparison, or be distracted by it, a meaningless visual counterpoint to whatever else was going on as we talked and drank.

What was the meaning of De Niro's smile? He, De Niro, smiled, but one had no idea what he was smiling about. Perhaps this is why, when I first met Farouq, I had been taken aback. I had subconsciously overinterpreted his smile, connecting his face to another's, reading it as a face to be liked but feared. I had read his face as that of the young De Niro, as a charming psychopath, for this most trivial of reasons. And it was this face, not as inscrutable as I had once feared, that spoke now: For us, America is a version of Al-Qaeda.

The statement was so general as to be without meaning. It had no power, and he said it without conviction. I did not need to contest it, and Khalil added nothing to it. "America is a version of Al-Qaeda." It floated up with the smoke, and died. It might have meant more, weeks back, when the one speaking was still an unknown quantity. Now he had overplayed his hand, and I sensed a shift in the argument, a shift in my favor.

And so, he changed tack. When we were young, he said, or I should say, when I was young, Europe was a dream. Not just a dream, it was the dream: it represented the freedom of thought. We wanted to come here, and exercise our minds in this free space. When I was doing my undergraduate degree in Rabat, I dreamed of Europe; we all did, my friends and I. Not America, about which we already had bad feelings, but Europe. But I have been disappointed. Europe only looks free. The dream was an apparition.

It's true, Khalil said, Europe is not free. The rhetoric claims freedom, but only the rhetoric. If you say anything about Israel, you have your mouth plugged with the six million. You're not denying it, I said, quickly, you're not actually questioning the figure, are you? That's not the point, Khalil said, the point is that it is against the law to deny it, and that it is also against an unwritten law to even bring it up in discussion. Farouq assented. If we try to speak to the Palestinian situation, we hear six million. The six million: it was a terrible tragedy, of course, six million, two million, one human being, it's never good. But what does this have to do with Palestinians? Is this Europe's idea of freedom?

He had not raised his voice, but the intensity of his words was palpable. Did the Palestinians build the concentration camps? he said. And what about the Armenians: do their deaths mean less because they are not Jews? What is the magic number for them? I'll tell you why the six million matter so much: it is because Jews are the chosen people. Forget the Cambodians, forget the American blacks, this is unique suffering. But I reject this idea. It is not a unique suffering. What about the twenty million under Stalin? It isn't better if you are killed for ideological reasons. Death is death, so, I'm sorry, the six million are not special. I am always frustrated that this number, this sacred number that cannot be discussed is used, like Khalil said, to put an end to all discussions. The Jews use it to silence the world. I really don't give a damn about the exact figure. All death is suffering. Others have suffered, too, and that is history: suffering.

Paulina came to clear the plates away, and we ordered another round of drinks. I asked Farouq if he cooked much for himself, or if he ate out. Neither, he said. The smoking kills my appetite, so I don't eat much. He smiled his De Niro smile and steered the conversation back. Have you read a man called Norman Finkelstein? I shook my head. Look him up if you have the chance; he is Jewish, but he has written a strong study of the Holocaust industry. And he knows what he is saying, because his own parents survived Auschwitz. He is not anti-Jewish, but he is against the profit making, and the exploitation that the Holocaust is used for. Do you want me to write the name down? You'll remember, you're sure? All right, read him, and tell me what you think.

A cellphone rang; it was Khalil's. He answered it, and spoke rapidly in Arabic. When he hung up, he said he had to leave. He and Farouq exchanged some words in Arabic, the first time they had done so in my presence. After he had gone, Farouq said, This is a good guy, you know. I can really say he is my best friend. He actually owns the phone shop, this one across the street, and several others in the city. So, he's my boss. But he doesn't believe in being boss, or acting like the boss. We are from the same town, Tétouan. He is so generous, you know; in fact, just now, as he was leaving, he went to the counter, and he just paid for everything, our drinks, your food. He's like that, he gives and doesn't think twice about it.

What I think is this, Farouq said, that Germany should be responsible for Israel. If anyone should bear the burden, it should be them, not the Palestinians. The Jews came to Palestine. Why? Be-

cause they lived there two thousand years ago? Let me give you
an example of what that is like. Khalil and I, we are Moroccans, we
are the Moors. We used to rule Spain. Now how would it be if we in-
vade the Spanish peninsula and say, Our forefathers used to rule here
in the Middle Ages, so it is our land: Spain, Portugal, all of it. It
makes no sense, does it? But Jews are a special case. Don't get me
wrong, I am not personally against Jews. There are many Jews in
Morocco, even today, and they are welcomed as part of the community. They look just like us, though, of course, they do better in business. I think sometimes that maybe I should become a Jew, just for
professional reasons. I'll be able to get everything done. What I am
against is Zionism, and this religious claim they make on a land
where someone else is already living.

I wanted to tell him that, in the States, we were particularly wary
of strong criticism of Israel because it could become anti-Semitic.
But I didn't, because I knew that my own fear of anti-Semitism, like
my fear of racism, had through long practice become prerational.
What I would impose on him would not be an argument, it would be
a request that he adopt my reflexes, or the pieties of a society different from the one in which he grew up, or the one in which he now
functioned. It would do little good to describe for him the subtle
shades of meaning evoked in an American ear by saying "Jews" instead of "Jewish people." I wanted also to take him to task for attack-
ing a religious ideal when his own central ideal was religious, but the
skein of argument was beginning to feel like futility piled on futility;
it was better to save my breath. So, instead, I asked him to tell me
about his family in Tétouan, and what life was like growing up there.
The café had by this time become quieter, and the cardplayers had
gone home. Even the rain seemed to have wound down for the night.
A few customers remained, like us, drinking, talking. When Paulina
came to our table again, she asked if I wanted more of the same, but
I thanked her and said I had had enough. Farouq ordered another
bottle for himself.

I am the third of eight children, he said, and my father was a soldier. It was a modest living for our family. If I am honest about it, it
was a very modest living. Soldiers were not paid much, and they did
not have a high status in the society. A hard man, my father, and he
was especially hard on me, because he thought I was not manly
enough; he's retired now. But things are even worse between me and
my eldest brother, who lives in Cologne and is very religious. Well,
my whole family is religious, and I'm actually the only one who has
drifted away; but my brother is too serious about religion. There's
him, my sister, then me, we are the first three. My brother thinks I'm
wasting my time on studies. He's a businessman, and that's what he
cares about. He doesn't understand why the studies are important to
me, he has no sense of an intellectual life, but it is more than misun-
derstanding it. He is hostile. I have a bad relationship with my father,
but it's much worse with my brother. My brother was married to a
German woman, but when he got his residency papers, he divorced
her, went back home, and brought over a Moroccan wife. Was that
the plan all along? I don't know. The man is a hypocrite.

I am closer to the rest of the family. Money difficulties prevent
me from visiting Morocco often, but I am close to my mother. She's
the most important person in my life, and I can bet yours is that important to you, too. It's just how mothers are. My mother is a little
worried about me; she wants me to get married, yes, but she's more
concerned that I stop smoking. Of course, she doesn't even know
that I drink. I write long letters to my younger brother, who is
twenty. This is one use of my studies: I don't tell my younger siblings
what to think, but I want to help them learn to think; I want them to
know that they can assess their own situations and come to their
own conclusions. I was the strange child, you see, I used to miss
classes so I could go elsewhere and read on my own. Taking classes
never taught me anything. Everything interesting was in the books; it
was books that made me aware of the variety of the world. This
is why I don't view America as monolithic. I'm not like Khalil in this

way. I know that there are different people there, with different ideas, I know about Finkelstein, about Noam Chomsky, and what is important to me is that the world realizes that we are not monolithic either, in what they call the Arab world, that we are all individuals. We disagree with each other. You just saw me in disagreement with my best friend. We are individuals.

I think you and America are ready for each other, I said. As we spoke, it was hard to escape a feeling that we were having a conversation before the twentieth century had begun or just as it had started to run its cruel course. We were suddenly back in the age of pamphlets, solidarity, travel by steamship, world congresses, and young men attending to the words of radicals. I thought of, decades later, Fela Kuti in Los Angeles, the individuals who had been formed and sharpened by their encounters with American freedom and American injustice who, by seeing the worst that America could do to its marginalized peoples, had had something in them awakened. Even at this belated date, in the antiterror regime, Farouq could still benefit from entering that inferno.

The moment had a naïve excitement about it, but if I were truly inviting him as a guest, I feared the logistics of such an invitation, were it to be accepted. But he quickly said, No, I don't like the place. I have no desire to visit America, and certainly not as an Arab, not now, not with all I would have to endure there. He had a look of distaste as he said it. I could have told him I had Arab friends, that they were fine, that his fears were baseless. But it would have been a lie. I, too, would not have wanted to visit the United States as a solitary North African Muslim with leftist beliefs.

There's a writer called Benedict Anderson, Farouq said, who wrote against the . . . what is this term, les Lumières? The Enlightenment? I said. That's it, Farouq said, the Enlightenment. Anderson talked about how it enthrones rationality but does not fill the gap left by religious faith. My view is that this gap should be filled by the

Divine, by the teachings of Islam. And I hold this as absolute and central even if I am not a good Muslim at the moment.

And what about Sharia? I said. I know that Sharia refers to more than its harshest punishments, so I can anticipate what you'll say. You'll say that it really is about the harmonious functioning of a society. But I do want to know what you think of these people who cut off hands, or stone women to death. The Qur'an is a text, Farouq said, but people forget that Islam also has a history. It is not static. There is the community as well, the Ummah. Not all interpretations are valid, but I'm proud of the fact that Islam is the most worldly religion there is. It concerns itself with the way we live in the world, with day-to-day life. You know the thing (and Farouq all of a sudden had a beatific look on his face, a look I hadn't seen on him hitherto), the thing is that I have a very deep love for the Prophet. I honestly love this man and the life he lived. A magazine did a poll recently: people voted for the most influential man in history. Do you know who was number one? Mohammed. Tell me, why was this?

But do you think you could live in Mecca or Medina? What happens to individual liberty in those places? If you moved to the central cities of Islamic faith, what would become of your cigarettes and your Chimay?

Mecca and Medina are special cases. Yes, I could live in the Holy Land. I would see it as a *paysage moralisé*. There's a spiritual energy in the topography, through which one can endure the physical limitations. I am drinking this now—he gestured to the bottle of beer—and I know that this is a choice I have made, and the consequence of this choice is that the wine of paradise will not be available to me. I am sure you know what Paul de Man says about insight and blindness. His theory has to do with an insight that can actually obscure other things, that can be a blindness. And the reverse, also, how what seems blind can open up possibilities. When I think about the insight that is a form of blindness, I think of rationality, of rationalism, which is blind to God and to the things that God can offer human beings. This is the failure of the Enlightenment.

And de Man, coincidentally, was a student in Brussels, at the same university I came to when I arrived from Morocco seven years ago. I had applied to do an M.A. in critical theory, because the department here was known for that. That was my dream, the way young people can have very precise dreams: I wanted to be the next Edward Said! And I was going to do it by studying comparative literature and using it as a basis for societal critique. I had to begin late, because my residency papers were being processed, and the university made me do all my course work in eight months, from January 2001 through August of that year. Then I wrote my thesis, which was on Gaston Bachelard's *Poetics of Space*.

The department rejected my thesis. On what grounds? Plagiarism. They gave no reason. They just said I would have to submit another one in twelve months. I was crushed. I left the school. Plagiarism? The only possibilities are either that they refused to believe my command of English and theory or, and I think this is even more likely, that they were punishing me for world events in which I had played no role. My thesis committee had met on September 20, 2001, and to them, with everything happening in the headlines, here was this Moroccan writing about difference and revelation. That was the year I lost all my illusions about Europe. Europe was supposed to be the perfect answer to the oppression by the king in Morocco. I was disappointed.

My foolish childhood dream was to have my Ph.D. at twenty-five. I finished my first degree in Rabat at twenty-one, and I knew my exact path. Well, I'm twenty-nine now. I transferred to the university in Liège, and I'm doing a part-time master's degree in translation. I commute there twice a week, sometimes three times, but, deep inside, I know that this is a course that has nothing to do with me. I am meant to be a scholar. I might apply for a doctorate, in translation. I want to write about Babel, about how the many languages came out of one—a religious idea, maybe, but I can do a scholarly study of it. It's not my first choice, but what can I do? The other door is closed now.

Farouq's eyes shone. The wound ran deep. How many would-be radicals, just like him, had been formed on just such a slight? It was time for us to leave. He had brought me too close to his pain, and I no longer saw him. In his place what I saw was the young Vito Corleone, who moved stealthily across the rooftops of Little Italy, making his way toward the house of the soon-to-be-usurped local godfather; this Vito whose will would carry him much further than he could imagine or desire, whose future would seem all out of proportion to that lithe young man who flowed swiftly from one low roof to another with only a single murderous action in mind.

Farouq drained his glass. There was something powerful about him, a seething intelligence, something that wanted to believe itself indomitable. But he was one of the thwarted ones. His script would stay in proportion.

# TEN

I was running across Lagos with my sister. We were doing a marathon, and having to push vagrants and street dogs out of our way. But I have no sister; I'm an only child. When I suddenly awoke, it was to total darkness. My eyes tried to adjust. From the warmth of the bed, the sound of traffic reached me. As always when one wakes up like this, it was impossible to tell the time. But a deeper terror immediately gripped me: I couldn't remember where I was. A warm bed, darkness, the sound of traffic. What country is this? What is this house, and who am I with? I reached out a hand; there was no one else in the bed. Was I alone because I had no partner, or because my partner was far away? I floated in the dark, anonymous to myself, lost in the sensation that the world existed but I was no longer part of it.

The first question that found its answer was about the partner: I had no partner, I was alone. The fact arrived, and it calmed me immediately. The distress had been in not knowing. Then other information came: I was in Brussels, Belgium, in a rented apartment, the apartment was on the ground floor of the building, and the rumble outside was from the garbage trucks. The trucks came on Fridays, before daybreak. I was someone, not a body without a being. I had slowly returned to myself from a distance. The effort of gathering this ballast for my identity, trivial-seeming ballast without which my heart might have given out, was exhausting. I fell back to dreamless sleep, and the trucks continued to rumble outside. When I finally woke up again, it was almost noon. The natural light that filled the room was diluted by rain. It was the seventh day of the rain, which had been nagging, trickling, falling without biblical grandeur. But its longevity reminded me of the only other rain I could recall that had lasted for days. There must have been others, but only that solitary incident stood out now in memory. I was nine at the time, so it was the year before I was sent away to boarding school.

That day had started with clear weather, hot, like any in the endless blur of hot days normal to us in all months of the year. I had come home from school at two, had lunch, and taken a nap, which was unusual for me. When I woke up, my mother had gone out, to the market, or to the bank. My father would not return from work for a few hours yet, and only my mama, my father's mother, was home. Her room was at the back of the ground floor of the house, in the section behind the kitchen, in the same part of the house where the study was. I went to see her, but she was still asleep. The electricity was out. If it hadn't been, I might have watched some television. I wasn't permitted to do so on school days, and the only things of interest on the weekends were the sports review shows: English soccer on Saturday evenings and the Italian league on Sundays. So the television rule was one I broke casually when my mother happened to be out on a weekday afternoon. Mama was hard of hearing. If she was downstairs, I could tell her I was going up to do my homework and easily watch two hours of television until the horn of my mother's car sounded at the gate. With the power cut, TV was out of the question and I was at a loss. I wandered back downstairs, to the kitchen, and opened the fridge. It didn't hum and no light came on. The bottles inside were beginning to sweat: the boiled water we drank, the fermented *ogi* for breakfast, the Coca-Cola and other minerals kept there in case we had guests.

The minerals were for parties and special events. When other families with their children came to visit, we served them, and the children always tussled over who got to drink Fanta—the most desired—or 7-Up or, at the bottom of the hierarchy, Coca-Cola. It was an absurd ranking. Some children believed Coke would make them darker, just as they believed that eating amala would make them darker. The younger ones would cry if the Fanta had all been taken and they were left with Coke. As a "half-caste," I had no conception of what it would mean to be darker; it was the least of my worries. And as an only child, I had formed my tastes simply, on the basis of what appealed to me. I liked Coke because nothing else tasted like it. The fizziness in the other drinks was never as convincing, and Fanta was too sickly sweet. But in our house, as with all good things in childhood, Coke was a controlled substance. I could no sooner just take a bottle of Coke out of the fridge than open up my father's whiskey cabinet. And so the temptation came at me on that hot day: I wanted a Coke. I didn't stamp my feet, or clench my fists: no one was present to view a petulant display. Mama was asleep and, in any case, she didn't have the say-so over the Cokes. I pushed the fridge door back and forth on its hinge.

Only my mother could give permission. I could wait for her return, but my desire was nothing rational; it would have been like asking her for permission to add my clothes to the washerman's pile instead of washing them myself. She would have looked at me, puzzled, and told me that I was no longer a child, and that I should think about how fortunate I was compared to other children. By the time I asked, I would have become embarrassed at the infantile nature of the request; her pretense at surprise would be unbearable for a proud boy like me. But these rules were all my father's. He had clear ideas about how not to spoil a child. The enforcement, though, had fallen to my mother, and if I resented the rules—which I only rarely did, as they were the only conception I had of childhood—if on rare occasions I ever resented the rules, I did so on my mother's account, and never took into consideration my father's part in it. In this way, I created a kind of innocence for him in my mind. But gradually, the dream of escaping these parental rules crystallized in my mind as the ideal of adulthood. There was no starting point for the rebellion, but I could mark an arbitrary one: that a grown-up was someone who, first and foremost, could drink a Coke at whim. And so, I shut the door of the fridge, and reopened it. I took out one of the clammy bottles and placed it in the sink with an unintentionally loud clink (Mama's room was next door).

I put the Coke back into the fridge and went outside. It was darker and cooler, and the clouds were starting to move. I swore that I would never forget the intensity of what I was feeling at that moment. I solemnly promised myself, electrified by the self-consciousness of oath taking, that, once I became an adult, I would drink Coke with impunity. In my imagination, this drinking took place in our kitchen: I saw a bigger version of myself walking casually up to the fridge and opening it. This grown-up self of mine takes a cool moment to think about what he wants, and he wants a Coke, always. He pulls it out, opens it with a bottle opener, and pours the hissing contents into a glass full of ice. This older me, this adult, does this once every day. Every blessed day: the thought of such frequency almost drove me mad with excitement. My heart raced at the thought of such a vengeance, and I longed to be done, there and then, with childhood. Still, I could not break the rule. I walked to the back of the house.

I removed the steel plate covering the well, and peered inside. It was more than ninety feet to the waterline. Were the spirits still there? The well diggers had given them alcoholic drinks, which my father had paid for. Had the spirits been merely placated, or had they been banished? It was too far a drop for the surface of the water to be visible. I looked hard and saw nothing, so I took a stone, holding it over the center, and I let it fall. It hit the side of the well with a flat sound, and then retorted with a splash. I thought perhaps I should go upstairs and do my long division. I took a larger stone and threw it, hard. It ricocheted several times until the invisible water gulped it loudly. I took off my rubber slippers and sat on the edge of the well, at first with my feet on the outside, then, one at a time, on the inside, so that both legs dangled into the darkness. I felt cool and danger-ous; but what if a spirit from the outside pushed me? The well was close to the perimeter fence. Something I had seen on television re-cently had convinced me that the spirits congregated in the corners of the perimeter fence, and so those four points were the only part of the compound I feared. I carefully brought both legs back to safety, replaced the plate, and went inside.

Upstairs, long division seemed out of the question. I put a searching hand into my shorts. I took off my shorts and briefs, and removed my T-shirt as well. I lay on my back, and fondled myself, but had no imagination, had no idea of what to do. My genitals lay squished in my palm. I suddenly remembered that I had seen a mag-azine once, years before, maybe when I was six or seven. The terrible excitement of it choked me, as did the notion that the magazine might still be somewhere in the house. I hastily pulled my clothes back on, and went downstairs to the study, and started searching, frantically but quietly, in the stacks of old magazines. It must have been something a wayward uncle of mine had left around, a glossy magazine (my memory could not have invented such details), and what it depicted was what I now desperately had to see again. I me-thodically went through the papers in the study, the old file folders with printed sheets and engineering graphs from my father's years in graduate school, the annual reports of the Nigerian companies in which my parents held stock. I was at it for the better part of an hour.

I flipped through a dusty paperback titled *Body Language,* a book of popular psychology from the seventies, but there was nothing of that kind of interest in it. I combed through all the binders in the bottom shelves, then gave up and went back upstairs. Then I took up the idea again, pushed by a longing that felt almost external to me, and looked under all the mattresses, mine, my father's, my mother's. I found nothing; I remade the beds. The exertion had left me winded and seething.

I went downstairs to the kitchen, and took out a bottle of Coke and went outside, again to the back of the house. The sky seemed to have cleared again. I sat on the steel plate, opened the bottle with my teeth, and sucked down the contents so fast that my throat hurt. I wiped my mouth, took the bottle to the storeroom, and took a warm bottle of Coke to put back in the fridge. It was a weeknight and my homework had not yet been done, and so I turned to that and, as I worked on it upstairs, I could hear Mama moving about downstairs. That was when it started raining, and not long afterward, I heard the car horn. I ran downstairs to open the gate. It was a torrential rainfall, and I was already soaked by the time I unlatched the padlock and swung the large metal doors open. The car came in, carrying my mother, the enforcer toward whom I wordlessly directed all the afternoon's anger. I wasted time closing the gate. I tilted my head back, and the rain diluted the sticky sweetness still in my mouth. Then I ran to my mother to bring in the bags of food she had bought. I would have preferred to stay in the rain and drink it and whip around in it. But I went inside and changed out of my wet clothes. The power supply hadn't returned, but it did so eventually, sometime before my father and his driver came back home at eight.

From that sudden beginning, the rain continued through the night, and through the next day, and the one after that. It was confusing, alarming in its relentlessness and intensity. We had known rain, but nothing like this. Even the concrete driveway of our house looked as if it was softening. Our wide gutters drained the water away, but out on the streets, life was a muddy mess. Many cars broke down in the inundated roads, and the commute to school took twice as long. I was morose. I didn't tell anyone what was wrong, and nobody asked. The well, which I didn't revisit, must have risen dramatically, and reflections might have become visible in its black water. It would have been strange to think—I didn't think so then, but it occurs to me now—that this flood wasn't worldwide. It seemed to have no boundaries, and was destined to last three solid days before it finally petered out.

The rain in Brussels was nothing so heavy, although the forecast said it would turn into a major storm by the weekend. It had become, in my thoughts, like a distant, drawn-out echo of that earlier childhood rain. But the story attached to that childhood rain was finished with, and of no import for the present. Part of it—the overheated desire, the oath—was good for a private joke, a thought that, when it flitted through my mind, amused me. I could no longer stand Coke, not its taste, not the rapacious company that produced it, or the ubiquitous screech of its advertising. For many years, I had been tempted to overinterpret the other events of that day, but what happened afterward, between my mother and myself, was due as much to any other day in my boyhood as to the day the rain began.

Looking out from my apartment and across the street, I saw a broken lightbulb and a newspaper lying in a puddle. The sidewalk pulsed with falling drops and, on the wall, someone had spray-painted the word ZOFIA and, in smaller letters, JE T'AIME.

# ELEVEN

I arrived too early at Aux Quatre Vents, where I was to have dinner with Dr. Maillotte. The sky, after seven days, was worsening, and I stood under the restaurant's awning, attempting to repair the damaged top spring of my umbrella. Across the street was the soaring west façade of Notre Dame de la Chapelle. The wind tortured everything in its path, knocking down garbage bins, shaking leafless trees, blowing walkers off course, but it got no quarter from the cathedral itself. The stone hulk was lashed by rain, that was all. As Dr. Maillotte would not be arriving for another half hour, I headed across the street, toward the church.

The doors were open, and the first impression, on entering, was of total silence. But soon afterward, my ears adjusted to the quietness of the space, and I could hear the organ being played softly. I looked down the nave, but no one was visible. I walked down the aisle on the south side of the cathedral, under cool and soaring bays. Nothing of the rain outside was audible and, as I moved closer to the front, the music became clearer. Usually in these churches, there were one or two staff members about, and occasionally a handful of tourists as well. So I was surprised to find myself completely alone, save for the unseen organist, in such a cavern; it was desolate even for a rainy Friday afternoon. I noticed, just then, a dissonance in the sound of the organ music. There were distinct fugitive notes that shot through the musical texture, like shafts of light refracted through stained glass. I was sure it was a Baroque piece, not one I had heard before, but with all the ornamentation typical of that period, yet it had taken on the spirit of something else—what came to mind was Peter Maxwell Davies's "O God Abufe"—a fractured, scattered feeling. It was at such low volume that, even as I heard the distinctly unsettling half step of a tritone repeated in the music, the melody itself was difficult to catch hold of.

Then I saw that there was no organist playing at all. The music was recorded and piped in through tiny speakers attached to the massive piers at the crossing. And I saw, also, the source of the fracture in the sound: a small yellow vacuum cleaner. The high-pitched hum from the machine had risen and mixed with the recorded organ music to create diabolus in musica. The woman who was cleaning did not look up from her work. She wore a bright green scarf, and a coat that reached down to the floor. She moved between the little wooden chairs of the north aisle. Instead of going into the crossing, I walked up the south aisle, toward the altar. The woman continued her work, fully absorbed, and the organ piece wove around the single, wavering hum of the vacuum cleaner.

A few weeks before, I would have assumed that the woman was Congolese. I had arrived in Brussels with the idea that all the Africans in the city were from the Congo. I knew the colonial relationship, I had a basic understanding of the history of the slave state there, and that had dislodged any other idea from my head. But then I went out one night to a restaurant and club on rue du Trône, a place called Le Panais. I spent the evening alone at my table, drinking and watching the young Congolese, all dressed up, fashionable, flirting with each other. The women wore afros or hair weaves, and many men wore long-sleeved shirts tucked into their jeans and looked particularly African, like recent arrivals. The music was American hip-hop, and the average age was twenty-five or thirty. It was a scene such as one would see in any city in Africa, or in the West: a Friday night, young people, music, liquor. After almost three hours, I paid for my drinks and was about to leave, and that was when the bartender came to talk to me. He asked where I was from, and we had a brief conversation; he was himself half-Malian and half-Rwandan. But what about the crowd, I wanted to know, were they all Congolese? He shook his head. Everyone was Rwandan.

The realization that I had been with fifty or sixty Rwandans changed the tenor of the evening for me. It was as though the space had suddenly become heavy with all the stories these people were carrying. What losses, I wondered, lay behind their laughter and flirting? Most of those there would have been teenagers during the genocide. Who, among those present, I asked myself, had killed, or witnessed killing? The quiet faces surely masked some pain I couldn't see. Who among them had sought deliverance in religion? I changed my mind about leaving just then and instead ordered another drink. I watched the couples, watched the parties of four and five, watched the young men who stood in trios, who were obviously absorbed in the moving bodies of the beautiful young women. The innocence on view was inscrutable and unremarkable. They were exactly like young people everywhere. And I felt some of that mental constriction—imperceptible sometimes, but always there— that came whenever I was introduced to young men from Serbia or Croatia, from Sierra Leone or Liberia. That doubt that said: These, too, could have killed and killed and only later learned how to look innocent. When I finally left Le Panais, it was late and the streets were silent, and I walked the three and a half miles home.

Looking now at the woman in the church, as she slowly folded the telescoping tube of the vacuum cleaner, I thought that she, too, might be here in Belgium as an act of forgetting. Her presence in the church might doubly be a means of escape: a refuge from the demands of family life and a hiding place from what she might have seen in the Cameroons or in the Congo, or maybe even in Rwanda. And perhaps her escape was not from anything she had done, but from what she had seen. It was a speculation. I would never find out, for she possessed her secrets fully, as did those women that Vermeer painted in this same gray, lowland light; like theirs, her silence seemed absolute. I walked around the choir and, when I passed her by in the north aisle, only nodded to her, before heading out again. But near the entrance, there was suddenly someone else. I started. I hadn't seen him walk up behind me: a middle-aged white man with a full beard. A vicar or sexton, I guessed. He ignored me, and went on his way across the south choir aisle with soundless footfall.

AT THE ENTRANCE OF THE RESTAURANT, TELEVISION NEWS WAS on, with the volume turned low. On the screen was an aerial shot of choppy waters, which captions identified as *la Manche,* the English Channel. I could just make out that a container vessel had run into trouble in the storm, and all twenty-six crew members had gone overboard on life rafts. The ship, rectangular and orange, looked like a toy, listing dangerously in the swelling sea, and, all around its inundated form, tiny orange life rafts bobbed. The camera cut to a weather report, which said that the storm was spreading across Europe and moving swiftly eastward. There was already serious damage in Germany: a collapsed bridge, swathes of snapped trees, and smashed cars. Then someone touched my arm. It was Dr. Maillotte. She kissed me on the cheek and said, It's never this bad, this is the strangest winter we've had in years; come, let us eat. Then she added, Wait, I forgot, you prefer English, yes? Okay, I'll remember, we'll speak English.

We sat near a big window that came down to floor level, on the other side of which the rain descended like a sheet. She said she had just had a meeting about a foundation she was involved with. I hate meetings, she said, some things are much easier if one person decides. It was easy to imagine what her style was like in the operating room, or at an official meeting. She broke off a piece of a bread roll, chewing quickly as she studied the menu and said, almost randomly, Did we talk about jazz on the plane? I think we did, no? But if you like jazz, I'll tell you about Cannonball Adderley. He was a patient of mine.

Her finely veined hands tore expertly into the bread. She looked much older, I thought, than when we had first met. Actually, she continued, it was his brother, Nat Adderley, who was my patient in Philadelphia. I had to take some gallstones out of him, and it was through Nat that I met Cannonball, and then Cannonball himself became my patient. He had high blood pressure, you see. Anyway, because of the Adderley brothers, we—my husband and I—met many of the notable jazzmen of the sixties. Chet Baker.

The waiter, a dead ringer for Obelix, arrived to take our orders: *waterzooi* for her, veal for me. She asked if I liked wine, I said yes, and she ordered a carafe of Beaujolais. Philly Joe Jones, the drummer, and Bill Evans, too. You know Art Blakey? Cannonball liked to introduce people to each other, so we met all kinds of characters through him. We went to too many concerts to count. Not as many after Cannonball died, in the mid-seventies. He had a stroke and, like all these other men, he was terribly young. Forty-two or forty-six, something like that.

I was happy to be there, and enjoyed the way she pulled each vignette like a rabbit out of a hat. The names of the jazz artists Dr. Maillotte was now listing meant nothing to me, but I could tell that she had gotten something extraordinarily meaningful out of having been part of, or rather having fallen into, that milieu.

I became aware of just how fleeting the sense of happiness was, and how flimsy its basis: a warm restaurant after having come in from the rain, the smell of food and wine, interesting conversation, daylight falling weakly on the polished cherrywood of the tables. It took so little to move the mood from one level to another, as one might push pieces on a chessboard. Even to be aware of this, in the midst of a happy moment, was to push one of those pieces, and to become slightly less happy. And your husband, I said, does he not come to Brussels as often as you? No, she said, he's much happier in the States. I think he slowly lost his connection to Belgium. For me, it's my friends that keep me coming back. And also the fact that I just can't stand American public morals. And you, do you go to Nigeria a lot? I don't, I said. My last visit happened two years ago, and that was after a gap of fifteen years; and it was a brief visit. Being busy all these years was part of it, and losing some of the connection, as you said, also plays a role. Also, my father died not long before I left, and I have no siblings.

Our food arrived. So, I guess English is only your second language, she said. What's the first? For a second, I thought I might tell her that German, not English, was my second language, the private language between my mother and myself until I was five, the language I later totally forgot. Though, even now, to hear a child call out in a department store *Mutter, wo bist du?* still cut me to the quick; it must have been the kind of thing I said myself, once upon a time. English came later, at school. But I didn't want to get into the intricacies of the story, so I told her that Yoruba was my first language. It's the second biggest of Nigeria's native languages, I said. I spoke only Yoruba until I began primary school.

Are you still fluent in it? Yes, I said, I can get by, though by now my English is much stronger. But I want to ask you something, I said. You've been away for a long time, so you're not a typical Belgian in any sense, but I wonder what you make of something a friend of mine said recently. He described Belgium as a difficult place for an Arab to be. My friend's specific trouble is about being here and maintaining his uniqueness, his difference. Do you think that's true? I don't know if you remember, but on the plane you described Belgium as color-blind. But that doesn't seem to have been the experience of Farouq—that's my friend's name—in the seven years that he has been living here. I think he even had his thesis rejected at the university, presumably because he wrote on a subject that the committee was uncomfortable with.

She had not touched her *waterzooi*. She continued chewing bread and spoke, in response to my question, dispassionately. Look, I know this type, she said, these young men who go around as if the world is an offense to them. It is dangerous. For people to feel that they alone have suffered, it is very dangerous. Having such a degree of resentment is a recipe for trouble. Our society has made itself open for such people, but when they come in, all you hear is complaints. Why would you want to move somewhere only to prove how different you are? And why would a society like that want to welcome you? But if you live as long as I do, you will see that there is an endless variety of difficulties in the world. It's difficult for everybody. I nodded. But it would have been different, I said, if only you'd heard him tell it. He's not a complainer, and I don't think he's full of resentment, not really. I think the hurt is genuine. Well, I'm sure it is, she said, but if you're too loyal to your own suffering, you forget that others suffer, too. There's a reason, she said, I had to leave Belgium and try to make my life in another country. I don't complain and, to be honest, I really have little patience for people who do. You're not a complainer, are you?

I ate, and my thoughts wandered over to her son, the one who had died. I wanted to hear her talk about him, and about the foundation that had been set up in his name, but I didn't dare ask. She finally put a spoon into the creamy dish in front of her. The restaurant was almost empty; it was an unusual time of day to be eating, late for lunch, and a few hours before dinner. So, she said, how long will you remain here? I leave tomorrow morning, I said. She said she would stay a few weeks yet, that she was planning to buy a little sports car, an antique. Something for her use as she spent more and more time in Belgium; and then she spoke about jazz again. Our afternoon passed easily. I hoped she wouldn't attempt to pay for the meal, and she didn't. She said, You must call me if you ever come to Philadelphia. We have a house near the woods, in the suburbs, which is wonderful in the summer, and even better in the fall. Again, as she spoke, I felt the sense of well-being surge through me, a feeling that, even then, I couldn't quite match up with her dismissal of Farouq's story. And be sure to get Cannonball's *Somethin' Else,* she said. That's the great one of all his albums, a true classic. I promised I would.

Walking from Place de la Chapelle, up through Sablon toward the museums, I wondered if I would run into the Czech, though I knew it was unlikely she was still in the city. The rain had subsided a little, but the wind picked up suddenly, turning my umbrella inside out. One of the ribs snapped, dislodging the top spring I'd been trying to repair earlier and leaving only half the umbrella functional. And though I was intent on getting out of the rain and getting home, I was arrested by a small monument set in a garden at the side of rue de la Régence, where that road met rue Bodenbroek. I had seen it before, in better weather, but had never stopped to look at it properly. It was a bronze bust of the poet Paul Claudel, set on a plinth on the side of the road like a shrine to Hermes.

Claudel had served as French ambassador to Belgium in the 1930s, and later went on to fame as a writer of Catholic plays, and as a right-winger. His support for the collaborators and Marshal Pétain during the war earned him much scorn, but W. H. Auden, himself a leftist agnostic, spoke kindly of him. Auden had written: "Time will pardon Paul Claudel, pardons him for writing well." And as I stood there in the whipping wind and rain, I wondered if indeed it was that simple, if time was so free with memory, so generous with pardons, that writing well could come to stand in the place of an ethical life. But Claudel, I had to remind myself, was far from being the only problematic figure among the hundreds of statues and monuments around the city. It was a city of monuments, and greatness was set in stone and metal all over Brussels, obdurate replies to uncomfortable questions. It was time, in any case, to go home, to leave Claudel with his wet bronze head, to leave, in the museum next door, Auden's Bruegel with its falling Icarus, and the unforgettable painting by an anonymous painter of a young girl with a dead sparrow.

I waited at the bus stop in front of the elaborate ironwork façade of the Musée des Instruments de Musique, and the bus, when it arrived, was nearly full. It was warm and damp inside, and everyone found it hard to breathe. We went through the city in that fogged-up interior, looking out with difficulty at the windy streets. I disembarked at Flagey. My umbrella was useless by then, and I threw it away. As I came onto rue Philippe, I found myself walking behind a woman pushing a pram. We were walking in single file between the buildings and some temporary barriers, flat panels of sturdy plastic anchored in concrete blocks that had been set up for a construction project. A sudden gust of wind lifted the panels, which were all tied to each other, and tipped them over, toward us. Immediately I sprang forward and broke their fall with my hands and my body. I staggered, but did not lose my balance. The woman, who was young and Mediterranean-looking, in too-tight jeans, was able to swerve her pram out of harm's way. I caught no sight of the child, who was swaddled and shielded from the rain with a translucent plastic sheet. The young mother thanked me, again and again, gasping. She seemed stunned at how quickly it had all happened. I waved it off, proud.

The wind persisted in its howling fury. The little street we were walking on had, a hundred years ago, been a stream, not a street. It had been covered over by city planners, and waterside houses suddenly found themselves looking out on traffic. But the water still coursed underground, along the entire length of the street, and that water was returning now, in the form of rain, heavy waters above and flowing waters below.

Instinctively saving a baby, a little happiness; spending time with Rwandans, the ones who survived, a little sadness; the idea of our final anonymity, a little more sadness; sexual desire fulfilled without complication, a little more happiness: and it went on like that, as thought succeeded thought. How petty seemed to me the human condition, that we were subject to this constant struggle to modulate the internal environment, this endless being tossed about like a cloud. Predictably, the mind noted that judgment, too, and assigned it its place: a little sadness. The water that had once flowed along the street we were walking on had run into an artificial pond in the middle of Flagey, a pond that had then been obliterated to create a traffic island, echoing the creation of land in the oldest myths, as a division between the waters.

Night had fallen. I entered the apartment and threw off my clothes and lay in bed in the darkened room, naked. Heavy drops tapped on the window. The weather report was right: in ever widening circles from where I stood, rain was lashing the land. It fell heavily all over the Portuguese district, on the shrine to Pessoa and on Casa Botelho. It fell on Khalil's phone shop, where Farouq had perhaps just begun his shift. It fell on the bronze head of Leopold II at his monument, on Claudel at his, on the flagstones of the Palais Royal. The rain kept coming down, on the battlefield of Waterloo at the outskirts of the city, the Lion's Mound, the Ardennes, the implacable valleys full of young men's bones grown old, on the preserved cities farther out west, on Ypres and the huddled white crosses dotting Flanders fields, the turbulent channel, the impossibly cold sea to the north, on Denmark, France, and Germany.

## PART 2

*I have searched myself*

# TWELVE

I made an effort to develop a mind of winter. Late last year, I actually said to myself audibly, as I do when I swear these oaths, that I would have to embrace winter as part of the natural cycle of seasons. Ever since I left Nigeria, I'd had a bad attitude about cold weather, and I wanted to put an end to that. The effort was surprisingly successful, and through October, November, and December, I was properly braced for winds and snow. One thing that helped was that I made a habit of overdressing. Without checking the daily weather, I would wear long johns, doubled socks, a scarf, woolen gloves, a long, thick, dark blue coat, and heavy shoes. But it was to be a year without a real winter. The blizzards for which I braced never came. There were a few days of cold rain, and one or two cold snaps, but heavy snow stayed away. We had a series of sunny days in the middle of December, and I was unnerved by that mildness, and when the season's first snow did eventually fall, it was while I was in Brussels, getting drenched by the rain there. The snow was in any case short-lived, melted away by the time I returned to New York in mid-January, and thus did the impression of unseasonal, somewhat uncanny, warmth persist in my mind, keeping the world, as I experienced it, on edge.

Those thoughts had returned even before I was properly back in the city. The pilot's voice crackling through the system—*We are now making our final approach for landing*—added to the anxiety of return because those ordinary and, by now, banal words seemed to carry some ghostly portent. My thoughts quickly became entangled with one another, so that, in addition to the usual morbid thoughts one normally has on a plane, I was saddled with strange mental transpositions: that the plane was a coffin, that the city below was a vast graveyard with white marble and stone blocks of various heights and sizes. But as we broke through the last layer of clouds and the city in its true form suddenly appeared a thousand feet below us, the impression I had was not at all morbid. What I experienced was the unsettling feeling that I had had precisely this view of the city before, accompanied by the equally strong feeling that it had not been from the point of view of a plane.

Then it came to me: I was remembering something I had seen about a year earlier: the sprawling scale model of the city that was kept at the Queens Museum of Art. The model had been built for the World's Fair in 1964, at great cost, and afterward had been periodically updated to keep up with the changing topography and built environment of the city. It showed, in impressive detail, with almost a million tiny buildings, and with bridges, parks, rivers, and architectural landmarks, the true form of the city. The attention to detail was so meticulous that one could not help but think of Borges's cartographers, who, obsessed with accuracy, had made a map so large and so finely detailed that it matched the empire's scale on a ratio of one to one, a map in which each thing coincided with its spot on the map. The map proved so unwieldy that it was eventually folded up and left to rot in the desert. Our view from the plane, as we banked over

Queens itself, brought all of that back to mind, and in this case it was the real city that seemed to be matching, point for point, my memory of the model, which I had stared at for a long time from a ramp in the museum. Even the raking evening light falling across the city evoked the spotlighting used at the museum.

On the day I had seen the Panorama, I had been impressed by the many fine details it presented: the rivulets of roads snaking across a velvety Central Park, the boomerang of the Bronx curving up to the north, the elegant beige spire of the Empire State Building, the white tablets of the Brooklyn piers, and the pair of gray blocks on the southern tip of Manhattan, each about a foot high, representing the persistence, in the model, of the World Trade Center towers, which, in reality, had already been destroyed.

THE DAY AFTER I RETURNED, STILL IN THE MENTAL FOG OF JET lag, and knowing that by seven in the evening I would start to get sleepy, I tried to keep thoughts of Monday from my mind. That my colleagues would be hostile toward me was an inevitability because I had taken all four of my vacation weeks at once. Using up vacation time like this was permitted, under the regulations of the program, but it was unusual, and considered bad form because it put the other residents under additional pressure. It was the kind of thing that would probably show up in a future letter of recommendation, disguised in the language of faint praise. In the course of the four weeks of my absence, many of the cases would have turned over, with the exception of the most serious admissions. There were bound to be several new patients.

The weeks to come were going to be difficult.

That was still a day away. On Sunday, I went down to the International Center of Photography in midtown. The main attraction there was a show on Martin Munkácsi. Admission was reduced for students, so I lied, flashing my expired medical school ID, and as I did so remembered how seriously Nadège had taken this practice. I had always countered her by saying that I was hardly earning more than a student, even if I was technically out of school. I had begun to use the expired ID more often, at first as a way to annoy her, and then, afterward, out of habit. Nadège came to mind because she had written to me while I was away. In the pile of printed mail waiting for me at the apartment when I arrived, there was the lime green envelope, addressed in her hand. The card was a sickly-sweet Nativity scene, and on the inside she had written a plain Christmas greeting.

The show was crowded and the prints unexpectedly lively. Munkácsi's journalism was dynamic; he liked sports poses, youth, people in motion. In these snaps—which were so carefully composed but always seemed to have been taken on the go—I could see the alertness that he brought to his other masterful work, such as the photograph of three African boys running into the surf in Liberia. It was from him, and from this picture in particular, that Henri Cartier-Bresson had developed the ideal of the decisive moment. Photography seemed to me, as I stood there in the white gallery with its rows of pictures and its press of murmuring spectators, an uncanny art like no other. One moment, in all of history, was captured, but the moments before and after it disappeared into the onrush of time; only that selected moment itself was privileged, saved, for no other reason than its having been picked out by the camera's eye.

Munkácsi moved from Hungary to Germany, where he would remain until 1934. He worked for the *Berliner Illustrirte Zeitung*, a weekly paper of photographs and advertising; it was for this paper that he had made his picture of the Liberian boys in 1930. The *Illustrirte Zeitung* had covered the First World War, and would, after Munkácsi's departure, cover the Second as well. In the ICP show, copies of the magazine, showing Munkácsi's work, had been placed in Plexiglas cases at waist height. A man in his sixties was studying the same case as I was, and we stood side by side, leaning over the clear case. His face was relaxed, and he wore a yellow windbreaker.

Seeing how intently I was studying the magazine, he said, without turning to look at me, that the spelling was a mistake—what was printed on the newspaper was *illustrírte* instead of *illustrierte,* he said—and that had been the case since the first issue. In that first issue, the gentleman said, it had been an error, but later, it became a kind of trademark for the magazine and was left unchanged. This was familiar to him, he said, because he remembered the magazine from his childhood. It had come to their house weekly when he was a little boy in Berlin.

Sensing my interest, the man spoke on, and our eyes moved over the surfaces of Munkácsi's photographs as he talked. There was one that showed a field of young Germans lying in the sun, which must have been taken from a zeppelin. The bodies, filling every available space, made a flat, abstract pattern against the field. The man spoke with the slowness of someone who was entering a memory, but it was not a foggy memory, and he spoke about it clearly, as though it had only just happened. I was thirteen when we left Berlin in 1937, he said, and New York has been my home ever since.

My guess of his age had been far off, and yet he looked nothing like an eighty-four-year-old. He was fit, and the way he moved his body was unimpeded by age. There was a lightness, too, in the way he spoke about his boyhood, almost as if he were talking about something else, something less frightening, something less littered with disaster. It wasn't until much later, he said, that they finally adopted *illustrierte* with the extra *e.* But this spelling, this is the one I knew in those days. Have you been to Berlin? I told him I had, and that I had enjoyed the city very much. I've never been back, he said, but I liked it a lot when I was there. It must have been an unimaginably different place back then, I said. I did not tell him that my mother and my oma had been there, too, as refugees near the end of the war and afterward, and that I was myself, in this distant sense, also a Berliner. If we had talked more, I would have told him only that I was from Nigeria, from Lagos. As it turned out, just then, his wife, or an old lady whom I presumed was his wife, came to join him. She looked much older than he did, and used a walker. With a smile and nod to me, he moved on with her to another part of the exhibition.

The mood of Munkácsi's photographs darkened as the 1920s became the 1930s, and the soccer players and fashion models gave way to the cool tensions of a military state. This story, told countless times, retains its power to quicken the heart; always, one holds out the secret hope that things will turn out differently, and that the record of those years will show wrongs on a scale closer to the rest of human history. The enormity of what actually happened, no matter how familiar it is, no matter how often it is reiterated, always comes as a shock. And that was what happened when, among the photographs of troops and parades at the opening of the Reichstag in 1933, there was the image, at once expected and unexpected, in the middle ground of a row of soldiers, of the new German chancellor. Walking close behind him, with his contorted nightmare of a face, was Goebbels. I happened to be looking at this picture at the same time a young couple was. I stood to the left of it, and they to the right. They were Hasidic Jews. I had no reasonable access to what being there, in that gallery, might mean for them; the undiluted hatred I felt for the subjects of the photo was, in the couple, transmuted into what? What was stronger than hate? I did not know, and could not ask. I needed to move away, immediately, needed to rest my eye elsewhere and be absent from this silent encounter into which I had inadvertently barged. The young couple stood close to each other, not speaking. I couldn't bear to look at them, or at what they were looking at, any longer.

The show turned on that axis. It became about something else, and couldn't be saved. There were other photographs, images from Munkácsi's successful career in the 1940s in Hollywood, stylish pictures of socialites and actors: Joan Crawford, Fred Astaire. But the afternoon was poisoned, and I wanted only to get home and sleep, and begin my year of work. I moved through the crowd toward the exit, and caught a last glimpse, as I passed the museum shop, of the old Berliner and his wife. His long-saved story of *illustrirte* had found the time and place for its airing; unimaginable how many small stories people all over this city carried around with them. It was only then that I noted that Munkácsi, the photographer of the so-called *Day of Potsdam,* into whose camera one seemingly ordinary moment in Berlin in 1933 was secreted away for future viewers, was himself Jewish.

I walked north on Sixth Avenue as far as Fifty-ninth Street. Then I took a turn, and walked on Broadway in the direction of Times Square, and passed the Iridium Jazz Club. No longer wanting to go to bed, trying to fend off jet lag, I called my friend to ask if he would come see the guitarist playing there that night. He expressed sarcastic shock that I would willingly pay for jazz but said he was already booked for the evening. And so I headed home, with the thought I would call Nadège: it would be around four in the afternoon in California, and she would be back from mass. But it wasn't time yet to open up the lines of communication. Months had passed, but it wasn't yet time. How strange the effect of those few months with her had been on me. Her card meant, perhaps, that things were thawing from her point of view, but I, for my part, remained unready. Nor was I prepared, now that I think of it, to admit to myself that I had made too much of our brief relationship. When I got home, I took a shower, drowsing under the warm water, and I got into bed; but right away got out again and called her, after all.

WE EXPERIENCE LIFE AS A CONTINUITY, AND ONLY AFTER IT FALLS away, after it becomes the past, do we see its discontinuities. The past, if there is such a thing, is mostly empty space, great expanses of nothing, in which significant persons and events float. Nigeria was like that for me: mostly forgotten, except for those few things that I remembered with an outsize intensity. These were the things that had been solidified in my mind by reiteration, that recurred in dreams and daily thoughts: certain faces, certain conversations, which, taken as a group, represented a secure version of the past that I had been constructing since 1992. But there was another, irruptive, sense of things past. The sudden reencounter, in the present, of something or someone long forgotten, some part of myself I had relegated to childhood and to Africa. An old friend came to me out of this latter past, a friend, or rather an acquaintance whom memory now made convenient to think of as a friend, so that what seemed to have vanished entirely existed once again. She appeared (apparition was precisely what came to mind) to me in a grocery store in Union Square late in January. I didn't recognize her, and she followed me for a while, tracing my steps around the aisles, to give me an opportunity to make the first move. It was only when I noticed that I was being shadowed, and was beginning to adjust my body into that skeptical awareness, that she came right up to where I was standing, in front of a display of carrots and radishes. She said a bright hello, waved, and addressed me by my full name, smiling. It was clear she expected me to remember her. I didn't.

She looked Yoruba, with a slight slant to her eyes and an elegant swoop to the jaw, and it was clear from the accent that that was where I should look for the connection between us. But I failed to find it. At the same moment that I confessed to having blanked out on who she was, she accused me of just that, a serious accusation, but jocularly expressed. She couldn't believe I had forgotten her, and she said my name several times in quick succession, as if to chide me. My lighthearted apology masked the irritation I suddenly felt. I feared for a moment that she would overextend the charade, and make me cajole her into saying who she was, but she introduced herself, and the memory was restored: Moji Kasali. She was the older sister (by one year) of a school friend, Dayo. I had met her two or three times in Lagos, when on school breaks I would visit Dayo at home. Dayo and I were rather close friends during the junior secondary years, but he hadn't stayed at NMS long, leaving at the beginning of the first senior secondary year, and transferring to a private school in Lagos. We made an effort to communicate with each other the following Christmas break, but when I visited him at home, the gateman turned me away, and when he returned my visit a week later, I wasn't home. We no longer had the NMS connection, and I was sure he'd made new friends. Our friendship faded. About a year later, I'd met him at some tennis courts in Apapa. He was with a girl, playing the man-about-town, and our conversation was stilted.

I was by then much taller than he was, but he was stout and had the stubbly beginnings of a beard. We promised once again to stay in touch with each other, and I remember telling him I was thinking of going to America, if I could find a way out, though, as it turned out, I didn't leave until a few years afterward. He was wearing dark glasses that day, which he didn't take off, though the sky was overcast; his girlfriend had on a white polo shirt and tight shorts, and looked bored, and was, as such, the instant object of my envy. That I had my own girlfriend didn't matter. Dayo's girl struck me as impossibly cool.

I took his address and phone number—he wrote them down, I recall, on the back of a religious tract someone had pinned to the fence—and not long afterward, I called him. Then there had been a party at his house, a wild one, with lots of drinking. The girl wasn't there by that point—they'd split up—and I had split up with my girl, too. Afterward, I lost Dayo's address and, in any case, by the time I came to the United States, three years later, I had no serious intention of writing to him, or anyone else. The promise to write had simply been a gesture of respect, an acknowledgment of the fact that once, when we were in our early teens, we'd been close, and even for a brief moment best friends.

I doubt I would have recognized him thirteen years later, in a grocery store, much less his sister. But now, the certainty with which she pinned me to my name, the ease with which she repeated it, made me think she'd thought of me but never expected to see me again. And perhaps I had been the unwitting target of a school-girl crush: the brother's friend, the sophisticated *aje-butter*, a self-confident older teen. On the earlier occasions that I had gone to Dayo's house, there had been one or two other school friends there as well, and she had ignored us, of course. Perhaps she was more interested in us than she'd let on. Maybe that memory remained now, as she stood with a box of muesli under her arm, and the embers of that memory were what made her catch my eyes, and hold them, as she asked me the expected questions: marriage, children, career. When I had answered, plain answers that I was careful not to deliver too brusquely, I felt it polite to ask her the same.

She was an investment banker at Lehman Brothers, she said. I acted suitably impressed, and made vague noises about how busy she must be. But I did not want the small talk to go on, so I looked every now and again at the basket in my hand, and nodded as she talked. Her brother was in Nigeria at the moment, she said. He'd gone to the U.K. for graduate school, at Imperial College, but had returned home and gotten married. Moji said she'd been in closer contact with him during the six years he'd been in London. We don't talk very often now, she said, he's got a kid, he runs his own civil engineering firm. But he's had some strange times. He had an accident in 1995, just before going for his master's. I suppose that's the biggest thing, really, that's happened to him since you left Nigeria. He was studying in the east at the time, in Nsukka, and he was in a bus crash, out on the highway at night. The bus ran into a motorcyclist who was riding without lights, and it careened off the road. Ten of the four-teen people onboard died instantly; another three were badly injured, and one of them died later. Dayo alone had walked away without injury. I think maybe he dislocated a shoulder or something, but nothing major at all. When you have such an experience as that, she said, everyone immediately thinks it would make you more religious. That wasn't the effect it had on him. He became more thoughtful, I guess. He went through life, for the next couple of years, in a kind of distracted daze. He spoke about the accident just once, after he came back to Lagos—that's when we found out it had happened. Maybe it was a news item buried inside the papers— ten killed in Nsukka crash, or something like that—so we might have heard of it, but we could never have imagined he would be involved. He simply kept it to himself until he came home on semester break; he's funny like that. My parents, of course, made him come to church for a special thanksgiving service. He went along with it. Then he put it out of his mind, filed it away like it had just been a bad dream and, if he revisited it, it wasn't in any public way. Me, of course, I was curious, and I used to badger him about it initially, but he just clammed up, and that was that. I've seen dead people at the scene of an accident—I guess everyone who lives in Nigeria has—but I'm sure it's different if you were in the accident yourself, or if that body lying by the side of the road could easily have been yours. So for a long time, everyone treated Dayo as if he was the luckiest person in the world, but I think his attitude was that it would have been luckier to be nowhere near the crash at all. Anyway, he's mostly past it now, and it was all so long ago. I'm sure that's more detail than you wanted.

We'd used up our common ground, and there seemed nothing left to chat about. She assured me that I would hear from her again, and marveled once more, in what had become a quite irritating way, that we had run into each other. I don't really believe in coincidences, she said. Something either happens or it doesn't, coincidence has nothing to do with it.

# THIRTEEN

At the beginning of February, I went down to Wall Street to meet Parrish, the accountant who was doing my taxes, but I forgot to bring my checkbook. Speaking with him just before I left home, I had asked if I should bring anything, and he'd said I should bring a check, so I could pay him. I had taken the checkbook out of its drawer and placed it on the table with my gloves and keys. But I then left it behind, and didn't realize I had done so until the 2 train came to the station. I was embarrassed at having to meet him empty-handed. But I was supposed to give him only two hundred dollars, and I had my bank card with me. I could get cash. It seemed vaguely illicit, putting cash in an envelope and sliding it across a table, but it was better than not paying him right away.

When I came out of the Wall Street station, I looked around for a cash machine. I hadn't been to that part of town since I had gone on my night walk there in November. Now, in daylight, with the sun pouring into the deep clefts formed by the sides of skyscrapers, the street's ominous character was tamed. It had become an ordinary street, a place of work, marred in the normal way by construction cordons and divots where the road was undergoing repair, and nothing at all like the Dantesque vision of huddled and faceless bodies I had experienced a few months earlier. After a short walk, I found a cash machine inside a pharmacy, but was unable to take money out of it because I typed in the wrong four-digit code for my card. So I tried again, and failed again. I tried five times, with different numbers, all of them wrong. I wasn't alarmed—which I would have been if I had thought the card was compromised—but rather, sad: I had simply forgotten the number. A thought flitted through my mind: how terrible it would be to blank out like this while seeing a patient. This was the ATM card I had used for more than six years, and it had always had the same code. I had used the card on my recent trip to Brussels and, indeed, I had been entirely dependent on it for that journey.

Now, as I stood in a little pharmacy on the corner of Water Street and Wall Street, my mind was empty, subject to a nervous condition; this was the expression that came to me as I stood there, as though I had become a minor character in a Jane Austen novel. Such sudden mental weakness, I thought (as the machine asked if I would like to try again, and I did, and failed again), was from a simplified version of the self, an area of simplicity where things had once been more robust. This was true of a broken leg, too: one was suddenly lessened, walking with an incomplete understanding of what walking was about.

I was already late for my meeting with Parrish, who had been recommended to me by a colleague. But I left the pharmacy and wandered around the area, and tried to calm myself down. It was cold out, the sunshine giving no warmth as a breeze came stiffly off the East River two blocks away. The clouds in the bright sky were small and numerous, and ruffled like breaking waves. I shivered, and tried to ignore the nervousness, hoping it would simply float away. I went

down to Hanover Square and twenty minutes later, having no defi-
nite number in mind, went to another machine, this one in the lobby
of a bank. I tried the withdrawal again, hoping that the memory in
my fingers, their familiarity with the pattern, might bail me out, as it
sometimes did in the case of phone numbers. I was surprised the
machines permitted so many attempts. In any case, all failed, and I
was left with a handful of printed receipts. I had kept thinking that
the number was 2046. But that wasn't it; that number came from the
title of the film by Wong Kar Wai. The number I was after was
something similar, had been picked even before the film was made,
but it was 2046 that kept echoing in my head.

When I finally sat down with Parrish, I told him that I had neglected to bring my checkbook. I said nothing about the cash machines. He was solemn, and as he adjusted his cuff links, I had the
feeling of having disturbed a carefully calibrated universe. I apologized, and assured him I would put the check in the mail right away.
He shrugged, and I signed the tax paperwork he had prepared for
me. I was awed by this unsuspected area of fragility in myself. It was
an insignificant portent of age, the kind I tended to smile at in others, the kind I took as a mark of vanity. I thought of the few white
curls that had sprung up and were now nestled in the black mass of
my hair. I used to joke about them, but I knew also that the entire
head of hair would someday change color, that the white strands
would multiply, and would win eventually, that if I lived to old age,
like Mama, there would be hardly any of the black ones left.

I went down Broadway, past the old Customs House, and down
to Battery Park. It was a clear day and I could see right across to
Brooklyn, to Staten Island, and the glimmering green figurine of the
Statue of Liberty. The Tetris-like line of buildings sat in the still afternoon air. The park brimmed over with the noise of children too
young for school. Their mothers fussed around them in the play-
ground. The creak-creak of the swings was a signal, I thought, there

to remind the children that they were having fun; if there were no creak, they would be confused. This had been a busy mercantile part of the city in the middle of the nineteenth century. Trading in slaves had become a capital offense in the United States in 1820, but New York long remained the most important port for the building, outfitting, insuring, and launching of slavers' ships. Much of the human cargo of those vessels was going to Cuba; Africans did the work on the sugar plantations there.

In profiting from slavery, the City Bank of New York was not unlike the other companies founded by merchants and bankers in the same time period—the companies that later became AT&T and Con Edison emerged from the same milieu. Moses Taylor, one of the world's wealthiest men, had joined the board of the City Bank in 1837 after a long and successful career as a sugar merchant. He became the president of the bank in 1855, and served in that capacity until his death in 1882. Taylor had helped fund the war effort on the Union side; but he had also made massive profits from brokering the sale of Cuban sugar in the port of New York, investing the profits of the sugar planters, facilitating the processing of the cargo at the New York City Customs House, and helping finance the acquisition of a "labor force." He had made it possible, in other words, for plantation owners to pay for the purchase of slaves; this he did in part by operating his own ships. He had six of them sailing the high seas. Taylor and other bankers like him knew exactly what they were doing, and their optimism paid off. The profit margins were irresistible: a fully outfitted slaving ship costing around $13,000 could be expected to deliver a human cargo worth more than $200,000. *The New York Times* noted in 1852, as the City Bank brought in its greatest profits, that if the authorities pleaded that they could not stop this profiteering, they were simply confessing their own imbecility, and that, if it was a matter of will, the moral guilt they were incurring was equivalent to that of slave traders themselves.

The circuit from the old Customs House to Wall Street, and then down to South Street Seaport, was a distance of less than a mile. The Customs House faced Bowling Green, which had been used in the seventeenth century for the executions of paupers and slaves. In a tarred space in the park, along an avenue bordered by sturdy, heavy-headed elms, Chinese women danced in formation. There were eight of them, all in casual clothes. One was young, maybe in her thirties. All the others had gray hair, and there was one who was especially old and wise-looking. Their calisthenics was accompanied by vaguely martial pop music blasted from a radio. The young dancer led the group. Her movements were exaggerated. Each time she swept her arms, the too-long sleeves of her baggy pink jacket tousled calligraphically. The others followed easily, through points, swoops, quarter turns in one direction, half turns in the other. She was graceful and beautiful. But when the music stopped and the dancers paused, she did not look beautiful. The beauty had all been in her movement.

Their pause let me hear the other sound present, that of an instrument being played at the opposite end of the park. I wanted to get closer to it, and so I walked under the arbor of elms, passing by rows of concrete chess tables, which were oases of order and invitations to a twinned solitude. But no one sat at them or played chess. Around the tables, where they sank into earth, moss grew, spreading up the concrete and into the ground so that it seemed as if the chessboards had grown roots. I walked under the trees, past the creak of children's swings and, as I moved closer to the end of the arbor, I could make out the sound of an erhu. The line was breathy and nimble, the precise nimbleness of an old-fashioned thing. How clear its sound in the park, how unlike the whine the same instrument made when it was played by a subway busker competing with the screech of subway trains.

When I reached the other side of the park, I saw that there were actually two erhu players, not one. They were playing in unison, seated together on a stone ledge, and standing, facing them, was a young woman singing. A small group near the musicians, three women and a man, all past middle age, talked and stretched. One of the women carried a child in her arms and played with it, and as she walked around slowly she pointed her feet to the grass ahead of her, first one, then the other. Her deliberate movements were like a delayed shadow of the dancers'. I sat in the grass for a long while listening to the erhu players and the singer. It was cold. The singer sang softly, matching the bowed strings note for note. The players nodded to each other at the accents. I thought of Li Po and Wang Wei, of Harry Partch's pitch-bending songs, and of Judith Weir's opera *The Consolations of Scholarship*, which were the things I could best connect to this Chinese music. The song, the clear day, and the elms: it could have been any day from the last fifteen hundred years.

The *Times* had said, in the obituary I read that day, that V. wrote of atrocity without flinching. They might have said, without flinching visibly, for it had all affected her far more deeply than anyone's ability to guess. I could hardly imagine the kind of raw pain her family—her husband, her parents—would be experiencing. I returned to the knoll in the park, where I had come in. The dancers had started again. Many of them, I now noticed, wore red or pink. I could not remember if red was lucky in Chinese culture. The thin sound of the erhu still slithered in among the drums of the dancers' tape player, and it seemed to summon to my mind's eye the long-ago spirits that V. had been so concerned to honor in her work. Turning away from the dancers, and taking in the expanse of the bay once more, I sat on a green wooden bench. A curious junco, black on its upper half and white on the lower, hopped up to my feet. It was tiny, and soon darted away. There was another man on the bench, dressed in a linen suit, with carefully polished shoes, and a straw hat: summer clothes on a winter's day. His shirt was yellow and his tie dark brown—my train of thought was suddenly interrupted by the laughter of the Chinese women behind us. His mustache was white and neatly trimmed. The man read *El Diario,* seriously and slowly. We sat there, the two of us, and I looked over the green park. We did not acknowledge each other's presence, though I had a sudden urge to tell him all about V.'s life, the depth of her work, her tragic death. We simply sat, and the day rolled down the knoll before us and drifted upward across the grass, and across the water, with its busy crisscrossing ferries, and southward, toward the Statue of Liberty.

When I got home, still not remembering the number for my ATM card, I refused to check the bank documents. I assured myself the number would return in its own time. Then I forgot all about the incident. The next day, Citibank called to tell me they had noticed a dozen failed attempts to withdraw money from my account. I was jovial with the clerk, and assured her that it was my encroaching senility that was responsible, not a thief; my card was fine, they needn't worry. But when I got off the phone I sat on my bed in the silence of my apartment. I had forgotten about the incident, but then it had become fresh again, and this time more heavily, and this time without witnesses or an official record. The strange feeling was harder to dispel, the memory of standing alone, standing in Wall Street, my memory gone, a pathetic old-young man padding about in the grip of some nervousness, while all around me the smart set made deals, talked on cellphones, and adjusted their cuff links. I recalled having seen a police officer from whose holster an automatic shone, and how I'd been taken with an odd sort of envy of that weapon, of its total lack of ambiguity, of its promise of danger. I imagined I had forgotten not just that number but all numbers, as well as all names, and why I was even there on Wall Street in the first place. I got up from the bed and checked the oven.

Later that day, it snowed, the first snowfall I had witnessed in the season. A furious sense of imbalance came over me as I watched the flakes tumble down and disappear on contact with the ground. Almost a full week afterward, when the cold front had retreated once again into the shadows of our unwintry winter, I still hadn't remembered the four-digit code. I finally looked it up among my documents, and recaptured what had been hovering, for no good reason, just out of reach.

# FOURTEEN

We've had a rough time of it, Dr. Saito said, welcoming me in. I've been sleeping here in the living room, on this pallet. We've had an infestation of bedbugs. Red coats they used to be called in this part of the country, do you know that name? We thought the exterminators had cleared it up, but it came back worse eight days later, and I've had to make an unpleasant choice between this room, with its noisy vents, and being eaten up by the little creatures. He gestured toward the slats above the window. They bite. Like this, one, two, three; breakfast, lunch, and dinner, along your arm; but I'm afraid I haven't much blood to spare anymore. Then he folded his hands and said he expected the exterminators to return in a few days.

But my spirits are up, so you've come at an excellent time. I was out earlier today to see the Chamber Music Society at Lincoln Center. They performed one of the Bach cantatas, the one about coffee. Do you know it? It was so well played that it seemed like a newly made work. It's about a father fretting over his daughter's choices. So at least we know nothing has changed through the centuries. Coffee was quite new then, and the elders were skeptical of this drug, and even more skeptical of the enthusiasm young people had for it. They would have been surprised to see how common it is now. And, I'll tell you, while I was sitting in the concert hall, it struck me that this was exactly like the problem with marijuana today. Coffee, coffee, the young woman sang, I simply must have coffee. Three times a day, or I will shrivel up!

I sat in an armless chair facing Professor Saito. It was good to see him vigorous, amused. It made me happy. His hands were coarsely veined, thin, and cold, and with both my hands I reached out and held both of his and massaged them. In the yellow-gray winter's light of his apartment, in the deep winter of his own life, this reaching out seemed the most natural thing to do. I'm sorry I've been away so long, I said, I've had a lot of work to do. He asked if I had just returned from Europe. No, I said, I came back in the middle of January, and I've had you on my mind since then. But the rotations have been unusually demanding. You'll see more of me in the next few months, now that things are stable again.

It's so noisy, and I think we can lower the heat now, if that is fine by you. He called out for the nurse-aide. Do you think we could lower the heat, Mary? Actually, I think we should turn it off for now, he said, adjusting the blanket around his knees. It has gotten very dry again, the heat makes it so dry in here. Whatever you'd like, she said. She seemed to have gained a lot of weight in the months since I had last seen her. But then I realized she was expecting a child, and was starting to show. I wouldn't have thought her young enough, as I had put her age somewhere north of forty. But the upper limits are perpetually shifting. A baby at forty is no great rarity anymore, and even fifty is not unheard of. I caught her eye, inclined my head in a gesture at her belly, and smiled. She smiled in return.

Mary, did the Sunday paper come in? Oh yes, good, maybe Julius would like to read to an old man? I told him I would be delighted to do so, and walked over to the dining table, where the paper sat on a pile of others. The apartment was dense with its various collections: the endless variety of South Seas masks on the walls, some of them in darkly polished wood, others brightly painted, the several months' worth of daily newspapers stacked on the table and near the door, the overstuffed bookshelves, from which hundreds of volumes called out for attention, the little figurines and puppets crammed on the desk facing the entryway. All that was missing, it occurred to me, were photographs: of family members, of friends, of Professor Saito himself.

I read the headlines from the *Times,* and the first two paragraphs of each story on the front page. Most of them were about the war. I looked up from the paper and said, It's almost too much to think about, all the intended and unintended consequences of this invasion. I think it's a terrible mess, and I can't stop thinking about it. Yes, Professor Saito said, but I felt that way about a different war. In 1950, we were deeply worried about the Korean situation. It was an endless tension, one that we never really believed would go away. So many people were called up into the military and, really, it wasn't so long after World War II. There were doubts about how far it would go, how long the stalemate would continue, who else would get involved. There was an unspoken nuclear fear, and that worsened, you see, when China entered the war. That unspoken fear became spoken. We Americans started wondering whether to use nuclear weapons again. But the war ended, as all wars eventually end; it exhausted itself. By the time Vietnam came around, it was a different pressure, at least for those of us who had been psychologically invested in Korea. Vietnam was a mental battle for the young, for the generation after ours. You go through that experience only once, the experience of how futile a war can be. You latch on to all the names of the towns, all the news. It didn't happen to me in World War II, that was a different experience, much more isolated, much more difficult. But as a free man in 1950, as a part of the campus scene, I experienced Korea more intensely. By the mid-sixties, the confusion of war was no longer a novelty for me. And now with this war, it's a mental battle for a different generation, your generation. There are towns whose names evoke a real horror in you because you have learned to link those names with atrocities, but, for the generation that follows yours, those names will mean nothing; forgetting doesn't take long. Fallujah will be as meaningless to them as Daejeon is to you. But look, I've veered off from the subject at hand, as I usually do. Bach really got my blood flowing, I think. Forgive my ramblings. Why don't you read me the rest of the headlines?

I expressed my delight in his ramblings. But as I read out stories about satellite radio and about civil unions in New Jersey, I became like one who was no longer there. My mind picked up an earlier thread in the conversation. When Professor Saito asked me not to stop at the second paragraph but to read the civil unions story all the way to the end, I did so, fully understanding the printed words but without engaging with them. Afterward, we discussed the story, and that, too, I did at a certain distance. It was a kind of party trick, to continue a conversation of this kind and remain the whole while perfectly distracted. It was like a film in which the soundtrack and the images were out of sync. Professor Saito expressed the view that the advances in equal rights for gays were welcome, and that, viewed from his lifetime of following such advances, the process looked inexorable. There was much to celebrate. But, he said, it has been slow. While I am happy for these couples now, I have a sense of how wasteful the struggle has been. It has been much too difficult to pass legislation of this kind. Future generations will perhaps wonder what took us so long. I asked him why New York State did not take the lead in passing such laws. Too many conservatives in Albany, he said, the political will isn't there to make it happen. It's all those people in the rural parts of the state, Julius, they think about these things differently.

I knew that Professor Saito had cared for a long-term partner, a man who had later died. I came by this information not through a conversation with him, but from a biographical profile I had seen in the alumni magazine at Maxwell. I had had conversations with him for three years without any idea about this vital part of his life and, when I did find out, there had been no reason to bring it up in conversation. But at no time did I have the impression that Professor Saito was trying to avoid talking about his sexuality. Indeed, there were two occasions on which it had come up. Once he had mentioned, in the course of saying something else, that he had known about his sexual orientation since he was three years old. The second time was, now that I think of it, a kind of bookend to the first: his prostatectomy, he had told me, had effectively killed off any sexual urges that had survived the other ravages of old age. But the strange thing he found, he had said at the time, was that this freed him to have more tender and uncomplicated relationships with people.

Professor Saito was like this, especially after his retirement: a curious combination of reticence and frankness. I wish I had asked what his late partner's name was. He would have told me. Perhaps some of the artifacts on display in the apartment—the Meissen porcelain in the curio cabinet, the Javanese puppets, the row of books on modern poetry—were the legacy of this other man, with whom Professor Saito had spent so much of his life. Or perhaps there had been a series of partners, each important in his own way. But in spite of myself, unable to be fully present to our conversation, I could not lead it in this new direction. I simply nodded, smiled, and spoke about other things. He noticed, perhaps, that my attention was flagging, and he said, as if he were waking someone who had fallen asleep, You're still young, Julius. You must be careful about closing too many doors. I had no idea what he was talking about, and I simply nodded when he said this, and watched his spidery hands slowly dancing around each other in that gloomy room.

The bedbugs were on my mind. New Yorkers had begun to speak more often about these tiny creatures in the past two years. The conversations, as befitted a troublesome occurrence in the private arena, had remained private, and the bedbugs were having an unlikely success. They were the unseen enemy that carried on their work, even as false alarms were raised about the West Nile virus, avian flu, and SARS. In the age of the dramatic epidemic, it was the old-fashioned bedbug, a minuscule red-coated soldier, that was least deterred. Of course, other illnesses were much more serious, and more of a drain on public resources. AIDS remained a devastating problem, especially for the poor, and for people who lived in the poorer countries. Cancer, heart disease, and emphysema were not pandemic, but were nevertheless of great importance among the causes of mortality. Even as the terms of transnational conflicts had changed, a similar shift was happening in public health, where, too, the enemies were now vague, and the threat they posed constantly shifting.

But bedbugs were not fatal, and were happy to stay out of the headlines. They were hard to fumigate into oblivion, and their eggs were almost impossible to kill. They did not discriminate on the basis of social class and, for that reason, were embarrassing. An infection in a wealthy home was just as likely, and just as difficult to get rid of, as one among the poor. Hotels at all levels of luxury suffered. If you had them, you had them, and ridding yourself of them permanently was difficult. And in that moment, as I contemplated these ideas, I suddenly felt sorrowful for Professor Saito. His recent encounter with the bedbugs troubled me more than what he had suffered in other ways: racism, homophobia, the incessant bereavement that was one of the hidden costs of a long life. The bedbugs trumped them all. The feeling was subconscious, contemptible. Had it been put to me so baldly at the time, I would have denied it. But it was there, an example of how an inconvenience can, because of one's proximity to it, take on a grotesque aspect.

These tiny, flat creatures, which had sought out human blood since before Pliny's time, were involved in a kind of low-grade warfare, a conflict at the margins of modern life, visible only in speech.

At the end of the afternoon, when I left Professor Saito's apartment, I decided to walk north through Central Park. The snow from three days previously had not melted. In the frigid air, it had hardened to create smooth, low hills across the fields. I kept to a snow-covered road that ran along a sturdy old wall. Footprints were visible, but there was no one else in sight. The light was so diffuse that almost no shadows were cast on the snow, and this gave one the feeling of levitation: white light above and white below. A flock of tiny birds—they might have been starlings—swirled around a tree in the distance. I had the distinct impression that the tangled branches, and the birds that wove expertly in and out of them, were made of the same dun brown substance, the latter different only because they were in an active state. At any moment, I thought, the jagged little branches would unfold their hidden wings and the entire crown of the tree would become a living cloud. The surrounding trees, too, would lose their heads, leaving sentrylike stumps behind, and in the sky above the park there would be a massive canopy of starlings. I walked along this soothing white road for a long time, until the cold cut through my gloves and scarf and compelled me to leave the park and take the subway the rest of the way home.

Later that night, looking through my medical textbooks for more on the bedbugs, I found only dry descriptions of etiologies, life cycles, and therapies. Steam laundering and cyanogas fumigation were discussed at length, but none of this got at what disconcerted me about these creatures. But by a remarkable chance, I found among my books a volume of field reports on epidemiology from the early twentieth century, one in a stack of outdated books that had been discarded by Dr. Martindale at his lab. I had idly picked up a few of those books without really looking at them, but now I found the report written by Charles A. R. Campbell in 1903, and in his writing I got a sense of the disgust and awe in which *Cimex lectularius* was then held.

Dr. Campbell's report superficially conformed to the period style for a medical bulletin, but it drew its real power from a gradual accumulation of assertions, which created an intense and oppressive image of the creature under study. One of the characteristics of the bedbug, Campbell wrote, is its cannibalistic nature. He presented evidence that engorged bugs were sometimes slit open and consumed by their young. He also described a half dozen experiments he had carried out, ostensibly in the interest of scientific research but which gave the impression of an obstacle course designed to prove the bedbug's hardiness and intelligence. Campbell would have been disappointed, I felt sure, had the bedbug failed to pass any of the trials he put it through.

In the experiments, bedbugs survived four months of isolation on a table in a sea of kerosene without food, they came through a deep freeze lasting 244 hours without being harmed, and were able to remain alive underwater for an indefinite period of time. The cunning of these insects, an awed Campbell wrote, is remarkable, and it appears that they have, to a certain extent, the power of reasoning. He described an experiment by Mr. N. P. Wright of San Antonio— "a very reliable citizen and close observer"—in which, as Wright moved his bed farther and farther from the sides of the room, the bedbugs climbed up the wall to the precise height from which they could jump and land on him. When he moved his bed closer, the bugs climbed only as high as was necessary. Campbell's report included a number of stories of this kind, in which bedbugs demonstrated a certain ingenuity in reaching a bed to which their access had been blocked.

I thought of the bugs in their countless millions in all the five boroughs of the city, of their invisible eggs, of their appetite, which was greatest at the hour before dawn. The problem began to seem less and less a scientific one, and I came to share Campbell's unease. The concerns were primeval: the magical power of blood, the hours given over to dreams, the sanctity of the home, cannibalism, the fear of being attacked by the unseen. My rational self was dismayed at these glib analogies, at this unexpected surrender to the kind of insecurity I mocked in others. Nevertheless, when I was done reading, I unmade my bed, switched off the lights, and, kneeling down, carefully examined the seams of the mattress with a flashlight. I found nothing, but of course this did not in itself guarantee a restful night.

# FIFTEEN

There had been a bombing at the biggest pet market in Basra, and the scene was filled with the feathers of parakeets, the cries of dying animals, blood-streaked debris, a mangled engine, a destroyed chair, and cages twisted as though they were made of twine. On the radio, the secretary of state began to discuss an upcoming offensive in the Shiite-controlled area of Baghdad. I went to the pet market and saw the carcasses of dogs lying next to human corpses. Women in black gowns cried and beat their breasts. There was one father who, dead, continued to clutch the vial of insulin he had been trying to take home to his daughter. I became very tired; *tired unto death* was the phrase that scrolled across my mind. I was in my white coat, and my tie was loosened at the neck. My mother was in the pet market. She wore a burka, and Nadège was there with her, wearing the same. My mother asked, What is worse than the bombs? Nadège said, Bedbugs! The two spoke to each other in Yoruba. My mother said, Listen to your sister, Julius. I was about to correct her.

It was one in the morning, and I had fallen asleep in my clothes. I undid my tie and changed, and drank water from the glass on the side table. Before I fell asleep, I had been reading the prologue of *Piers Plowman*. Of its long, alliterative descriptions, all I now retained was the image of William Langland wandering around the world, seeing the various work and struggle of humanity, then settling on one of the Malvern Hills and looking at a brook. He became drowsy, "slumbered into sleep," and in his dreams a magical vision of reality appeared to him, and it was just as I began to read that section that I had fallen asleep.

The light of a streetlamp trembled from behind the curtains. I was hungry but had no appetite. There was a pork chop in the fridge and, as I ate it, standing with the fridge door open, the siren of an ambulance went by in the night. I opened the window, and the air entered in a single gust, as though it had been waiting for admission. The pulsing in my mind matched the flickering pattern of the street-lamp against the curtain. Below, the world was bare, and showed little sign of Langland's "fair field full of folk." I took two aceta-minophen and went back to sleep. The following day was the Satur-day of a call-free weekend, and I could sleep in, untroubled by dreams. When I awoke, I decided I would run errands and, if the day was right for it, visit the old professor later in the afternoon.

THE DOORMAN IN HIS BUILDING USHERED ME IN. THE ELEVA-tor was humid and smelled of sweat. Mary, heavily pregnant, let me into the apartment. Everything was dark and gray inside. He's very sick, she said. He's in the bedroom, come this way, he'll be happy to see you. But when we got there, I saw a man darken the door and go inside ahead of me. He was the doctor. Mary signaled me to wait. I went into the living room and sat down, under Dr. Saito's ring of Polynesian masks. I could hear voices from the bedroom. When the doctor came out, he had a genial expression. His face creased in smiles as he nodded at me and left. I went inside to see Professor Saito, who lay huddled on the bed, tiny and white and weaker than I had ever seen him. His eyes, though they were rheumy and almost closed, were the only part of him that seemed fully there. His voice seemed to be coming not from his mouth, which in any case moved little, but from somewhere else in the room. The timbre was pinched, and he took many breaths. Nevertheless, he spoke lucidly.

Ah, yet another doctor is here, he said. I feel popular. But, Julius, I don't know what you do in Africa, but I must say, I'm ready to go into the forest. I am ready to go in. It is time for me to enter the forest and lie down, and let the lions come for me. I've done enough, I think, I've had a good life, and I'm in such terrible pain just now. Who might say ninety years is not enough? It is time. I sat down next to him and held his small, cold hand in mine. He was tired, and I left him, so that he could rest. I told him I would return soon.

Later that day, not wishing to be alone with the image of Death hovering in the room with its cheap suit and bad manners, I called my friend, and went over to his place. His daughter, a bright nine-year-old named Clara, who otherwise lived with her mother, was visiting. But she's out wandering, he said. His living room had two windows, one west, facing onto Amsterdam Avenue, the other south into a small courtyard, boxed in on all four sides by brick, concrete, and by the small windows of his neighbors' apartments. Those windows lit up one after the other with warm evening lights. There was a tall tree in the middle of the otherwise empty courtyard, bare and with a dense network of branches. I doubted that it got much sunshine, but it looked healthy enough.

That's a tree of heaven, my friend said. I know because I, too, got curious about it, and looked it up. Botanists call it an invasive species. But aren't we all? Once, down in the courtyard, I got a smell quite similar to coffee from one of the broken-off branches. The species was first brought over from China a long time ago, in the 1700s, I think, and apparently it liked American soil so much that it grew freely and wildly in almost every state, often displacing native species.

He went into the kitchen, and returned with a bottle of Heineken for me. It's the shade, you see, he said. It casts shade over other plants, cutting off their sunlight. A tree of heaven will grow anywhere, practically: abandoned lots, back gardens, sidewalks, streets, beaches, unused fields, even right inside boarded-up buildings, even in a sunless courtyard choked with academics. Well, what's so bad about that? I said. A tree's a tree, isn't it? Can't have too many trees in the city. It's not so simple, he said. The tree of heaven reduces local biodiversity. It's thought of as a pest, no good for timber or wildlife, and not even all that great for firewood.

While he spoke, I stood by the facing wall, which had a massive bookcase, and I looked at the endless rows of volumes, including a rich section on African and African-American literature. There was an overflow of books on the floor, and on the coffee table, I noticed a copy of Simone Weil's essays. I picked it up. My friend turned from the window. She's wonderful on the *Iliad,* he said. I think she really gets what force is about, how it motivates action and loses control of what it has motivated. You really should take a look at it sometime.

I had hoped for grace, I said, not for immortality. I had hoped for a graceful, strong exit for this professor of mine. I so badly wanted the old man to give me words of wisdom, I said, not this nonsense about lions. Maybe it's still possible. Maybe the next time I see him, he'll recite something from *Gawain,* or from some Middle English lyric. But maybe I'm being foolish. Instead of being thankful for the relationship, I'm attempting to design it to my own specifications. But, you know, I had hoped that, even as his body broke down, that intricate mind of his, one of the best I've ever known, would soldier on.

My friend looked at me, and said, I wonder why so many people view sickness as a moral test. It has nothing to do with morals or grace. It's a physical test, and usually we lose. Then he clapped his hand on my shoulder, and said, My man, suffering is suffering. You've seen what it does, you see it every day. It might not be especially comforting to you now, but what you just said about the graceful and strong exit reminds me again of something I often think about. For many years, I've thought that the manner and timing of one's death should be a matter of choice. And I really don't think it should be limited to situations when terminal illness has made one's suffering and death imminent. That it should be extended to seasons of life in which one is healthy. Why wait around for the decline? Why not preempt fate?

My friend had by now gone to stand by the window. I remained on the sofa and watched the low sun cut a black silhouette out of him, so that it almost seemed as if I were being addressed by his shadow, or by his future self. There were sparrows flitting about in the distance, attempting to find a place to rest for the night, darting in and out of the network of coves formed by the bare trees and the interlocking arches of the university's buildings. As I reflected on the fact that in each of these creatures was a tiny red heart, an engine that without fail provided the means for its exhilarating midair maneuvers, I was reminded of how often people took comfort, whether consciously or not, in the idea that God himself attended to these homeless travelers with something like personal care; that, contrary to the evidence of natural history, he protected each one of them from hunger and hazard and the elements. For many, the birds in flight were proof that we, too, were under heaven's protection, that there is indeed a special providence in the fall of a sparrow.

My friend waited for me to say something, but I didn't, so he continued. The idea is contrary to the ethics, not to speak of the laws, of our time, but I cannot help but think that in thirty or forty years, when I've taken what joy life has to offer me, and come around to making the choice I have just described, it will have become, if not exactly popular or uncontroversial, at least much more common. Think about contraception, fertility drugs, and abortion; think about these decisions we make so easily about the beginning of life; think about our admiration of figures who chose their own ends: Socrates, Christ, Seneca, Cato. I suppose you don't like how your professor said what he did about the lions, but you shouldn't think of it as an insult to Africans. You know it wasn't meant that way. What he seems to be saying is that, in a better world, the delirium and pain could be avoided. He could walk with his dignity intact into the forest, as he envisioned it, and never be seen again.

He had paused again, standing perfectly still and continuing to look outside. The birds were hardly visible now. Then, in a low voice, almost as if he were talking to himself or regarding his body from a posthumous point of view, he said, The reality, Julius, is that we are alone out here. Perhaps it's what you professionals call suicide ideation, and I hope it doesn't alarm you, but I often paint a detailed picture in my mind of what I would like the end of my life to look like. I think of saying goodbye to Clara and other people I love, then I picture an empty house, perhaps a large, rambling rural mansion somewhere near the marshes where I grew up; I imagine a bath upstairs, which I can fill with warm water; and I think of music playing all through this big house, *Crescent,* maybe, or *Ascension,* filling the spaces not taken up by my solitude, reaching me in the bath, so that when I slip across the one-way border, I do so to the accompaniment of modal harmonies heard from far away.

# SIXTEEN

It had been several weeks since I had seen Professor Saito. At the end of March, I called him up, and a woman, not Mary but someone else, told me he had died. I gasped the words *Oh, Christ* into the phone and hung up. Afterward, sitting in my quiet room, I felt the blood moving around inside my head. The curtains were drawn open and I could see the tops of trees. The leaves were just beginning to come to life after an indifferent winter and, on all the trees on our street, the tips of branches were swollen, the tight, green buds looking as though they might open at any moment. I was shocked, saddened, but I was not completely surprised. Avoiding the drama of death, its unpleasantness, had been my inadvertent idea in not going there.

I called his place again—no longer his place, the thought occurred to me—and the same woman answered. I apologized for having hung up on her, explained who I was, and asked about funeral arrangements. She said, in too prim a tone of voice, that there would be a small private ceremony and that it would be for family only. There might be, she added, a memorial much later on, in the fall perhaps, organized at Maxwell College. I asked her if she knew how I could get in touch with Mary. She didn't seem to be familiar with the name and, as she was eager to get off the phone, our conversation ended.

I didn't know whom to call. He had meant so much to me but, I realized, our relationship had been so private or, rather, outside a network of other connected relationships, that hardly anyone else knew about it, or about how important it had been to us. I had a moment of peculiar doubt just then: perhaps I had overvalued the friendship, and the importance of it had been mine alone. I knew this was the shock speaking to me.

It was nine-thirty in the morning, and three hours earlier than that in San Francisco. I was surprised that Nadège answered the phone. I apologized again and again when I heard the sleepiness in her voice. It's Professor Saito, I said, he died. You remember my old English literature professor, Professor Saito. He died of cancer, and I just found out. He was so kind to me. I'm sorry, is this a bad time to call? She said, No, it's fine, how are you? And as she said this, I heard a man's voice say, Who is that? And she, responding to him, said, Just give me a second. Later in the morning, she called me and said that it was best if she told me the truth, that it was simpler for everyone that way: she was engaged to be married. He was Haitian-American, someone with whom she'd been family friends for a long time. They would be married in late summer. It was best, she said, if I refrained from calling. Just for now; that would be best.

I had the ulcerous sensation of too many things happening at once. What did she think I wanted from her? But I knew she had freed me from the faint hopes I had been harboring. It helped bring a concrete end to what had, in any case, ended long before. I was annoyed only at how long it had taken, and how much wasted thought had gone into it; annoyed, too, that it would surprise me at all that she'd moved on so quickly and so decisively. So my griefs interfered with each other. I put Bach's Coffee Cantata into the stereo that afternoon and lay in bed. It was a recording by the Academy of Ancient Music. The music, rhythmic and jocose, had no entry into my mind, but I let it play on, recognizing its beauty without feeling it. Then I thought perhaps Purcell would be better, more soothing, so I put in "An Evening Hymn": a beautiful score, for tenor and six viols, but that was too lugubrious, and I was insensible to it as well. So I lay there in silence, watching dust motes, until I decided to get up, and run an errand I had been putting off—a package I had been meaning to send—and keep the self-pity at bay.

I walked into Morningside Park. There was snow on the ground still, in dirty patches. It was a world of brown and black, gray and white. My pace was reluctant. Then I stopped: I had the distinct sensation of being watched. In a tree, I saw a hawk. Or, rather, he saw me. His predatory glare pricked the back of my neck, and I turned round to discover him, all intent, on a low branch not more than twenty feet away from where I stood. The park was empty, and the sun was ineffectual, invisible, hiding. He was a strong bird, big, in his presence an embodiment of an extreme elaboration of the evolutionary process. I wondered if he was, perhaps, kin to Pale Male, the celebrated hawk in Central Park who had nested on a Fifth Avenue building, or if, indeed, he was Pale Male himself. He regarded me less with disdain than with disinterest. We looked at each other, and looked, until, spooked, I lowered my eyes, turned around, and carefully, evenly, walked away from him, the whole while feeling those eyes boring into me.

When I came out of the park just north of Central Park North, not many people were about. There were two men in a doorway near the entrance of the post office, one of whom I had seen before. He had dirt-encrusted brown hair that fell about his face like fine ropes. His beard was bushy, flecked with white, and the odor of unwashed weeks emanated from him; his feet, bare and splayed out in front of him in his sitting position, were ashen. The second man, who was clean and much younger, and who was unfamiliar to me, was on one knee, holding the older man's foot. When I got closer, I saw that they were talking, quietly and congenially, as though they were at a dinner table in a restaurant. They spoke Spanish, and laughed every now and again, seemingly unaware that their interaction was taking place in public, oblivious to my staring. The clean man was clipping the dirty man's toenails. He did it with such attentiveness that I couldn't help guessing that the man he was caring for was an older relative of his; his father, perhaps, or an uncle.

I entered the post office. It was late, almost closing time. Unable to find a customs form for my package, I joined the dishearteningly long line, but just then, one of the postal workers redivided the lines, opened a new window, and asked if anyone was sending an international package. I suddenly found myself at the head of a line. I thanked her, and moved toward the window. I told the man behind the glass, a pleasant, bald, middle-aged man, that I wanted a customs form. I filled it out with Farouq's address. The memory of my conversations with him had convinced me to send him Kwame Anthony Appiah's *Cosmopolitanism*. I sealed the envelope, and the postal worker showed me various booklets of stamps. No flags, I said, something more interesting. No, not these, and certainly not these. I finally opted for a beautiful set featuring quilts from Gee's Bend, Alabama. He looked up at me and said, I know. And he added, after a pause, I know, my brother. Then he said, Say, brother, where are you from? 'Cause, see, I could tell you were from the Motherland. And you brothers have something that is vital, you understand me. You have something that is vital for the health of those of us raised on this side of the ocean. Let me tell you something: I am raising my daughters as Africans.

There was no one in line behind me, and the postal window was partially concealed by a column. Terry (that was the name on the ID card around his neck) finished processing my parcel, and asked if I was going to pay for it with cash or a credit card. See, brother—Julius, I said—okay, Brother Julius, the thing is, you're a visionary. It's the truth. I can see that in you. You're someone who has traveled far. You're what we call a journeyer. So let me share something with you, because I think you'll get it. He placed his hands on the metal scale in front of him, inclined his head toward the window, and, lowering his voice to just above a whisper, began a recitation: We are the ones who received the boot. We, who are used for loot, trampled underfoot. Unconquered. We, who carry the crosses. Yes, see? Our kith and our kin used like packhorses. We of the countless horrific losses, assailed by the forces, robbed of choices, silenced voices. And still unconquered. You feel me? For four hundred and fifty years. Five centuries of tears, aeons of fears. Yet still we remain, we remain, we remain the unconquered.

He held the last line in a meaningful pause. Then he said, You know it? I shook my head. It's one of mine, he said. I'm a poet, see. I call that one "The Unconquered." I write these things down, and sometimes I go down to the poetry cafés. That's my gift, you see, poetry. If you liked that, he said, listen to this one: The catalogue of pain, that comes with cocaine, is not from us. They made it, they made the stuff, they made us tough, it was they, the bringers of pain, who brought the rough times, where once all things were calm. And now what we need, you feel me? We need to seed a new balm, a new creed. From within. From our ancestors. For our children. For our future.

Again, moved by his own words, he fell into silence. Brother Julius, he said, with great feeling, you're a visionary, keep hope alive. I think we should see some poetry together. I can see that you instinctively get it. We must be a light for this generation. This generation is in darkness, you feel me? I know you understand. Do you write, yourself? I took the card he slid under the glass. It was printed in gold ink on off-white stock. TERRENCE McKINNEY, WRITER/PERFORMANCE POET/ACTIVIST. No, I said. I wouldn't exactly call myself a writer. Well, drop me a line sometime, he said. We can go to the Nuyorican Poets Cafe. I'd like to talk to you. Sure thing, I said.

It was, in the circumstances, the simplest thing I could say. I made a mental note to avoid that particular post office in the future. When I came out of the building, the younger of the two Spanish-speaking men I had seen earlier had left. The bearded man who'd just had his toenails clipped sat in the golden glow of the sun, which had now come out, and the day became much warmer than I had anticipated. The light fell straight down from the corner of the building across the street. He lay there half asleep in the pool of light, transfigured. Beside him were three empty liquor bottles. I had paid for my postage with cash, and had some change. I gave the drunk two of the three dollars in my pocket. There was a feral cat behind him, seeking shade from the sudden brightness. *Gracias,* the man said, stirring. When I had walked three steps beyond him, I came back again and gave him the last dollar, and he smiled at me through broken teeth. The cat struck with its paw at its own shadow in the concrete.

I got on the subway at 110th Street. I disembarked at 14th Street, and cut across to the East Side, and I walked all the way down the Bowery, with no particular destination in mind, past the innumerable shops selling lamps and restaurant equipment, shops that, from the outside, resembled exotic aviaries. I finally came to a busy square on East Broadway. It was only a short walk from the part of China-town that was most popular with tourists, but it felt like an entire world away, for here no tourists were to be found and almost no one, in fact, who was not originally from East Asia. The signs on the shops, restaurants, businesses, and advertisements were in Chinese characters, and only occasionally were these supplemented with En-glish translations. In the middle of the square itself, a square that was hardly more than a traffic island bounded by the crossing of seven streets, there stood the statue that, from a distance, I guessed was of an emperor or an ancient poet but that turned out to be Lin Zexu, the nineteenth-century antinarcotics activist. The severe monument commemorating this hero of the Opium Wars—he had been appointed commissioner in Guangzhou in 1839, and was much hated by the British for his role in impeding their drug traffic—was the one around which now pigeons flocked. They streaked it with gray guano, enriching the dried white material they had earlier left on the dark green finish of the statue's robes and head. A few people ate ice cream or fried snacks as they sat on the benches of the traffic island, or walked around the statue enjoying the sunshine. Little sign remained of what the neighborhood had been in the early 1800s: an open-air market for livestock and horses, a district of flophouses, tattoo parlors, and saloons.

Everyone in sight seemed to be Chinese, or could be easily taken for Chinese, excepting me and one other person—a man stripped to the waist, and vigorously wiping his arms and chest with a rag. There was an unearthly shine to his body, as though he were already doused in oil, but whether he was applying the shine, or trying to remove it, I could not tell. He was silhouette dark, and his body bore signs either of long hours at the gym or of a lifetime of physical labor. No one paid any attention to him as he meticulously went about this task, which he soon interrupted to pick up the bicycle lying at his feet. He moved the bicycle out of the sun, so that he was more securely in the shadow cast by Lin Zexu's monument. He then resumed his wiping, or application, of the oily material. His entire body glistened, neither more nor less than when he started, and he himself was like a bronze statue. The man then stuffed the rag into the back pocket of his jeans and, as one suddenly struck by a forgotten errand would do, jumped on the bicycle and sped away down one of the smaller streets, weaving in and out of traffic as he did so, until I could no longer see his bright black back among the throng in the direct glare of the sun.

Presently, I, too, went down one of the side streets, an even smaller and more congested one, along which prewar buildings jostled vertiginously, each with an elaborate fire escape that it offered like a transparent mask to the world. Electric wires, wooden poles, abandoned buntings, and a thicket of signs clotted the façades all the way up to the tops of the four- and five-story buildings. The shop windows advertised dental products, tea, and herbs. Large bins were filled to the brim with gnarled ginger and medicinal roots, and there was such a complete motley of goods and services that, after a while, to see a shop window full of hanging carcasses of roast duck succeeded by another one crammed with tailors' dummies, yet another full of fluttering printed leaflets in a half dozen sun-bleached variants of red, and that in its turn followed by a jumble of bronze and porcelain Buddha figures, came to seem a natural progression. Into this last shop I entered, to escape the dizzying activity of the tiny street.

The shop, of which I was the sole customer, was a microcosm of Chinatown itself, with an endless array of curious objects: a profusion of bamboo cages as well as finely worked metal ones, hanging like lampshades from the ceiling; hand-carved chess sets on the ancient-looking bar between the customer and the shopkeeper's bay; imitation Ming Dynasty lacquerware, which ranged in size from tiny decorative pots to round-bellied vases large enough to conceal a man; humorous pamphlets of the "Confucius say" variety, which had been printed in English in Hong Kong and which gave advice to those gentlemen who wished to find success with women; fine wooden chopsticks set on porcelain chopstick stands; glass bowls of every hue, thickness, and design; and, in a seemingly endless glass-fronted gallery high above the regular shelves, a series of brightly painted masks that ran through every facial expression possible in the dramatist's art.

In the midst of this cornucopia sat an old woman, who, having looked up briefly when I came in, was now fully reabsorbed in her Chinese newspaper, preserving a hermetic air that, it was easy to believe, hadn't been disturbed since horses drank water from the troughs outside. Standing there in that quiet, mote-filled shop, with the ceiling fans creaking overhead, and the wood-paneled walls disclosing nothing of our century, I felt as if I had stumbled into a kink in time and place, that I could easily have been in any one of the many countries to which Chinese merchants had traveled and, for as long as trade had been global, set up their goods for sale. And, right away, as though to confirm this illusion, or at least to extend it, the old woman said something to me in Chinese and gestured outside. I saw a boy in a ceremonial uniform walk by with a bass drum. He was presently followed by a row of men with brass instruments, none of them playing, but all walking solemnly in step, marching down the narrow street, which seemed magically to have cleared itself of shoppers for their passage. The old woman and I watched them from the eerie calm of the shop, in which only the ceiling fans were audible, and row after row of these members of a Chinese marching band marched past, with their tubas, trombones, clarinets, trumpets: men of all ages, some with jowled faces, others looking as if they were just reaching puberty, with the first black traces of peach fuzz on their chins, but all with the most profound earnestness, carrying their golden instruments aloft, row after row, until, as if to bookend them, there marched past at the last a trio of snare drums and a final massive bass drum carried by an enormous man. I followed them with my eyes until the procession trickled beyond the last of the bronze Buddhas that sat looking outward from the shop's window. The Buddhas smiled at the scene with familiar serenity, and all the smiles seemed to me to be one smile, that of those who had stepped beyond human worries, the archaic smile that also played on the lips on the funeral steles of Greek kouroi, smiles that portended not pleasure but rather total detachment. From beyond the shop, the old lady and I heard the first series of notes from the trumpet, playing for two bars. Those twelve notes, spiritual cousins of the offstage clarion in Mahler's Second Symphony, were taken up by the entire band. It was a chromatic, blues-inflected figure that must have had its first life in a mission hymn, a dirge that was like a tempest heard from far away, or the growl of waves when the sea is out of sight. The song wasn't one I was able to identify but, in all respects, it matched the simple sincerity of songs I had last sung in the school yard of the Nigerian Military School, songs from the Anglican songbook *Songs of Praise,* which were for us a daily ritual, many years before and thousands of miles away from where I stood in that dusty, sun-suffused shop. I trembled as the throaty chorus of brass instruments spilled into that space, as the tuba ambled across the lower notes, and as the whole sound came into the shop like shafts of interrupted light. And then, with almost imperceptible slowness, the music began to fall in volume as the band marched farther and farther into the noise of the city.

Whether it expressed some civic pride or solemnized a funeral I could not tell, but so closely did the melody match my memory of those boyhood morning assemblies that I experienced the sudden disorientation and bliss of one who, in a stately old house and at a great distance from its mirrored wall, could clearly see the world doubled in on itself. I could no longer tell where the tangible universe ended and the reflected one began. This point-for-point imitation, of each porcelain vase, of each dull spot of shine on each stained teak chair, extended as far as where my reversed self had, as I had, halted itself in midturn. And this double of mine had, at that precise moment, begun to tussle with the same problem as its equally confused original. To be alive, it seemed to me, as I stood there in all kinds of sorrow, was to be both original and reflection, and to be dead was to be split off, to be reflection alone.

# SEVENTEEN

In the spring, life came back into the earth's body. I went to a picnic in Central Park with friends, and we sat under magnolias that had already lost their white flowers. Nearby were the cherry trees, which, leaning across the wire fence behind us, were aflame with pink blossom. Nature is infinitely patient, one thing lives after another has given way; the magnolia's blooms die just as the cherry's come to life. The sun coming through the petals of the cherry blossoms dappled the damp grass, and new leaves, in their thousands, danced in the April breeze, so that, at moments, the trees at the far border of the lawn seemed insubstantial. I lay half in shadow, watching a black pigeon walk toward me. It stopped, then flew up and out of sight, behind the trees, then came back again, walking awkwardly as pigeons do, perhaps seeking crumbs. And far above the bird and me was the sudden apparition of three circles, three white circles against the sky.

In recent years I have noticed how much the light affects my abil-

ity to be sociable. In winter I retreat. In the long and sunny days following, in March, April, and May, I am much more likely to seek out
the company of others, more likely to feel myself alert to sights and
sounds, to colors, patterns, moving bodies, smells other than the
ones in my office or at the apartment. The cold months make me feel
dull, and spring feels like a gentle sharpening of the senses. In our little group in the park that day, we were four, all reclining on a large
striped blanket, eating pita bread and hummus, picking at green
grapes. We kept an open bottle of white wine, our second of the afternoon, hidden in a shopping bag. It was a warm day, but not so
warm that the Great Lawn was packed. We were part of a crowd of
city dwellers in a carefully orchestrated fantasy of country life. Moji
had brought *Anna Karenina* with her, and she leaned on her elbow and
read from the thick volume—it was one of the new translations—
only occasionally interrupting herself to participate in the conversation. And a few yards away from us was a young father calling out to
his toddler who was wandering away: Anna! Anna!

There had been a plane traveling at such a height above us that
the grumble of its jets was barely audible over our discussion. Then
only its faint contrail remained, and just as that faded, we saw the
three white circles growing. The circles floated, appearing to fall upward at the same time they were falling down, then everything resolved, like a camera viewfinder coming into focus, and we saw the
human shape within each circle. Each person, each of these flying
men, steered his parachute, to the left and to the right, and, watching
them, I felt the blood race inside my veins.

Everyone on the lawn was by now alert. Ball games stopped, chatter became loud, and many arms pointed upward. The toddler Anna,
astonished as we all were, held on to her father's leg. The parachutists
were expert, floating toward each other until they were in a kind
of shuttlecock formation, then drifting apart again, and steering
toward the center of the lawn. They came closer to earth, falling
faster. I imagined the whoosh around their ears as they cut through

the air, imagined the tight focus with which they were bracing themselves for landing. When they were at a height of some five hundred
feet, I saw that they were dressed in white jumpsuits with white
straps. The silken parachutes were like the enormous white wings of
alien butterflies. For a moment, all surrounding sound seemed to fall
away. The spectacle of men fulfilling the ancient dream of flight un-
folded in silence.

I could almost imagine what it was like for them, surrounded by
clear blue spaces, even though I've never skydived. Once, on a simi-
larly fine day a quarter of a century ago, I had heard a boy's cries. We
were in the water, more than a dozen of us, and he'd drifted away
toward the deep end. He couldn't swim. We were in a large swimming pool on the campus of the University of Lagos. As a child, I had
become a strong swimmer at my mother's insistence, and somewhat
to my father's dismay, since he was himself afraid of water. She had
taken me to lessons at the country club from the time I was five or
six and, a good swimmer herself, she had watched without fear as I
learned to be at home in the water; from her I had learned that fearlessness. I haven't been in a pool in years but, once, my ability had
made a difference. It was the year before I went away to NMS; I had
saved another's life.

This boy, of whom I now remember nothing other than the fact
that he was, like me, of mixed race (in his case, half-Indian), was in
mortal danger, drawn into increasingly deeper areas of the pool the
more he struggled to keep his head above water. The other children,
shocked into inaction by his distress, had remained in the shallow
end, watching. There was no lifeguard present, and none of the
adults, assuming any of them was a swimmer, was close enough to
the deep end of the pool to help. I don't remember deliberating, or
considering any danger to myself, only that I set off in his direction
as fast as I could. The moment that has stayed in my mind is of having not yet reached the boy but having already left the crowd of children behind. Between his cries and theirs, I swam hard. But caught

in the blue expanse around me and above, I suddenly felt like I was no closer to him than I had been a few moments before, as though water intervened intentionally between where he was in the shadow of the diving structures and where I floated in the bright sunshine. I had stopped swimming, and the air cooled the water on my face. The boy flailed, briefly breaking the surface with frantic arms before he was pulled under again. The strong shadows made it difficult for me to see what was happening. I thought, for an instant, that I would always be swimming toward him, that I would never cross the remaining distance of twelve or fifteen yards. But the moment was to pass, and I would become the hero of the day. There was laughter afterward, and the half-Indian boy was teased. But it might easily have been a tragic afternoon. What I hauled the short distance to the diving platform might have been a small, lifeless body. But almost all that day's detail was soon lost to me, and what remained most strongly was the sensation of being all alone in the water, that feeling of genuine isolation, as though I had been cast without preparation into some immense, and not unpleasant, blue chamber, far from humanity.

For the parachutists, the distance between heaven and earth began to vanish more quickly, and the ground suddenly rushed upward to meet them. Sound returned, and they landed, one after the other, neatly, in billowing clouds, to the whoops and whistles of the picnickers in the park. I applauded, too. The parachutists slipped out from under their tents, crouching, and signaled to each other. Then they rose like victorious matadors, gesturing to the crowd, and were rewarded with our happy cries and louder applause.

Then it stopped. Above the noise, we heard the blaze of sirens on the east side of the park. Four police officers came racing over the ropes around the perimeter of the lawn and ran toward its center. One was white, one Asian, and the other two were black, all as ungainly in their movement as the parachutists had been balletic. We began to boo, safe in our numbers, and were pushed back from the congratulatory circle we had formed, so that they could arrest the daredevils. Someone at the far end of the circle shouted "Security theater!" but the wind had picked up, and it swallowed her voice.

The parachutists did not resist arrest. No longer encumbered by their wings, they were led away by the police. The crowd began to cheer again, and the parachutists, all young men, grinned and bowed. One of them, taller than the other two, had a full ginger beard that glinted in the sun. The parachutes remained in a glossy heap in the grass and, when the wind picked up again, seemed to give off trembling exhalations. And so we watched the parachutes breathe for a while, while the men were led away. Then, but only after what seemed like a long time out of ordinary time, we came out of the marvelous and resumed our picnic. Something had appeared in the sky, defying nature. My friend, who seemed to have read my thoughts, said, You have to set yourself a challenge, and you must find a way to meet it exactly, whether it is a parachute, or a dive from a cliff, or sitting perfectly still for an hour, and you must accomplish it in a beautiful way, of course.

Moji, Dayo Kasali's sister, lay prone, a straw hat over her head. Lise-Anne and my friend were well matched, I thought. I had never met her, but he had assured me that she was his ideal companion. There was a balance in his seriousness and her natural lightness. She already understood him, which was more than could be said for his last several girlfriends. His love of philosophy was equaled by the way he (as he once put it to me) practiced biology. My friend was often forgiven his inconstancy; the willingness of women to forgive him came with his being the suave creature he was. For him to be understood, as she seemed to instinctively understand him, was rarer.

Near us, a wisteria's boughs hung low, the petals on its purple blooms reticulated and busy with resurrection. There were some tulips, Sultans of Spring, I supposed, with large silken petals that were like ears. Bees collided again and again with the flowers, tracing flight paths all around us. On our way into the park, Moji had said to me that she was more worried than ever about the environment. Her tone was serious. When I responded that I supposed we all were, she corrected me, shaking her head. What I mean is that I actively worry about it, she said, I don't think that's generally true of other people. I think I waste things, I have bad habits like most of the Americans around me. Like most people in the world, I suppose. My awareness of it has intensified in the past couple of months, she said.

I had attempted to meet the issue in the right way. I asked her if she worried about things like air travel. I knew that she went to Nigeria at least once a year. Wasn't she concerned about the environmental effect of jet fuel, and all that? She responded that she was. Then our conversation trailed off when Lise-Anne and my friend, walking a few steps behind, caught up with us again, and she began to tell us about life in Troldhaugen, where she'd grown up. Now, as I watched park workers fold up the parachutes, I remembered that brief earlier exchange with Moji. I had heard the environmental concern often enough to know how earnest a priority it was for some people, but I did not, as yet, feel it seriously in my bones. I had not experienced a fervor over it. I did not pause to consider whether to use paper or plastic, and I only ever recycled out of convenience, not out of some belief that recycling made a real difference. But already, I was starting to respect those who were fervent. It was a cause, and I was distrustful of causes, but it was also a choice, and I found my admiration for decisive choice increasing, because I was so essentially indecisive myself.

Moji lifted the hat off her face, and a bee that had been troubling her reassessed the situation and flew off in the direction of the nearest bloom. The sky had turned a darker blue, and the air was cooler. She brushed her cheek with her hand. I looked at her, and found her puzzling. She was too tall, and her eyes were small. Her face was dark, so dark that it had faint purple notes in it, but she was not beautiful in the way I expected dark women to be. You know what I know about bees? she said all of a sudden, breaking into my thoughts.

That the name Africanized killer bees is a piece of racist bullshit. Africanized killers: as if we don't have enough to deal with without *African* becoming a shorthand for murderous. She leaned forward to pluck a grape from its stem on the plate. She was wearing a tank top, and I caught sight of the dark curve of her breast.

Around the country, I said, bees are dying and the scientists don't know why. I've always found bees inscrutable. They are obsessed in ways that elude humans, and now they are falling prey to mass death. It has something to do with weather patterns or pesticides, I think, or perhaps some genetic change is at the heart of it. Already, one in every three bees has died, and more are to follow; the percentage is increasing all the time. For so long, I said, they have been used as machines for making honey, their obsession was turned to human advantage. Now they are proving adept at dying, too, dying from some terrible disorder in the order Hymenoptera.

There were nods and smiles. Lise-Anne looked at me with some admiration, and my friend mocked me with his eyes. Moji said she'd read something about the phenomenon, that it was called colony collapse disorder. It is quite widespread by now, she said, common all over Europe and North America, even as far as Taiwan. And isn't it something also to do with genetically modified maize? My friend put his head in Lise-Anne's lap, and said, That sounds like something out of imperial history: colony collapse disorder! The natives are restless, Your Majesty, we can't hold on to these colonies much longer. Lise-Anne said, Do any of you know *El Espíritu de la Colmena*? It's a film by a man named Erice, made in the seventies. In that film, bees represent, I don't know what, but it seems that, in a violent and sad time in Spanish history, they represented a different way of thinking, a way of thinking and being that was specific to bees, but that was related to the human world. There are some scenes in that film that, really, are under my skin now. I think of the ones where the father—he has two young daughters, and one of them is called Ana, just like that little girl who was over there a moment ago—the scenes where the father is kind of shell-shocked, or in the cage of some memory he cannot talk about, and just works at the beehive. Those scenes are very moving, they are without dialogue or plot, but they are effective. Anyway, I don't know what my point is, but maybe bees are sensitive, unusually sensitive, to all the negativity in the human world. Maybe they are connected to us in some essential way that we haven't figured out yet, and their death is a warning of some sort to us, like the canaries in a coal mine, sensitive to an emergency that will soon be apparent to dull, slow human beings.

I hadn't seen Erice's film, but the collapse of the bee populations made me think of something else, which I now connected to what Lise-Anne had just described. The lack of familiarity with mass death, with plague, war, and famine, seemed to me a new thing in human history. These last few decades, I said to my friends, in which wars flare up in patches instead of being all-consuming, and agriculture no longer evokes elemental fear, and the seasonal variations in weather are not harbingers of starvation, is an anomaly in human history. We are the first humans who are completely unprepared for disaster. It is dangerous to live in a secure world. Look at this harmless and beautiful stunt by the parachutists. We know that they are in the right, right for having made something memorable for us, at some personal risk, but the police are charged with keeping us safe at all times, empowered to secure us with the force of arms, and protect us even from pleasure. I often think of the long nineteenth century, which, in all parts of the world, was one interminable bloodbath, an orgy of continuous killing, whether in Prussia or in the United States, or in the Andes or in West Africa. Butchery was the norm, and nations went to war on the slightest pretexts. And it went on and on, interrupted by brief pauses for rearmament. Think of the epidemics that wiped out ten, twenty, even thirty percent of populations in Europe: I read somewhere recently that the city of Leiden lost thirty-five percent of its population in a five-year period in the 1630s. What could it mean to live with such a possibility, with people of all ages dropping dead around you all the time? The thing is that we have no idea. In fact, when I read it, it was as a footnote in an article talking about something else, an article about painting or furniture.

Families that lost three of their seven members were not at all unusual. For us, the concept of three million New Yorkers dead from illness within the first five years of the millennium is impossible to grasp. We think it would be total dystopia; so, we think of such historical realities only as footnotes. We try to forget that other cities in other times have seen worse, that there isn't anything that immunizes us from a plague of one kind or another, that we are just as susceptible as any of those past civilizations were, but we are especially unready for it. Even in the way we speak about what little has happened to us, we have already exhausted ourselves with hyperbole.

I'd been going on. It was Lise-Anne who saved me from myself by changing the subject. She said, But, Julius, you're a shrink. I've always wondered about that. I'm obviously crazy, or I wouldn't be with this guy over here. So never mind the bees or the plague and all that. Who's the craziest person you've treated recently? I bet you get some really whacked-out ones. Or are you sworn to secrecy? We promise not to tell anyone.

I indulged them, and told them stories about my patients, about the alien visitations and government surveillance, the voices in the walls, the suspicions of family conspiracies. There is always a fund of humorous tales from the horror of mental illnesses, particularly in the ranks of the paranoid. I called on these stories now, even passing off some of my colleagues' patients as my own. My friends laughed as I recalled a case in which the patient had "successfully" jammed signals from other planets, carefully lining every window in her apartment with aluminum foil, placing receptors elaborately woven from paper clips in the soles of her shoes, and always carrying a small piece of lead in each pocket, even when she was asleep. Paranoid schizophrenia lent itself especially well to such narratives, and the sufferers of the disease were good storytellers because they engaged in world building. Within the parameters of their own realities, these worlds were remarkably consistent: they looked crazy only from the outside.

Do doctors actually use the word *crazy*? Moji asked. We most certainly do, I said. Some people, in fact, are simply nuts, and that's what we write down in the chart. I did this just last week. Forty-nine-year-old salesman: I talked to him for a few minutes and wrote down, as he spoke: The patient is as crazy as a sack full of ferrets. Another patient I once diagnosed: Just plain nuts. I think you'd be surprised at what doctors actually say when no one is looking.

Do you know that shop near TriBeCa, Lise-Anne said, We Are Nuts About Nuts? Well, my friend said, I know I definitely am. There are actually lots of insane people in this town, maybe the majority of New Yorkers. Well, no, he went on, I don't mean that. But, really, everyone just finds a way to cope, no one is completely free of mental problems, so I say let everyone sort themselves out. Insanity is used as an excuse for suppressing dissent, just as it has always been. Julius, I'm sure you know all about this: there used to be floating prisons in medieval Europe, ships of fools sailing from port to port, collecting the undesirables. People whom we would think of as a little depressed today were put through exorcisms. It was all about removing the contaminants from society.

And if we're talking about real insanity, my friend went on, and I'm not going to pretend that doesn't exist, if we're talking about deep down, in-the-gut disjunction between actual reality and a sort of personally invented reality, well, there's been plenty of that in my own family. What you said about Leiden, well, in a way, my family was Leiden. My father went crazy and became a cocaine fiend. Or maybe it was the other way around, maybe the cocaine came first. Anyway, he's out there in South Carolina somewhere right this minute, looking to score some blow. That's what he lives for. Understand that I use the word *father* in a loose sense. I haven't seen the man in four years, and the times I saw him, I wish I hadn't. My mom, on the other hand: six children from five different men. That's kind of crazy, too, isn't it? I mean, how do you not quit doing that after the third or fourth kid? I've got an older brother who's doing time for dealing. And that's without mentioning my uncle Raymond. Uncle Ray was a mechanic in the Atlanta area. He had a wife and three kids. Salt-of-the-earth type, never strayed, never did drugs. Then, when I was eleven, he lost his mind over God only knows what, and he went into the backyard and shot his brains out. His youngest kid, my cousin Yvette, who was seven at the time, found him.

A silence fell on the group. I knew the story. This was the appalling family background my friend had had to overcome to go to university and to graduate school, and to become an assistant professor in the Ivy League. Now, having spoken, he had a peaceful expression on his face. Ahead of us, in the lengthening shadows of afternoon, the parachutes had been folded and were being carted away on vehicles belonging to the Department of Parks and Recreation. The stuntsmen would probably get slapped with a charge of reckless endangerment and be fined. I suppose, Moji said at length, that the things black people have had to deal with in this country— and I don't mean me or Julius, I mean people like you, who have been here for generations—the things you've had to deal with are definitely enough to drive anyone over the edge. The racist structure of this country is crazy-making.

Oh, man, Lise-Anne said, don't give him excuses! We all laughed, with some relief. Lise-Anne was immediately likable. In contrast, I was struck by Moji's brittleness, the defensiveness she seemed to have so readily at hand. Speaking of her boyfriend, whom I had not met yet, she'd demanded of me: Are you trying to find out if he's black? I was startled. I assured her that no, I had no such interest. It was trite, it suggested a sort of unformed mind to me. But I found it appealing, and even sexual, and I suddenly imagined us together in a sexual situation. She was no Nadège; this attraction was of a different valency. I wasn't even certain if I could term it attraction. But there was something interesting in the mood she gathered around her like a robe. She was forthright, she spoke freely, she was always spoiling for a fight, and yet she gave the impression of being an observer, a close watcher of people and words.

On our way out of the park, my friend and his girl broke off, and took a cab uptown. I walked along Central Park West with Moji. Again, I did most of the talking. I tried, again, to draw her out on the subject of recycling. She responded in yeses and nos, as though she knew well that I was prattling, filling in the silence. A pigeon with dark feathers, possibly the same one we had seen early in the afternoon, though I doubted it, hopped along the stone wall along the west side of the park, as if it were following us, then took sudden flight, and vanished into the trees for good. I asked her once more about her boyfriend, pretending to be interested. His name was John Musson. She had nothing to say about him. The spring night diminished what we said, absorbing our energy, so that after a while we merely walked along in silence. Once or twice I glanced up at her face, which just then seemed so focused, and so unpretty, and so complete in its allure. I was having such a difficult time reading her. Traffic growled low alongside us, the sound of impatient, churning engines, and gasoline smoke adding menace to the park's perfumed world. At the subway on Eighty-sixth Street, I let her go.

THE PRACTICE OF PSYCHIATRY IS PARTLY ABOUT SEEING THE world as a collection of tribes. Take a set of individuals who have brains that, with regard to how they map reality, are more or less equal: differences among brains in this set, this ostensibly normal group, this control group, which constitutes the majority of humanity, are small. Mental well-being is mysterious, but this group is fairly predictable, and what little science has discovered about brain function and chemical signaling applies broadly. The right hemisphere processes in parallel, the left processes serially, and messages are passed more or less efficiently between the two by the corpus callo-sum. The whole organ nestles inside the skull, steadily improving at a range of astonishingly complex tasks, while getting worse at a few others. This is our picture of normality. Anecdotally the differences tend to be exaggerated—for important social reasons, people like to think that other people are totally unlike them—but these differ-ences are, in reality, for most functions, rather small.

But take another set of individuals, a more distant tribe, and among these the brains differ from those of the first set in some chemically and physiologically significant way. These are the men-tally ill. The mad, the crazy: people who are schizophrenic, obsessive, paranoid, compulsive, sociopathic, bipolar, depressed, or some grim combination of two or more of these: these people all belong to-gether, they ought to be classed with each other. Or so we think—and this is the rationale for the medical practice of psychiatry. If they are ill enough, they show up at the hospital, willingly or otherwise, and are given drugs, admitted willingly or otherwise. But within this tribe, it has often struck me, the differences are so profound that, really, what we are looking at is many tribes, each as distinct from the others as it is from the tribe of the normal.

In my duties as a medical school graduate and psychiatric resi-dent, I was licensed to be the healer, and nudged those who were less normal toward some imaginary statistical mean of normalcy. I had the costume and the degree to prove it, and I had the *DSM-IV* at my side. My task, if I were to state it as grandly as possible, was to cure the mad. If I could not cure them, which was more often than not, I did my best to help them cope. I had struggled all through medical school not to lose sight of this grand statement, the dream that lay beneath our science and praxis. These ruminations were entirely private, of course, and one of the lessons I learned most swiftly as a medical student was that the larger picture was sacrificed, more out of habit than out of necessity, to the small detail. We were taught to distrust philosophy; our teachers favored the potent neurotransmitter, the analytical trick, the surgical intervention. Holism was looked down on by many professors, and in this the best students followed their lead.

We were all deeply sensitive to the suffering of our patients, but I was one of a tiny minority, as far as I could tell, who thought incessantly of the soul, or worried about its place in all this carefully calibrated knowledge. My instinct was for doubts and questions. The management of most cases became straightforward for me after three years of residency. How bewildering everything had been, to begin with, a great sea of unmasterable knowledge, full of tricky passes and opportunities to fail. But, as though all at once, I found that I was a competent psychiatrist. I was also by this time getting a better idea of what I might do afterward: which fellowships to apply for, from whom to seek letters of recommendation. I had gradually given up the ambition for academic practice and research, and my future seemed to be in a large, nonacademic city hospital, or perhaps a small practice in the suburbs. This was fine by me, as I had never really had the appetite for the kind of competition academia entailed.

In mid-April, our department chair left for private practice. His replacement, a transplant from Hopkins named Helena Bolt, a leading expert on ADHD, was generous and much easier to work with. Her presence made a difference to the entire department. There had been a scandal: a year previously, the chair, Professor Gregoriades, had been accused of using a derogatory term in reference to some Asian patients. The accusation had not been made publicly or formally, but from what those who discussed the story claimed, the sources were credible. Though most of us never did find out what actual word, if any, had been used, it was a bad scene, especially for the handful of Korean-American and Chinese-American interns in the program. It was a serious charge, and undoubtedly played a role in his moving to a different program. With his departure, some of the negative energy and malcontentment in the department dissipated.

Gregoriades had, in truth, never been anything but civil with me. He was a brilliant scholar with a national reputation, a finalist for a Lasker Award, a member of the American Academy of Arts and Sciences, an honoree of the American Psychiatric Association; the professional achievements said something about him distinct from his personality, something that commanded respect. In any case, I had never minded his somewhat cold manner, and had even entertained thoughts, earlier on, of getting to know him better, of working on a strategy to get into his good graces, for the possible benefit doing so might have been for my career. That was something I'd decided not to follow through on, but the idea had been there. Eminence, pedigree, connections: had I been entirely free of those concerns, I would probably not have come to Presbyterian. Still, he was of a different generation, or so it was said. He was less sensitive to the new nuances of political correctness. No doubt people would have been less sanguine about the situation had he been accused of racially abusing black students, or Jewish ones.

Professor Bolt, his replacement, was better than polite. Through her, we younger physicians got some genuine insight into what a compassionate practice might look like, twenty-five years into a university- and hospital-based career. She had a publications list several pages long, had had professional successes only a little less glittering than Gregoriades', and was reputed to be a smart manager. But what was most apparent was that she also genuinely cared about the direct care of patients. She wanted to design policy around what we could do to improve their outcomes. The change was imperceptible at first, but by a month after Bolt's arrival, a recurring subject in the shift room chatter was about the way our work culture in the department had changed. It was to the good. And it was especially satisfying to me, with my stubbornly held and somewhat naïve vision, as

I approached the end of my training, of what psychiatry really ought to be about: provisional, hesitant, and as kind as possible.

Talking to my friend and the others in the park about residency, I had focused, as I'd had to in the context, on comic vignettes. There is a long marriage between comedy and human suffering, and mental illness, in particular, is easily played for laughs. But I had dozens of cases that would have been ill-suited for the purpose, and sometimes it is hard to shake the feeling that, all jokes aside, there really is an epidemic of sorrow sweeping our world, the full brunt of which is being borne, for now, by only a luckless few.

I READ FREUD ONLY FOR LITERARY TRUTHS. HIS SHORTCOMings had, after all, been so thoroughly exposed that, in the popular culture almost as much as in the profession of psychiatry, he was understood almost primarily through his critics: H. J. Eysenck had taken him to task for his psychotherapy, Popper for his science, Friedan for his attitude to women. The criticism, in general, was not unjust. So I read him, not as a professional seeking professional insight, but as I would read a novel or a poem. His work was a good counterweight to the pharmacological bias of modern practice. The historical aura was attractive, too: he had, after all, been sought out even by Mahler. The argument could be made that, even allowing for his excesses and misreadings, he illuminated psychoanalysis—which, let no one forget, was his original discovery—more vividly than would even the most meticulous of modern practitioners.

His writings on grief and loss, I found, remained useful. In *Mourning and Melancholia* and, later, in *The Ego and the Id,* Freud suggested that, in normal mourning, one internalizes the dead. The dead are fully assimilated into the living, a process he called introjection. In mourning that does not proceed normally, mourning in which something has gone wrong, this benign internalization does not happen. Instead, there's an incorporation. The dead occupy only a part of the one who has survived; they are sectioned off, hidden in a crypt, and from this place of encryption they haunt the living. The neatness of the line we had drawn around the catastrophic events of 2001 seemed to me to correspond to this kind of sectioning off. There had been great heroism, of course, though, as the years passed, it had become clear that aspects of this heroism were overstated. There was firmness of purpose, too, in the language of the president, there was certainly political squabbling, and there was a determination to rebuild right away. But the mourning had not been completed, and the result had been the anxiety that cloaked the city.

Set against this bigger picture, the many smaller ones: in the spring, I saw an old gentleman. Mr. F., of Westchester County, was eighty-five years old and, save for some cataracts, was in remarkably good physical health. For a few months, his family had assumed that he was sliding into Alzheimer's disease: his attention wandered, his memory failed, and often he seemed to be lost in the moment. He said less and less, and when he did talk, he seemed to be interested only in old memories, some of which he mixed up. But eventually the neurologist found that there was no medical reason to believe he had Alzheimer's; she had sent him up to us in Milstein, and her suspicion was proved correct: Mr. F. was depressed.

He was a Navy veteran of the Second World War, and had seen action in the Pacific. But he'd come home and married his sweetheart, and they'd had a large family—five children—all of them raised on his income as a factory worker in Albany, and hers as a nurse-aide and substitute teacher. His wife had died in 1999, and he'd moved in with the second of his three daughters a year later; it was while living there, in White Plains, that he began to eat and sleep badly, lose weight, sink into low moods, and experience a racing of his thoughts that he described, with great difficulty—he was a reticent man—as an effort to keep from drowning. When he came in, in his veteran's cap and a blue windbreaker, he had that faraway look of those who had somehow gotten locked inside their sadness.

I saw him only twice (he went on to psychotherapy), but I remember how, after that second session together, by which time I had gotten a fairly comprehensive medical history from him, I explained to him how the various medications might work. I was telling him that it was unlikely he would see any improvement in his mood for about a month when he interrupted me, raising his hand gently. I stopped midsentence, and Mr. F. said, with sudden emotion in his voice, Doctor, I just want to tell you how proud I am to come here, and see a young black man like yourself in that white coat, because things haven't ever been easy for us, and no one has ever given us nothing without a struggle.

# EIGHTEEN

At a light on 124th were two men in their twenties, fragments of whose conversation floated around me as we crossed the street. He come up, word? said one. He come up yo, said the other, I thought you knew that nigga. Shit, said the first, I don't know that motherfucker. They acknowledged me, and I them, then they turned right and went down the street, toward the south. They walked effortlessly, lazily, like athletes, and I marveled at their prodigious profanity for a moment, then forgot about them.

About ten minutes later, as I came around the little road that runs above Morningside Park (before it becomes Morningside Drive proper), I noticed sudden movement in the shadows up ahead. My jumpiness hadn't been necessary, and I smiled and relaxed when I saw who it was: the two young men at whom I had nodded earlier. They didn't return the smile, but loped toward me, their every step seemingly calculated to save energy. They walked past me on either side without speaking to each other and as though they hadn't seen me. Each appeared to be intent on his own thoughts. There had earlier been, it occurred to me, only the most tenuous of connections between us, looks on a street corner by strangers, a gesture of mutual respect based on our being young, black, male; based, in other words, on our being "brothers." These glances were exchanged between black men all over the city every minute of the day, a quick solidarity worked into the weave of each man's mundane pursuits, a nod or smile or quick greeting. It was a little way of saying, I know something of what life is like for you out here. They had passed by me now, and were for some reason reluctant to repeat that fleeting gesture.

We were in the day's last light, and the street was largely in shadow. It was unlikely they would have recognized me again even in strong daylight. Still, I was unnerved. And it was in the middle of that thought that I felt the first blow, on my shoulder. A second, heavier, landed on the small of my back, and my legs gave way like sticks. I fell to the ground. I don't recall if I cried out, or if opening my mouth I was unable to make a sound. They began to kick me all over—shins, back, arms—a quick, preplanned choreography. I shouted, begging them to stop, conscious of a man on the ground being beaten. Then I lost the will to speak, and took the blows in silence. The initial awareness of pain was gone, but now came the anticipation of how much it would hurt later, how bad tomorrow would be, for both my body and my mind. My mind had gone blank except for this lone thought, a thought that made my eyes sting, a prospect more painful, it seemed, than the blows. We find it convenient to describe time as a material, we "waste" time, we "take" our time. As I lay there, time became material in a strange new way: fragmented, torn into incoherent tufts, and at the same time spreading, like something spilled, like a stain.

There was no mortal fear. Somehow it was clear that they did not intend to kill me. There was an ease to their violence, and even though no gun had been brandished and no explanations given, I

knew that they were in control. I was being beaten, but it was not severe, certainly not as severe as it could be if they were truly angry.
"They" were not two, as I had thought: a third had joined them, and
there was laughter, easy laughter, interspersed with profanities.
When my eyes came into focus, I saw, or had the impression, that
they were much younger than I had guessed before, that they were
no older than fifteen. And the words, fluent, spiking in and out of
their laughter, seemed somehow distant from the situation, as if they
were addressing someone else, as if this were like all the other times
I had encountered those words: never hostile, never directed at me,
as innocent as when these same words had been foreshadowed at the
crossing. They were intended, now, to humiliate, and I shrank from
them. My hand was raised against curses, too, as the blows kept coming, though less quickly. The boys continued to laugh, and one of
them stepped on my hand one last time, especially hard. The world
darkened. They left, sprinting, their basketball shoes thudding and
squeaking against the ground.

They left, and time's shape was restored. They'd taken my wallet
and my phone. I sat on the road in silence, bewildered, thinking it
could have been worse, thinking, too, that it had been inevitable.
Above me, the evening lights of apartments came on, and there was
still a little light in the sky; incoming night was poised between daylight and electric light; the light shining from interiors I could see
but not reach seemed to promise that life was continuing. People
were returning home from work, or preparing dinner, or finishing
the last fragments of the afternoon's tasks. People; but there were
none on the street, just the dry wind falling through the trees. I sat
in the street looking into a nettle-choked ditch. The intricacy of the
weeds startled.

It could have been worse: an infuriating thought, a false thought,
because what had happened was worse, worse than safety and an un-
violated body. Then pain came streaming in, physical pain, as if the
ambient temperature had suddenly risen and a dry heat was spread-

ing to all parts of my body. The tears fell from my eyes. It hurt to breathe. I guessed at a broken rib or two, though that turned out not to be the case. The knuckles of my left hand were covered in sand and blood, and there was a gash across the back of the same hand, beyond the wrist; this was the hand I had lifted to protect my head as I lay curled on the asphalt with my knees brought up and head lowered. My mouth was numb, as after a visit to the dentist. It wasn't my mouth, I thought as I moved my tongue around inside it, this uncooperative, alien, ugly mouth.

I saw someone, at last, at the far end of the street. It wasn't the far end, just two blocks down. The person was small, slow, like a memory approaching. Picking myself up, brushing my clothes clean, I began to walk, limping a little, gritting my teeth, feeling the ugliness spread across my face. But this person bought my disguise. It was an elderly man in overalls. He walked past, and did not notice, or did not care to notice, that I had just been beaten.

Walking back, I stayed in the shadows for as long as I could. It wasn't far. The boys had melted away into the park, and were probably far away, somewhere deep in Harlem, by now. The lobby was empty, the elevator free. I entered my apartment and stood before the bathroom mirror for a long time. I touched my jaw, traced a finger gently up onto the cheek. It hurt, swollen to a furious purple. I removed my clothes, first the filthy black coat, then the pristine powder-blue shirt rumpled underneath it. The shirt, which I rarely wore, was a gift from Nadège. Clarity returned: I must clean the wounds (a hospital visit did not seem necessary), and I must make a report. My credit cards, too: that was the first call to make, to limit the financial damage. Then the campus police, who would put up a sign by the elevator announcing (as so often before, in all the previous instances when I wasn't the victim) that someone had recently been attacked in the neighborhood, and that the suspects were male, black, and young, of average height and weight.

I opened the window and looked out. It was total darkness now, and the sky was a charcoal gray, the darkness interrupted closer to ground level by distant halogen lights. The buildings across the street were apartments, mostly occupied by students and faculty of the various institutions of the neighborhood, Teachers College, Union Theological Seminary, the Jewish Theological Seminary, and Columbia Law School. In one of the apartments, the one almost directly level with mine, a young woman faced a wall. She was wearing a shawl, and bowed her head repeatedly, davening in the yellow light of a standing lamp. A few floors above her, on the flat roof of the building, a large chimney belched out gray smoke in a wide plume. The smoke was like a slowed-down explosion, silent, billowing, being absorbed at its edges into the deeper darkness of the sky. My own apartment was dark. I had made some tea, and I drank it as I watched the woman pray. Others are not like us, I thought to myself, their forms are different from ours. Yet I prayed, too, I would gladly face a wall and daven, if that was what had been given to me. Prayer was, I had long settled in my mind, no kind of promise, no device for getting what one wanted out of life; it was the mere practice of presence, that was all, a therapy of being present, of giving a name to the heart's desires, the fully formed ones, the as yet formless ones.

It had been only two hours. I trembled from the shock, still gasped inwardly at the suddenness of it; but already, it felt in some way like a school yard scuffle. Had I sailed through a brief moment when, like an old man welcoming death, I had accepted the next blow and the next? No, I hadn't. I had felt only the fear of pain and the love of being free of pain. But how could I have missed this! I'd thought, lying in the dirt. How could I have been less than completely aware of how good it was to be injury-free?

Now every cliché by which the assault could be minimized hurried to claim space in my head. These things happen, it was only a matter of time, count your blessings, and, yes, it could have been worse—and such bile rose into my throat at these thoughts. Three personal days from work would be enough to restore my equilibrium, I thought, and I would try to be frank about the reasons for my time away, for my staying out of sight. In the meantime, I would have to reach out to my friend for help with some practical things. He, at least, would not make more of the event than was necessary.

I had listened to others' stories of being mugged. A colleague on the service had had her purse snatched. One of the nurses—a burly, soft-spoken Portuguese-American—had had his jaw broken by a gang, and they had left his wallet, his watch, his gold chain, and taken only his iPod. He'd needed seventeen stitches across his face. Violence for sport was no strange thing in the city; but now: me. I had cleaned the wounds on my shoulders, arms, and legs, mostly numerous small bruises that would heal quickly. My disfigured mouth and my hand troubled me most. As I examined the bruises, a herd of thoughts clattered through me: Why had this same body hale so often hurried past its lovers?

The woman had stopped praying. She ran her fingers through her fair brown hair, and took the tallit from her shoulders, pausing for a moment as though she'd forgotten something. Then she folded it, and switched off the lamp.

THE YOUNG WOMAN WAS UNCERTAIN, THINKING HARD BEFORE she said each word. The man sitting next to her, to whom she had looked for confirmation, shook his head and corrected her. No, that's World Health Organization. Try it again, do you see? That is World. Trade. Organization. Yes, that's trade. Do you remember the word for trade?

He pointed, and trilled a pair of fingers on the page. She mulled it over awhile, then gave another answer in Chinese, which sounded similar to the first. This one pleased him more, and he asked her if she would like to review the list from the beginning. I was at a small table, alone, drinking coffee, picking out their conversation from the fugue of voices in the diner. They were at the bar across from me, drinking Cokes. The student was Asian. Her inky black bangs cut straight across her face, and she moved a stack of flash cards from one hand to the other, restless. Her teacher, not much older than she was, was a blond man in a tracksuit.

I pretended to look out at the street. The shadows were long, the light yellow, and, on the sidewalk, two women with high heels and large shopping bags embraced. The negotiation between the blond teacher and his student was that of a new relationship, with the roles set already but a certain formality still prevailing. She laughed every now and again, and he corrected her pronunciation. She seemed to be struggling to draw what little she knew of the language to the surface. Her eyes searched, oblivious of being seen. His manner seemed more self-conscious. He was aware of the incongruity between his features and his task, aware of carrying out that task in a public space. He seemed to be presenting his credentials, addressing not her alone, but anyone within earshot who might pause for a moment at the sight of a white man teaching Chinese to an Asian woman. He sounded a little pleased with himself. He repeated the phrases again, and, in a quick upward glance, caught my eye in the storefront glass of the diner.

The diner was on Broadway, between Duane Street and Reade Street, and close to the Brooklyn Bridge–City Hall subway station, opening into a park that, by the standards of lower Manhattan, was tranquil. That morning it was busy with office workers, park workers, and the odd tourist, but the volume hardly rose above a hum. People came up the stairs out of the station and made their way to work; those on the early shift were already out in the park, taking their first coffee break of the day. An unlit neon sign that said COMIDA LATINA swung outside the café, and inside the restaurant workers cleaned out steam-heated chargers. These would shortly be filled up with yellow rice, fried plantains, chow mein, barbecued spare ribs, and the various Dominican, Puerto Rican, and Chinese dishes that places like these set out for the lunch-hour rush. It wasn't a big place, but it was easy to tell that it did good business, no doubt because of its proximity to the massive buildings all around, and the countless civil servants who daily streamed in and out of them.

It had been two weeks, and everything else had healed. As it turned out, I hadn't needed to go to the hospital for my mouth. But my left hand troubled me. What had felt like a minor bruise now seemed to have been a bruise of the bone, and turning a doorknob, or lifting a full cup of coffee, hurt. Mostly, I kept the hand in the pocket of my coat. Across the street, in front of the largest of the federal buildings, there had formed a snaking queue. No one lined up in front of a federal building early on a weekday morning unless they had to. When I came out of the diner, I saw that the crowd seemed to be an immigration crowd, as opposed to a jury-duty crowd, which was the other possibility at such a building. The air was of nervous anticipation, a palpable effort to project readiness for the interrogations ahead.

I walked across the street so that I would pass directly along the line. A group of Bangladeshis—the tiny silver-haired matriarch in *salwar kameez,* the young man dressed in wool coat and brown slacks, the young woman in a calf-length skirt, the young children bundled up—all seemed to be fumbling with their papers. There appeared to be an unusual number of interracial couples standing in line. One pair, I guessed, was African-American and Vietnamese. The security officers were, their uniforms revealed, also from Wackenhut, the same private firm contracted to control the immigrants in the detention facility in Queens. As each expectant family reached the front of the line, they were instructed to remove jewelry, shoes, belts, coins, and keys, so that the official fear of terrorism played along, like a bass figure, to the private fear of being found wanting by an immigration officer once they got upstairs.

From where I stood, I could see, behind the diner, the massive AT&T Long Lines building on Church Street. It was a windowless tower, a giant concrete slab rising into the sky, with little more than a few ventilation openings, which resembled periscopes, to indicate that this was a building rather than a dense brick fabricated by a gargantuan machine. Each floor was at least double the height of that found in a normal office building, so that the whole tower, intimidating though it was, came to only twenty-nine stories. The military aspect of the Long Lines building was intensified by the thickened corners, elongated shafts with which the building mimicked the form of a castle's keep flanked by gatehouse towers, and which concealed the elevators, ductwork, and plumbing. Those few workers who used the building, I imagined, must after a few years become moles, their circadian rhythms completely distorted, their skin depigmented to the point of transparency. Long Lines, which I continued to stare at, as though it had drawn me into a trance, seemed like nothing so much as a monument or a stele.

I was drawn out of my thoughts by the voice of a security officer: You can't stand here, move along, sir. I moved, and came down to the side street. The line had extended that far, to the distant edge of the building. Nearby, another man, who seemed to be a janitor, was helping a Hispanic family group, a mother and two children, who seemed to be lost. Trying to understand what they were asking for, he repeated the mother's pronunciation of *passport* as *passiport*. The older of her boys was just beginning to sprout his first unruly facial hairs. He looked bored, or perhaps embarrassed. Near the front of the line, a young woman raced out of the glass doors, and threw herself at a waiting group, hugging them and weeping. A young man, perhaps her husband, had come out with her, and the people they met outside beamed, embraced each other, and exchanged high fives. An older woman in the group began to weep, and the young woman said, loud enough for all to hear: Now you see who I get it from, from my mama. The other people in line, wishing the same good luck for themselves, possibly made even more tense by someone else's demonstration of relief, perhaps discomfited by the emotionalism, watched and looked away, and watched again. The janitor near me smiled, shook his head, and explained to the Hispanic family how to get to the passport office.

There was a small security island in the middle of the side street, and just across from it, surrounded by the huge office buildings, was a patch of grass. It wouldn't have drawn my attention at all, if I hadn't seen a curious shape—sculpture or architecture, I couldn't tell right away—set into the middle of it. An inscription on the monument, for that is what it turned out to be, identified it as a memorial for the site of an African burial ground. The tiny plot was what had been set aside now to indicate the spot, but in the seventeenth and eighteenth centuries, the site had been large, some six acres, as far north as present-day Duane Street, and as far south as City Hall Park. Along Chambers Street and in the park itself, human remains were still routinely uncovered. But most of the burial ground was now under office buildings, shops, streets, diners, pharmacies, all the endless hum of quotidian commerce and government.

Into this earth had been interred the bodies of some fifteen to twenty thousand blacks, most of them slaves, but then the land had been built over and the people of the city had forgotten that it was a burial ground. It had passed into private and civic ownership. The monument I saw was designed by a Haitian artist, but I was unable to take a closer look, because it was closed to public access, for renovation, as a sign informed me, in preparation for the summer tourism season. In the green grass and bright sun, in the shadow of government and the marketplace, standing a few yards from the cordoned-off monument, I had no purchase on who these people were whose corpses, between the 1690s and 1795, had been laid to rest beneath my feet. It was here, on the outskirts of the city at the time, north of Wall Street and so outside civilization as it was then defined, that blacks were allowed to bury their dead. Then the dead returned when, in 1991, construction of a building on Broadway and Duane brought human remains to the surface. They had been buried in white shrouds. The coffins that were discovered, some four hundred of them, were almost all found to have been oriented toward the east.

The squabble about the construction of the monument did not interest me. There was certainly no chance that six acres of prime real estate in lower Manhattan would be razed and rededicated as holy ground. What I was steeped in, on that warm morning, was the echo across centuries, of slavery in New York. At the Negro Burial Ground, as it was then known, and others like it on the eastern seaboard, excavated bodies bore traces of suffering: blunt trauma, grievous bodily harm. Many of the skeletons had broken bones, evidence of the suffering they'd endured in life. Disease was common, too: syphilis, rickets, arthritis. In some of the palls were found shells, beads, and polished stones, and in these scholars had seen hints of African religions, rites perhaps retained from the Congo, or from along the West African coast, from which so many people had been captured and sold into slavery. One body had been found buried in a British marine officer's uniform. Some others had been found with coins over their eyes.

There had been, in the 1780s, a petition by free blacks in defense of their dead. Black corpses were frequently singled out by cadaver thieves, who passed them on to surgeons and anatomists. The petition, in palpably pained language, laments those who under cover of night "dig up the bodies of the deceased, friends and relatives of the petitioners, carry them away without respect to age or sex, mangle their flesh out of wanton curiosity and then expose it to beasts and birds." The civil powers recognized the justness of the cause and, in 1789, the New York Anatomy Act was passed. From that time forward, as was done in Europe, the needs of surgical anatomy were to be met by the cadavers of executed murderers, arsonists, and burglars. The Act added, to the sentence of death for criminals, the further retribution of the medical profession; and it left the buried bodies of innocent blacks in peace and neglect. How difficult it was, from the point of view of the twenty-first century, to fully believe that these people, with the difficult lives they were forced to live, were truly people, complex in all their dimensions as we are, fond of pleasures, shy of suffering, attached to their families. How many times, in the course of each of these lives, would death have invaded, carrying off a spouse, a parent, a sibling, a child, a cousin, a lover? And yet, the Negro Burial Ground was no mass grave: each body had been buried singly, according to whichever rite it was that, outside the city walls, the blacks had been at liberty to practice.

The security island near the monument was unmanned. I stepped across the cordon, and into the grassy plot. Bending down, I lifted a stone from the grass and, as I did so, a pain shot through the back of my left hand.

# NINETEEN

I needed clothes for the ceremonies of my father's burial in May 1989. As these things, and many other simple tasks, confused my mother in those days, most of the rites and the practical matters were taken care of by my father's sister, my aunt Tinu. A few weeks before the burial, she took me to a tailor's shop in Ajegunle, a sprawling slum of rusted roofs and open sewers, where the children were all poor and some of them were visibly malnourished. These children stared when my aunt and I emerged from her car because, from their point of view, we would have represented unimaginable wealth and privilege, an impression strengthened by my "whiteness." The shop itself had an efficient air; its interior, lit only by natural light, was clean, and redolent of blue chalk. There were swatches of Dutch wax prints on the floor, semimatte squares of loud color that interrupted the gray shine of the concrete, and the tailor flattered me as he took measurements with his swiftly unfurled tape measure, as though it were the most natural thing in the world to congratulate someone on

the length of his inseam or the breadth of his shoulders. He was perhaps trying to comfort me, having had a quiet word beforehand with
my aunt, who had told him the purpose of our visit. He called out
mysterious numbers to his assistant, numbers that would later be
transmuted into clothing, a white shirt and dark suit for the burial, a
*buba* and *sokoto* in indigo-dyed, hand-spun cloth for the funeral after-
party.

The sensation of being in the tailor's shop was, even in those circumstances, pleasant. I liked the smell of new cloth and, for me, the
intimate wonder of getting measured for clothes was like that of getting your hair cut, or feeling the warm back of the doctor's hand nestled against your throat as he checked your temperature. These were
the rare cases in which you gave permission to a stranger to enter
your personal space. You trusted the expertise proffered, and enjoyed the promise that the opaque maneuvers of this stranger's
hands would yield a result. The tailor, simply by doing his job that
day, comforted me.

The funeral took place on a sunny day, in the afternoon, not on a
rainy morning, not in wretched weather, as I suppose I expected fu-
nerals to be, as I still expect them to be. I recall now that Mahler,
buried in Grinzing in 1911, was given the kind of quiet, private funeral he wanted, no speeches by the graveside, no religious readings,
no florid poetry on the gravestone, just the name, Gustav Mahler.
And, fittingly, it rained all through it until, as Bruno Walter tells it,
the body was interred and the sun came out.

My father was buried on a particularly hot day, an unfuneral day.
My new clothes, which were dark blue, not black, chafed, at the neck
especially, and standing outside in the heat made me especially aware
of the discomfort. The crowd jostling at Atan Cemetery was large, a
somber crowd but, on account of its size, not without a touch of fes-
tivity. Many of the people present seemed to be friends and business
associates of my grandfather, who was active in politics. Many of

them had traveled from Ijebu-Ile and other towns in Ogun State to show their respects for my grandfather, who, though he held no formal political office at that time, had been a state commissioner in the seventies, and was still widely viewed as a kingmaker and power broker.

My experience of death was limited, less than limited. No one I knew well had died. But, as my father was interred that afternoon, I thought of someone else who had died, or had probably died. She was a young girl, around my age, I guessed. I was in the front seat, being driven to school, when the driver knocked her down. It happened in a poor neighborhood, probably her neighborhood, or near it, if she was walking to school. The girl was about eight or nine, and was dressed in a school uniform, which I distinctly remember was a pale lime green dress. I remember well that we'd seen her cross in front of the car once, in stalled traffic, a skinny girl, though not unhealthily so, merely gangly. Then she crossed again, and we hit her. The situation, our situation, was dangerous for a minute, as some men from the neighborhood appeared. The driver was dragged out of the car, after he hesitated awhile behind his wheel, and at first it seemed he would be beaten up. But then, perhaps suddenly realizing how grave his situation was, he was all business, clearing the area, carrying the child and putting her in the backseat. She was conscious but mute. We drove her to a hospital nearby, going so recklessly fast that we'd have hit another child if there'd been one in the way. The driver sweated, though it was a cool harmattan morning. The hospital was, or had until recently been, a residential house, now converted, with a neon cross placed outside it on the street. The girl was unconscious by this time, and I had a feeling, a feeling of certainty that even now I cannot explain, that she hadn't merely fallen asleep or become comatose, but that she'd died. The driver, in a state of great agitation, carried her into the hospital. Please save me, I remember him repeating, to the nurses who had rushed outside to meet us. I remained in the car. I don't remember it being a long wait, twenty minutes, maybe, after which he came out, solemn, and we continued our drive to school in silence.

I didn't think about the little girl later that day, or the day afterward, or at any time at all afterward, I didn't talk about her to my parents or to anyone else. The driver did not mention the episode either. She came back to mind only four or five years later, at my father's funeral, at the graveside as the priest said prayers over his coffin, and I began to think in a general way about death. By then it was as though the little girl in the pale green school uniform, dead on a cool morning, a funereal morning, was something I had dreamed about, or heard in a telling by someone else.

After the burial, there had been a party at home. It wasn't the large, buoyant party there might have been had father died at seventy-five, nor was it the entirely joyless ritual of frying akara that would have been the case had he died at forty. My father had died at forty-nine, and he'd been successful by the important standards: a good career as an engineer, a wife and son, a fine house. And so, there was a party, to celebrate his life, and lunch was cooked for the few dozen members of the family, and close friends, professional associates, members of the church, and neighbors, but colors were somber, there was no live music, and there was no alcohol. People sat in the living room, and outside under the rented canopy.

Some of the guests had brought young children, and the children ran around the tables, laughing, while the adults spoke in low tones and commiserated with each other. Memory fails me, but I believe that, for most of that afternoon, my mother was alone in her room, and my grandparents, and my aunt and uncle, received most of the guests. I had a role to play, my aunt had told me, and so I was to remain in the airless living room, too, uncomfortable in my scratchy *buba* and *sokoto,* and be as polite as possible to the many old men and women who insisted that I surely recognized them, who, in trying to comfort me, the orphan, invented in their heads a relationship with

me that had little basis in reality, and that did not extend beyond that
occasion in any meaningful way. From many of them, I heard reiterated the idea that I was to take care of my mother, that I was to become the man of the house now, which struck me even then as an
unhelpful commonplace.

The children, for some reason hard to control that day, got increasingly boisterous, and when, in the middle of a chase, one of
them reached out a hand and accidentally overturned a serving
charger full of jollof rice onto the concrete floor, three of the others
fell into a laughing fit. No amount of shushing or threats was suffi-
cient to make them stop, and their laughter rose and bubbled across
the somber gathering, causing deep embarrassment to their livid
parents. Once or twice, the sound subsided, but then one of them
would begin again, and the other three would not be able to resist
joining in, and their raucous, heaving laughter went on for minutes.
One of the houseboys was instructed to take them to the back of the
house, from which, for at least another five minutes, we could hear
them chuckling as though possessed. This incident caused the as-
sembled adults obvious discomfort, but it amused me, and it is
impossible for me, even now, to think of the events of that day,
wreathed as they were in sorrow, without feeling a certain gratitude
to those children, all younger than eight, who fell under the momentary spell of mirth and let air into a room that the rites of death had
been asphyxiating.

I WAS ALREADY FOURTEEN, NOT ALL THAT YOUNG, WHEN MY FA-
ther was buried. The memory of the day wasn't secure, because it was
a public event and was as such taken over by other people's concerns.
His death had been private: there had literally been a deathbed
(which struck me at the time, because I had only ever thought of the
expression as a metaphor). But it was the burial I remembered more,
and not the death. Only at the graveside had I felt that absurd sense

of finality, the sense that he wouldn't be getting better, or returning after a few months: the feeling hollowed me out. And while I had the elevated thoughts of someone who was about to become a man, while I nurtured stoicism in myself, and a determination to handle the grief in the right way, I also fell to more childish instincts, so that, at the graveside, part of what I remembered, part of the reel that played in my mind as my father's body was prayed over, included the ghouls and zombies from Michael Jackson's *Thriller.*

In later years, it was the date of the burial, not that of the death, that I marked as an anniversary. I almost always remembered the former, and on May 9 of this year, I was on the 1 train on the way to work when it came to mind that he had been committed to earth for exactly eighteen years. In that time, I had complicated the memory of the day, not with other burials, of which I had attended only a few, but with depictions of burials—El Greco's *Burial of the Count of Orgaz,* Courbet's *Burial at Ornans*—so that the actual event had taken on the characteristics of those images, and in doing so had become faint and unreliable. I couldn't be sure of the color of the earth, whether it really was the intense red clay I thought I remembered, or whether I had taken the form of the priest's surplice from El Greco's painting or from Courbet's. What I remembered as long, sorrowful faces might have been round, sorrowful faces. Sometimes, in waking dreams, I imagined my father with coins on his eyes, and a solemn boatman collecting them from him, and granting him passage.

THERE WAS A MAN, I REMEMBER, ON THAT DAY OF THE EIGH-teenth anniversary, who was moving around the subway cars. He was inspecting the vents above the automatic doors. He wore a dark blue MTA uniform, and carried some sort of counter with him, into which he pressed numbers and which emitted intermittent beeps. I watched him closely, imagining him a spiritual messenger, an angel of some sort, though whether for good or ill, I couldn't tell, and so fo-cused was he on his task that his methodical examination of each vent did nothing to dissuade me from the fanciful ideas working themselves into my head. I looked up at the vents as we hurtled past the uptown stations, 125th, 137th, 145th, I thought of the final terri-ble moments in the camps, moments that no one has survived to give firsthand testimony of, when the Zyklon B was switched on and all the human captives breathed in their deaths, and how, while all this was happening in the early forties, my oma was on her way north to Berlin as a refugee, bewildered and frightened as everyone around her was. These were the conversations I would have wished to have with her: about the young men in her town who'd marched off to war, and never come back, or those who had come back eventually—like my opa, about whom I had been told almost nothing—or those who'd been rounded up and sent to Mauthausen-Gusen.

At 157th, an Asian girl who had been drowsing suddenly got up, skittish, doelike, and sprang out of the subway car before the doors closed. Someone else came in and, for a brief, startling moment, I thought I recognized one of the boys who had mugged me. But I was mistaken. They had, of course, been floating in and out of my dreams, and the idea, so distasteful to me at the time, that it could have been worse now seemed the most sensible one. But in those dreams, I fought back. I was more badly injured, but I also beat them to the point of bloodiness. One of them fell, and I set on him, punching his face until it became like red paper under my fists, until he lost one of his eyes. When I woke, the pain of hitting him would become congruent with the ache at the back of my left hand.

I left my seat and went to speak with the MTA official as he was about to push open the door connecting our car to the next. He looked like a Guyanese or Trinidadian Indian—there was a touch of African ancestry in him, I guessed—though he could also have been directly from the Indian subcontinent itself. I asked him about his work. He was an air-conditioning specialist, carrying out temperature checks on the cars. He was friendly, and seemed surprised anyone had noticed him at all.

It is amazing, he said, how a little variation, too hot or too cold, can lead to complaints. We have efficient HVAC systems—that stands for heating, ventilation, and air-conditioning—and in the summer, we try to keep things ten to fifteen degrees cooler than it is outside. We are constantly checking them, so it is a big operation. But of course no one notices the temperature unless it becomes uncomfortable, when the nozzles get blocked, or there's a local breakdown in the system. And, he added with a laugh, you don't ever notice your oxygen until it's gone: something goes wrong with the HVAC, even for fifteen minutes, and people are ready to riot.

# TWENTY

I was invited to John Musson's apartment for a party. It was in Washington Heights, just a little ways north of the hospital. The apartment overlooked the Hudson, Moji said, when she called me, and had a remarkable view, of water and trees and the George Washington Bridge, I simply had to come see it. She did not live with him, having her own apartment in Riverdale in the Bronx, but she spent many nights at his place, she said, and she was co-host of this party. I hadn't seen her since our day out in the park, but she had called me three or four times, and we had had brief, friendly conversations, usually late at night. Once, she had abruptly asked me how my mother was doing. I was silent, then told her that I didn't know, that we weren't in touch. Oh, that's too bad, she said, in a weirdly cheerful tone of voice. I remember meeting her. She was such a nice person.

In the days leading up to the gathering, I suppose I made some effort to edge out of it, but then the date arrived, in the middle of

May, and I found that I was without a good excuse and would have to attend. That day, I left work early, around five-thirty. I had time to kill, so instead of taking the subway, I decided to walk. I came around from Harkness to the intersection of Broadway and St. Nicholas, and the streets, as expected at that hour, were invaded in every lane and in both directions by impatient drivers. Mitchel Square Park, where the two main streets crossed, a vantage point of less than an acre, was dominated by a gently rising rock outcrop, from which one could read the overlay of buildings that had brought the medical campus to its current form. The new constructions not only sat close to the older buildings but were in many cases grafted right into them, shiny and strange as prosthetic limbs. Milstein, the central hospital building, was an amalgam of Victorian stone and a recent triangular frontage of glass and steel that gave it the aspect of a glittering pyramid in a dour and stately setting.

Such juxtapositions were common to the many buildings around, and the same layering extended to their names, which recounted the history of institutions that had begun as civic establishments and gradually become dependent on philanthropic and corporate bene-factors. In the ornately carved stone lintel of one of the older build-ings were the words BABIES AND CHILDREN'S HOSPITAL 1887; next door to it, in modern sans-serif font and glossy blue paint, was MOR-GAN STANLEY CHILDREN'S HOSPITAL. From Mitchel Square Park—dedicated to veterans of the First World War and named for a New York City mayor who had died in the war—I could see the Mary Woodard Lasker Biomedical Research Building, the Irving Cancer Research Center, the Sloane Hospital for Women, and the Russ Berrie Medical Science Pavilion. Parked in front of the Children's Hospital was yet another donation, an ambulance of the FDNY Fire Family Transportation Foundation. Some of these were older, many were recent endowments, but all established the powerful link be-tween modern medical care and memorials on the one hand, and memorials and money on the other. A hospital is not a neutral space, it is not a purely scientific space, nor is it the religious one it had been in medieval times; the reality now involves commerce, and the direct correlation between donating large sums of money and having a building named in memoriam. Names matter. Everything has a name.

On the great rock of the square, some boys were playing on skateboards, negotiating the gentle but craggy gradient up and down, and laughing. I read the plaque at the 166th Street entrance memorializing Mitchel. He had been the city's youngest mayor when he was elected to office at the age of thirty-four, at the beginning of the war, and his death in Louisiana four years later, while he was flying with the Army Aviation Corps, had occasioned a great outpouring of public grief. As I read the plaque, musing on the strange middle name Purroy, a man in a large Yankees jacket came into the park. He stood next to me, and asked for two dollars for the bus, but I refused him wordlessly, and went back out to Broadway. Just north of the park, beyond the bronze and granite World War I memorial, its three heroes arrested forever in battle—one standing, one kneeling, the third slumped in mortal injury—the temper of the neighborhood changed, and the hospital campus, as though the past had suddenly transformed into the present, gave way to the barrio.

Almost immediately, there were fewer of the white medical professionals who had been milling about the entrance to Milstein, and the streets were full now of Dominican and other Latin-American shoppers, workers, and residents. Someone coming toward me waved, exuberant. It was a tall, middle-aged woman with an infant, but I didn't recognize the face. Mary, it's Mary, she said. I worked with the old fellow, you remember? She shook her head with the surprise of having seen me. I reminded her of my name. And it was indeed her; she lived up in Washington Heights now, and was going to begin a nursing program at Columbia once her little boy went to day care. I congratulated her, and felt in myself an amazement at how quickly life went through its paces. We spoke a little about Professor

234 / Teju Cole

Saito. The old man was good, you know, she said. He always enjoyed your visits so much, I don't know if he told you. It was difficult to see him go like that, to see him have it so difficult at the end. I thanked her for having taken care of him. Her baby started crying, and we bid each other goodbye.

From the intersection of 172nd Street, the George Washington Bridge came into view for the first time, its lights soft yellow points in the gray distance. I walked past small shops selling knickknacks, the sprawling window display of El Mundo Department Store, and the perpetually popular restaurant El Malecon, to which I occasionally came for dinner. Across the street from El Malecon was a massive and architecturally bizarre building. It had been built in 1930, and was known back then as the Loews 175th Street Theatre. Designed by Thomas W. Lamb, it was filled with glamorous detail— chandeliers, red carpeting, a profusion of architectural ornament within and without—and the terra-cotta elements on the façade drew from Egyptian, Moorish, Persian, and Art Deco styles. Lamb's stated aim was to cast a spell of the mysterious on the "occidental mind," with the use of "exotic ornaments, colors, and schemes."

Now the building had a marquee sign, with white letters on a black background, that read: COME ON IN OR SMILE AS YOU PASS. It had become a church, but the gilded-age excess remained. This religious function had begun in 1969, and the theater, renamed the United Palace, still hosted several congregations. The best-known and longest-running of them was the one shepherded by the Right Reverend Frederick Eikerenkoetter. Reverend Ike, as he was popularly known, preached prosperity and lived in the princely manner befitting, in his view, a faithful servant of God's word. Parked in front of the church, and weirdly congruent with its false Assyrian battlements and decontextualized pomp, was his green Rolls-Royce, one of several luxury cars he owned. His church, the United Church Science of Living Institute, once numbered in the tens of thousands.

It was sparser now. But, still, the people gave freely, as they had done since the sixties.

The theater, America's third largest when it was built, seating over three thousand, had hosted films as well as vaudeville shows in its earlier incarnation. Al Jolson had played there, as had Lucille Ball, and back then it had been surrounded by expensive restaurants and luxury goods shops. Now, from the doorway of El Malecon, in the waning light of a Friday evening, it looked quiet. The jumble of architectural styles failed, more than seventy-five years on, to resolve themselves into anything meaningful. Even in its best days, it must have looked alien in the environment. It looked more so now, still reasonably well maintained, but utterly out of place, its architecture a world away from that of the small shops, its grand columns and arches irrelevant to the fatigued immigrants who rarely raised their heads to look above street level. The spell had faded.

The door of a parked minivan opened. A young boy stuck his head out, and vomited into the gutter, and from within the minivan, the reassuring voice of a woman spoke to him. The boy vomited again, then he looked up, with a cherubic expression, and caught my eye. I walked on, farther up Broadway, drawn, it seemed, into the fast-changing face of the neighborhood. There was another ornate building at the 181st Street corner. And here was the old competitor to the Loews 175th Street Theatre, the Coliseum, which, in its own time, before the Loews was built, was the third largest theater in the country. A brief and sad claim to fame: to have once been the third largest. Now, greatly altered, it had become the New Coliseum Theatre, and it shared space with a large pharmacy and a hodgepodge of other storefronts; only above its first floor were there hints of the 1920s architecture.

I turned left at 181st, and walked down to Fort Washington, past the A train station and the Fort Washington Collegiate Church, and then to Pinehurst, which was connected to 181st not directly but by a long and narrow flight of stairs rising into a small wooded tangle that opened out into the street proper. The stairs, vertiginous and reminiscent of the much longer stairs leading up to Sacré-Coeur in Montmartre, were in the shade of trees, fringed on both sides with dense, weed-choked plots, and bifurcated by a double rank of iron railings in a manner that evoked a funicular railway; I half-expected a tramcar to come chugging down the left side while I walked up the right. The stairs brought me out into the dead end of Pinehurst, a different world from the busy street life a few dozen yards below: residential buildings, a richer, whiter neighborhood. And so I proceeded among the whites, entering their quieter street life, feeling for minutes that I was the only person walking around a depopulated world, and reassured only by occasional signs of life: an old lady at the end of the block carrying a bag of groceries, a pair of neighbors in conversation in front of an apartment building, and the appearance, one after the other, of glimmering lights from within the windows of lovely brick houses set back from the street. To my right was Bennett Park, still and silent, animated only by the occasional fluttering of the American flag and the black POW flag hoisted below it. Pinehurst ended at 187th, and that brought me around to Cabrini, which ran alongside the river.

Following Cabrini a few hundred yards farther, to its farthest extent, would have brought me to Fort Tryon Park, in which was nestled, like a jewel in velvet, the Cloisters museum. I remembered my last visit to the museum, when I had come with my friend. We'd stood in the walled garden, which overlooks the Hudson. There was a large espaliered pear tree, shaped into a kind of green candelabrum against the stone wall, its branches, ramified like those on the Tree of Jesse, had been forced through the years by the attentions of gardeners into right angles and a single, two-dimensional plane. At my feet were the various herbs typical to a monastery plot—marjoram, parsley, marshmallow, garden sorrel, leek, red valerian, sage. They grew freely, thriving so well that we talked about how wonderful it would be to have a kitchen garden identical to this one.

I remember how, on that day, I knelt down close to the herb plot and inhaled its thin fragrance. The plot contained soapwort and liverwort, herbs that had been given their names by the old wisdom of simpling, or sympathetic herbal medicine, a quasi-mystical art by which the medicinal properties of plants were related to their physical appearance. Liverwort was thought to be good for liver ailments because its leaves evoked the shapes of the lobes of the liver; lungwort, likewise, was good for breathing complaints because its leaf was shaped like a lung; and soapwort was valued for its dermatological uses. This is where the search for meaning had led our medieval ancestors: to the certainty that God, who made all of creation, had scattered clues to the useful functions of created things in those things, and that only a little vigilance was necessary to decode those clues. Simpling was but the most basic of this kind of learning; the search for Signs, as undertaken by the sixteenth-century German humanist Paracelsus, was a further extension of the same idea.

For Paracelsus, the light of nature functioned intuitively, but it was also sharpened by experience. Properly read, it informed us what the inner reality of a thing was by means of its form, so that the appearance of a man gave some valid reflection of the person he really was. The inner reality is, indeed, so profound that, for Paracelsus, it cannot help but be expressed in the external form. On the other hand, as in the case of artists, unless the work of art addressed the question of an inner life, its external Signs would be empty. And so, Paracelsus developed a fourfold theory around how the light of nature is manifest in individual men: through the limbs, through the head and face, through the form of the body as a whole, and through bearing, or the way a man carries himself.

We are familiar with this theory of Signs in the debased forms of phrenology, eugenics, and racism. However, this sensitivity to the play between inner spirit and outer substance also underpinned the success of many of the artists of Paracelsus's time, not least the wood sculptors of southern Germany. By showing an extreme attentiveness to the properties of wood, and to how those properties might be translated into sculptural character, they created enduring works of art, precisely of the kind that lined the rooms and halls of the Cloisters. Riemenschneider, Stoss, Leinberger, and Erhat brought a complicated material knowledge of lindenwood to bear on their carving of it, and their attempts to marry the spirit of the material with its visible form, craftlike though it is, is after all not so different from the diagnostic struggle that doctors are engaged in. This is particularly true in the case of those of us who are psychiatrists, who attempt to use external Signs as clues to internal realities, even when the relationship between the two is not at all clear. So modest is our success at this task that it is easy to believe our branch of medicine is as primitive now as was surgery in Paracelsus's time.

On that day, with these thoughts of Signs and simpling in mind, I had tried to give my friend an account of my evolving view of psychiatric practice. I told him that I viewed each patient as a dark room, and that, going into that room, in a session with the patient, I considered it essential to be slow and deliberate. Doing no harm, the most ancient of medical tenets, was on my mind all the time. There is more light to work with in externally visible illnesses; the Signs are more forcefully expressed, and therefore harder to miss. For the troubles of the mind, diagnosis is a trickier art, because even the strongest symptoms are sometimes not visible. It is especially elusive because the source of our information about the mind is itself the mind, and the mind is able to deceive itself. As physicians, I said to my friend, we depend, to a much greater degree than is the case with nonmental conditions, on what the patient tells us. But what are we to do when the lens through which the symptoms are viewed is often, itself, symptomatic: the mind is opaque to itself, and it's hard to tell where, precisely, these areas of opacity are. Ophthalmic science describes an area at the back of the bulb of the eye, the optic disk, where the million or so ganglia of the optic nerve exit the eye. It is precisely there, where too many of the neurons associated with vision are clustered, that the vision goes dead. For so long, I recall explaining to my friend that day, I have felt that most of the work of psychiatrists in particular, and mental health professionals in general, was a blind spot so broad that it had taken over most of the eye. What we knew, I said to him, was so much less than what remained in darkness, and in this great limitation lay the appeal and frustration of the profession.

I FOUND THE RIGHT BUILDING, AND JOHN SPOKE TO ME ON THE intercom, and let me in. I took the elevator up to the twenty-ninth floor. He was at the door, wearing an apron. Come on in, he said, it's nice to meet you in person finally. There were quite a few people there already. John was a hedge fund trader, quite wealthy already, to judge from the house, which was spacious and rather richly decorated with mid-century modern furniture, an assortment of kilim rugs, and a Fazioli grand piano. I estimated he was about fifteen years older than Moji was. There was something forced in his gregariousness, and the ruddy pink cheeks and salt and pepper goatee did not appeal to me. Moji came up to me, and we embraced. What's with the bandage? she said. You've taken up boxing or what? I mumbled something about slipping on a threshold, but she had already gone into the kitchen. From there she called out, asking what I wanted to drink. I shouted an answer, unsure of what it was even before the echo of my voice faded, as my mind was still on how beautiful she looked, how desirable and, of course, unavailable.

BY ABOUT 2:00 A.M., MANY PEOPLE HAD LEFT, AND THE PARTY quieted down. Someone replaced the electronic dance music that had been playing on the stereo with a recording of Sarah Vaughan with strings. The dozen or so guests that remained were all sprawled on the sofas. A few were smoking cigars; the smell was pleasant, seductive, a baritone fragrance that evoked feelings of equanimity in me. One couple slept in each other's arms, and a girl with heavy black eye shadow was curled up on the carpet near them. Moji and John were deep in conversation with an Italian physicist. He was from Turin. His wife, a woman from Cleveland, whom I had met earlier, was also a physicist. There had been something about both her delayed reaction in conversation and the slightly odd way she spoke that had made me wonder if she was deaf. Naturally, it wasn't possible to ask, and I let the matter slide. I had spoken to her and her husband for a while. She'd been happy to get into a discussion about Italo Calvino and Primo Levi with me; he'd seemed bored and, on the pretext of going to refill his drink, had drifted away.

I stepped out onto the terrace, which I had been wanting to do all evening: the view was a marvel, as Moji had promised. It wrapped around the apartment on two sides and, from up there on the twenty-ninth floor, I could take in, in a single glance, the dwellings of millions. The way the tiny lights winked across the miles of air made me think of all the computers in all those homes, most of them sleeping now, with their single lights silently toggling between on and off. I was on my third glass of champagne. The day felt far away, and my spirit was soothed. There was, too, the pleasant sensation of flirting with Moji, not with any expectation, but for the pleasure of it. And I noticed, this time, less tension, less conflict, in my interaction with her. I was glad I had come.

The glass door clicked open behind me, and John came out onto the balcony. He also had a full champagne glass in his hand. His cheeks were flushed with drink. I complimented him on his generosity, and on his beautiful apartment. There was a row of bonsai trees, maybe a dozen plants in all, along the plate-glass window in the living room. They could not have been more different from ordinary houseplants. Each bonsai tree, stocky, ancient, and gnarled, had been growing since before we were born, and each had within its trunk and roots the genetic secrets that would ensure that it would outlive us all. I had been admiring them earlier, I told him. He asked me if I had noticed the one tagged *Acer palmatum.* That little baby is a hundred and forty-five years old, he said. Some call it the Japanese maple, and it can grow, I don't know, seventy feet, eighty feet. But this game is not about size now, is it? Did you notice how its leaves are like those of the marijuana plant? He chuckled. I was put off, but even he couldn't spoil my mood.

AFTER I LEFT JOHN'S PLACE, I STOPPED BY A DINER AT 181ST AND Cabrini for a coffee. I drank it quickly, then walked farther down Cabrini to 179th, and negotiated my way around to the George Washington Bridge. I wanted to see, closer at hand, the sun rising over the Hudson. The city was still asleep. In the diner, I had seen one man with a tattoo that covered most of his arm resting his head on his knuckles. When I came out, I saw another man, Dominican or Puerto Rican, in a parked car, who was either asleep or staring blankly at the GPS device in front of him. The reflection of the sun turned half of the windshield into a bright metallic field. When I got on the pedestrian walkway on the Fort Lee–bound side of the bridge, I saw, ahead of me and on the other side of the median, a stalled, maroon-colored car. It was one of the large American models from the late eighties, possibly a Lincoln Town Car, and it had plowed into a guardrail. The accident must have happened not more than fifteen or twenty minutes before I got there; the fire truck and police cars were just arriving. They pulled up in silence, clustering along the length of the bridge; there was almost no traffic, and they hadn't needed their sirens. I could see that both of the car's front doors were open, and that the windows had been smashed. The front end of the car was crumpled, and there was glass on the road, and blood as well, pooled on the pavement like an oil leak. I walked a few yards more, and could now see the car from the east.

On the concrete ledge near the car, with the rising sun gliding up the sky behind them, sat a couple. They were silent, bewildered, taking in the bad dream of a Saturday morning. From the distance, they looked Filipino, or perhaps Central American. As I walked onto the overpass, the firemen had just reached them, all business. The bright red of the fire truck was like a gash across the empty road. Where could all the blood near the car have come from? The man and woman both had leg injuries but didn't seem to be bleeding profusely. It was surreal, as surreal, in my memory of it now, as anything I had ever seen. This vision of needless suffering colored what else I saw of the sunrise, the river, and the quiet morning roads in the hour that followed, when, coming down from the bridge, I walked down Fort Washington until it met 168th Street, at the medical campus, and from there walked on Broadway, through the littered, sleeping barrio, all the way down, through Harlem, then on to Amsterdam and Columbia University's quiet campus. I saw my neighbor Seth— it had been months, I don't think I had seen him once since he'd told me of his wife's death—and I stopped to greet him. He was, with the building superintendent's assistance, dragging the second of two large mattresses out to the front of the building. Have to buy new ones, he said. He appeared to be reading something on the surface of the mattress, which had been propped up against the front of the building. Then he turned around and, by way of explanation, said, These ones have been invaded by bedbugs.

Seth asked if I had seen any sign of them in my own apartment, and I said I hadn't. But then I remembered that, before he left about two weeks earlier, my friend had mentioned trying to rid his place of them. His tenure application at Columbia had been unsuccessful, and he had left New York, bedbugs and all, for a teaching position at the University of Chicago. Much to my surprise, the new girlfriend, Lise-Anne, had gone with him. And it was at that particular moment, speaking with Seth in the front of the infected mattresses, that I had an inkling of how acutely I would feel the absence of my friend.

EACH PERSON MUST, ON SOME LEVEL, TAKE HIMSELF AS THE CALI-bration point for normalcy, must assume that the room of his own mind is not, cannot be, entirely opaque to him. Perhaps this is what we mean by sanity: that, whatever our self-admitted eccentricities might be, we are not the villains of our own stories. In fact, it is quite the contrary: we play, and only play, the hero, and in the swirl of other people's stories, insofar as those stories concern us at all, we are never less than heroic. Who, in the age of television, hasn't stood in front of a mirror and imagined his life as a show that is already per-haps being watched by multitudes? Who has not, with this consider-ation in mind, brought something performative into his everyday life? We have the ability to do both good and evil, and more often than not, we choose the good. When we don't, neither we nor our imagined audience is troubled, because we are able to articulate our-selves to ourselves, and because we have, through our other deci-sions, merited their sympathy. They are ready to believe the best about us, and not without good reason. From my point of view, thinking about the story of my life, even without claiming any espe-cially heightened sense of ethics, I am satisfied that I have hewed close to the good.

And so, what does it mean when, in someone else's version, I am the villain? I am only too familiar with bad stories—badly imagined, or badly told—because I hear them frequently from patients. I know the tells of those who blame others, those who are unable to see that they themselves, and not the others, are the common thread in all their bad relationships. There are characteristic tics that reveal the essential falsehood of such narratives. But what Moji had said to me that morning, before I left John's place, and gone up on the George

Washington Bridge, and walked the few miles back home, had nothing in common with such stories. She had said it as if, with all of her being, she were certain of its accuracy.

Of the ten or so people who had stayed over at the apartment on the night of the party, I had risen earliest. It was around six, and the sun was up already. I tiptoed over the slumbering bodies on the floor of the living room, and went into the kitchen. I made some tea, and tiptoed back, and sat on the glassed-in terrace, overlooking the Hudson. Moji came to join me, sitting in the other low, padded chair.

How did you sleep? I said, and was about to ask her about the physicist from Cleveland, whether she was deaf, as I suspected, but Moji looked out over the river, narrowing her eyes. Then she turned to me and said, in a low and even voice, emotional in its total lack of inflection, that there were things she wished to say to me. And then, with the same flat affect, she said that, in late 1989, when she was fifteen and I was a year younger, at a party her brother had hosted at their house in Ikoyi, I had forced myself on her. Afterward, she said, her eyes unwavering from the bright river below, in the weeks that followed, in the months and years that followed, I had acted like I knew nothing about it, had even forgotten her, to the point of not recognizing her when we met again, and had never tried to acknowledge what I had done. This torturous deception had continued until the present. But it hadn't been like that for her, she said, the luxury of denial had not been possible for her. Indeed, I had been ever-present in her life, like a stain or a scar, and she had thought of me, either fleetingly or in extended agonies, for almost every day of her adult life.

Moji went on in this vein for what was probably six or seven minutes. She told me who else had been at the party that night, and she described her precise memory of what had happened: we had both been drinking beer, she was close to passing out, and I had taken her to another room and forced myself on her. For weeks afterward, she said, she had wanted to die. I had refused to look at her, she said, and her brother Dayo knew that these things had happened, not that they had discussed it, but it was inconceivable that, in the shadows and absences of the night, he would not have known, and she hated him, she said, for having done nothing to protect her. And now, here we were, all grown up, and she still carried this hurt, which seeing me again, and seeing that I had lost none of my callousness, she said, had renewed and had brought back to her a distress comparable in intensity to what she had suffered in those weeks, only this time, she said, she had tried, for reasons unclear even to her, to keep her pain hidden and put a happy face on the situation. She had tried to forgive, she said, and to forget, but neither had worked.

Moji's voice, which had never increased in volume, had by now taken on a strained, shattered tone, as if she were getting hoarse. You'll say nothing, she said. I know you'll say nothing. I'm just another woman whose story of sexual abuse will not be believed. I know that. Look, bitterness has been eating away at me all this time, because this was so long ago, and it's my word against yours, and you'll say it was consensual, or that it never even happened at all. I have anticipated all your possible answers. This is why I've told no one, not even my boyfriend. But he sees through you anyway, you, the psychiatrist, the know-it-all. I know you think he's a buffoon. But he's a better man than you. He is wiser, he understands life better than you ever will. That is why, without me having to tell him anything, he knows what a malign influence you have been on my life.

I don't think you've changed at all, Julius. Things don't go away just because you choose to forget them. You forced yourself on me eighteen years ago because you could get away with it, and I suppose you did get away with it. But not in my heart, you didn't. I have cursed you too many times to count. And maybe it is not something you would do today, but then again, I didn't think it was something you would do back then either. It only needs to happen once. But will you say something now? Will you say something?

Other people had woken up, and were beginning to move around inside the apartment. Moji stopped speaking, and kept her eyes focused on the shimmering Hudson. I thought she would begin to cry but, to my relief, she didn't. Anyone who had come out onto the porch at that moment could not have imagined that we were doing anything other than enjoying the play of light on the river.

The just risen sun came at the Hudson at such an acute angle that the river gleamed like aluminum roofing. At that moment—and I remember this as exactly as though it were being replayed in front of me right now—I thought of how, in his journals, Camus tells a double story concerning Nietzsche and Gaius Mucius Cordus Scaevola, a Roman hero from the sixth century B.C.E. Scaevola had been captured while trying to kill the Etruscan king Porsenna and, rather than give away his accomplices, he showed his fearlessness by putting his right hand in a fire and letting it burn. From this act came his nickname, Scaevola, the left-handed. Nietzsche, according to Camus, became angry when his schoolmates would not believe the Scaevola story. And so, the fifteen-year-old Nietzsche plucked a hot coal from the grate, and held it. Of course, it burned him. He carried the resulting scar with him for the rest of his life.

I went inside, and greeted the risers. Five minutes later, I left. It wasn't until several days afterward that, looking up the story elsewhere, I saw that Nietzsche's contempt for pain had been expressed not with a coal but with several lit matchsticks that he had placed in the center of his palm and that, as they began to burn his hand, an alarmed school yard prefect had knocked to the ground.

# TWENTY-ONE

Monday was my first full day in private practice. The practice, which my senior partner, David Ng, has run for fourteen years, is on the Bowery. It's a pleasant office, on the third floor of a prewar building, with windows that open out to a clear view of lamp shops across the street, and the uncluttered sky above them. There has been no sign of this year's bird migrations yet, but I know they will come. At quiet moments, I will be able to take the auspices to my heart's content. It has been a busy month: only last week, I moved into a small apartment on West Twenty-first Street. The view there isn't good, but it is a desirable neighborhood (as the realtor reminded me ad infinitum) and I am within walking distance of the office. A few weeks ago, I had the hand surgery I had been putting off. The pain is gone.

My fellowship ended with the end of summer, and I opted to work with Ng, though there were more lucrative offers farther from the city, of which the most attractive was in a group practice in Hackensack, New Jersey. It would have meant more money, the tranquillity of the suburbs, the things that more money can buy; but in the end it hadn't been a difficult choice. Remaining here in the city is the only choice that makes emotional sense to me; my own instincts aided me, as did the professional advice of Dr. Bolt, the head of our service. Dr. Martindale, with whom I shared authorship of a couple of research papers, had tried to convince me to remain in academia, but it became clear a long time ago that the university setting is not for me.

I have begun to organize my office. The office is bare, for the most part, but I have brought in a few books, and my computer has been set up, with a pair of small speakers that I can use to listen to music in between appointments. I have already bookmarked on the computer one of the New York classical music stations, feeling more tolerant now of the announcers than I used to. A new sofa came in on Friday, and the smell of its fabric, a curious combination of lemon and dust, dominates the room, but none of the patients has complained yet. On the door outside is a beveled brass nameplate that Ng had made before I even arrived.

On the corkboard behind my chair is pinned a postcard of Heliopolis that I discovered by chance in a used bookshop two or three weeks ago. It is yellowed with age, and depicts a street shadowed by a building to the right. The building has what looks like a medieval European bell tower, with two pairs of columns on each side. Two men, tiny figures, walk along the side of the building. They are dressed in white robes. Another man, only a little larger, stands in the middle of the empty street, looking out at the photographer. He is also in an ankle-length white robe, but on top of his he wears a black jacket. To the right of this man, the street is patterned with the converging, silvery lines of a street tram and, near the horizon line, there are two trams. Their upraised, articulated elements, which connect them to overhead wires, make them look a little like houseflies. To the left of the otherwise bare street is a smaller, or perhaps simply more distant, building, and one of the towers of this building is topped with an onion dome. The postcard, which is undated, simply reads, in small white print on the photograph, "9108 Le Caire, Heliopolis." It is not a picturesque card. The sky is washed out, the shadows are dark, the composition of no great interest. It looks like something someone has forgotten, not something anyone would intentionally tack onto the corkboard. But I cannot shake the feeling that the small man in the black jacket and white robe, whose face is invisible because of the shadow of the street, plays the role of witness, and watches me while I work, and, indeed, it was this little figure who had first compelled me to pick up the card. Only later had I noticed that it depicted Baron Empain's Heliopolis.

While I was listening to the radio yesterday afternoon in a lull between seeing new patients, I was alerted to the performances this week at Carnegie Hall. The Berlin Philharmonic Orchestra is playing three concerts under Simon Rattle. I went online and bought myself a ticket to the evening's performance. Tonight is the final concert of the three, *Das Lied von der Erde,* which I'll miss because it is sold out. Mahler's mind was perpetually on last things: *Das Lied von der Erde,* with its pained notes of farewell and its bittersweet sound world, was largely written in the summer of 1908. The year before, in 1907, vicious politics of an anti-Semitic nature saw him forced out of his directorship at the Vienna Opera. This disappointment had come on the heels of a great shock earlier, in July 1907, the death from scarlet fever of the elder of his two daughters, five-year-old Maria Anna. When the Metropolitan Opera engaged him for the 1908 season, he brought his wife, Alma, and younger daughter over to New York. There had been a respite, a moment of glory and some satisfaction. He thrilled audiences with his conducting and innovative programming until the board pushed him out in favor of Toscanini.

Last night, I attended the performance of the Ninth Symphony, which is the work Mahler wrote after *Das Lied von der Erde.* So strong is

Mahler's sense of an ending that his many musical stories of the end almost come to dominate what went before. He made himself a master of the ends of symphonies, the end of a body of work, and the end of his own life. Even the Ninth wasn't his very last work; fragments of a Tenth Symphony survive, and it is even more funereal than the preceding works. From Mahler's sketches, the work was completed in the 1960s by the British musicologist Deryck Cooke.

I found myself thinking of Mahler's last years as I sat on the uptown-bound N train last night. All the darknesses that surrounded him, the various reminders of frailty and mortality, were lit brightly from some unknown source, but even that light was shadowed. I thought of how clouds sometimes race across the sunlit canyons formed by the steep sides of skyscrapers, so that the stark divisions of dark and light are shot through with passing light and dark. Mahler's final works—*Das Lied von der Erde,* the Ninth Symphony, the sketches of the Tenth—were all first performed posthumously; all are vast, strongly illuminated, and lively works, surrounded by the tragedy that was unfolding in the life. The overwhelming impression they give is of light: the light of a passionate hunger for life, the light of a sorrowful mind contemplating death's implacable approach.

The obsession with last things was not just apparent from his late style. It had been there right from the beginning of his composing career, as far back as the Second Symphony, which was an extended musical exploration of death and resurrection. Had he, in later years, written only *Das Lied von der Erde,* it would have been thought a fitting final statement, one of the great ones, to stand with Mozart's Requiem, Beethoven's Ninth, and Schubert's last piano sonata. But to have followed *Das Lied,* as he did, with the equally immense Ninth Symphony the following summer, in 1909, was to become, through the force of his will, the genius of prolonged farewells.

The concert was part of a series celebrating the city of Berlin. I bought my ticket for yesterday's concert too late, and I was up in the fourth tier above ground level. The hall, a beautiful conch shell of a space, with a ceiling studded with fixtures and recessed lighting, was packed. The person next to me, a beautiful woman, dressed in an expensive coat, stank; it was a strong smell, something between saliva and alcohol, and I guessed it wasn't a matter of inadequate hygiene, but rather an overapplied perfume. It occurred to me to change my seat, but that proved impossible. She fanned herself briskly, and the smell dissipated. Her companion, a tall, tanned man in a blue suit and a checked white shirt, a European-looking type with merry gray eyes, soon arrived. The concertmaster emerged from the wings to applause, and the orchestra began to tune, first with the oboist sending out a clear A, and then the sounds of the string instruments drawing themselves out of beautiful cacophony into the unison.

The last concert Gustav Mahler himself ever conducted was in Carnegie Hall, in February 1911. It contained none of his own music: he led the New York Symphony Orchestra, which later became the New York Philharmonic, in the world premiere of Busoni's *Berceuse Élégiaque*. On that day, he was in a fever, and he conducted only against the advice of his personal physician, Dr. Joseph Fraenkel; the fever must have burned unbearably within him that evening, as he conducted Busoni's piece, set to the following words: "The child's cradle rocks, the hazard of his fate reels; life's path fades, fades away into the eternal distance."

Again the oboist played an A, and this time the woodwinds tuned, and they were joined by a flurry of strings. At last a signal came from the stage, and a hush fell on the hall. Almost everyone, as almost always at such concerts, was white. It is something I can't help noticing; I notice it each time, and try to see past it. Part of that is a quick, complex series of negotiations: chiding myself for even seeing it, lamenting the reminders of how divided our life still remains, being annoyed that these thoughts can be counted on to pass through my mind at some point in the evening. Most of the people around me yesterday were middle-aged or old. I am used to it, but it never ceases to surprise me how easy it is to leave the hybridity of the city, and enter into all-white spaces, the homogeneity of which, as far as I can tell, causes no discomfort to the whites in them. The only thing odd, to some of them, is seeing me, young and black, in my seat or at the concession stand. At times, standing in line for the bathroom during intermission, I get looks that make me feel like Ota Benga, the Mbuti man who was put on display in the Monkey House at the Bronx Zoo in 1906. I weary of such thoughts, but I am habituated to them. But Mahler's music is not white, or black, not old or young, and whether it is even specifically human, rather than in accord with more universal vibrations, is open to question. Simon Rattle, smiling, his curly hair bouncing, came onstage to applause. He acknowledged the orchestra, and then the lights dimmed further. The silence became total and, after a moment of anticipation, Rattle gave the downbeat, and the music began.

The first movement of the Ninth Symphony is like a great ship slipping out of port: weighty but nevertheless entirely graceful in its motion. In Rattle's hands, it began with sighs, a series of hesitations, a repeated falling figure that stretched out at the same time that it became more frenzied. I was listening, as always, both with my mind and with my body, entering into the familiar details of the music, discovering new details in the score, points of emphasis and articulation that I had not noticed before, or that had been brought to the fore, for the first time, by the conductor. Rattle, as I watched, was conducting Mahler, but he was also communicating—at least to me, as a longtime partisan of that music—with other performers of the same: Benjamin Zander, Jascha Horenstein, Claudio Abbado, John Barbirolli, Bernard Haitink, Leonard Bernstein, Hermann Scherchen, Otto Klemperer, and not least Bruno Walter, who had premiered the piece in Vienna a year after Mahler's death, and two years before the beginning of the First World War. These were the names of mostly European men, many of them now dead, names that had, in the fifteen years since I came to the United States, come to mean so much to me, each name connected to a specific mood and inflection—balanced, extreme, sentimental, pained, consoling—on the symphony's vast score. Simon Rattle, as he shaped the sound of the first two movements, guiding the orchestra through the frenzies and the lullabies, was staking his claim as one of the titans in this piece. The third movement, the rondo, was loud, rude, and as burlesque as it could conceivably be.

Then, out of a calmness that seemed to have all in the auditorium holding their breaths, the sweet, hymnlike opening of the final movement, carried by the string instruments, filled the hall. I was stunned: I had never before noticed how similar the melody in this movement was to "Abide with Me." And that revelation steeped me in the deep sorrow of Mahler's long but radiant elegy, and I felt I could also detect the intense concentration, the hundreds of private thoughts, of the people in the auditorium with me. How strange it was that, almost a hundred years ago, right there in Manhattan, just a short walk away from Carnegie Hall, at the Plaza Hotel, on the corner of Fifty-ninth Street and Fifth Avenue, Mahler had been at work on this very symphony, aware of the heart condition that would soon take his life.

In the glow of the final movement, but well before the music ended, an elderly woman in the front row stood, and began to walk up the aisle. She walked slowly, and all eyes were on her, though all ears remained on the music. It was as though she had been summoned, and was leaving into death, drawn by a force invisible to us. The old woman was frail, with a thin crown of white hair that, backlit by the stage, became a halo, and she moved so slowly that she was like a mote suspended inside the slow-moving music. One of her arms was slightly raised, as though she were being led forward by a helper—as though I was down there with my oma, and the sweep of the music was pushing us gently forward as I escorted her out into the darkness. As she drifted to the entrance and out of sight, in her gracefulness she resembled nothing so much as a boat departing on a country lake early in the morning, which, to those still standing on the shore, appears not to sail but to dissolve into the substance of the fog.

Mahler had worked, without self-pity, through his illness, through the catalogue of sufferings, and in his gargantuan compositions had worked elegy finely into elegy. He liked to say, with characteristic gallows humor, that *Krankheit ist Talentlosigkeit*—illness is a lack of talent. He made his own death matter—there was one of his great talents—so that it almost seemed as though he really died like a dragon breaking down a wall, as is said of certain great Chinese poets. His funeral was to be in Vienna, in Grinzing Cemetery. And so, after he'd gotten the definitive sentence of death—a streptococcal blood infection, secondary to an earlier diagnosis of infective endocarditis, a condition devastating to the heart valves—from Dr. Fraenkel, who had arrived at the diagnosis in consultation with Dr. Emanuel Libman, chief of the medical service at Mount Sinai Hospital, Mahler had undertaken the arduous final journey home. He'd gone first by boat from New York to Paris, where he unsuccessfully tried an experimental serum at the Institut Pasteur, then by train, in great discomfort, to Vienna, where the crowds welcomed and extolled him, whom before they had treated so cruelly, following his motorcade as though he were Virgil returning to Rome to die. And die he did, a week later, at midnight on the eighteenth of May, 1911.

The music stopped. Perfect silence in the hall. Simon Rattle was stock-still on the podium, his baton still in the air, and the musicians, too, were still, their instruments up. I looked around the hall, at the illuminated faces, all flooded with that silence. The seconds stretched on. No one coughed, and no one moved. We could hear the faint sound of traffic in the far distance outside the hall. But inside it, not a sound; even the hundreds of racing thoughts had stopped. Then Rattle brought his hands down, and the auditorium exploded with applause.

ONLY WHEN THE DOOR CLICKED BEHIND ME DID I REALIZE what I had done. I had used the emergency exit, which led directly from the fourth tier to the fire escape outside the building. The heavy metallic door that had just slammed shut had no external handle: I was locked out. There was to be no respite from the rain and the wind because I had also left my umbrella in the concert hall. And, added to all this was the fact that I was standing not on an exit staircase, as I had hoped, but on a flimsy fire escape, locked out on the unlit side of Carnegie Hall on a stormy evening. It was a situation of unimprovable comedy.

The slick wirework was all that separated me from the street level of the city, some seventy feet down. The lights directly below were visible between my feet, and my head and coat were already wet. My fellow concertgoers went about their lives oblivious to my plight. It was farther than the distance of a shout, even in clement weather; at night, with rain lisping through the streets, it was futile. And a few minutes before this, I had been in God's arms, and in the company of many hundreds of others, as the orchestra had sailed toward the coda, and brought us all to an impossible elation.

Now, I faced solitude of a rare purity. In the darkness, above the sheer drop, I could see the lights of Forty-second Street flashing in the visible distance. The railings of the fire escape, which were probably precarious at the best of times, were slicked with water and inimical to the grip. I moved carefully, taking step after premeditated step. The wind pushed around the building noisily, and I took some grim comfort in the idea that, if I were to fall from that height, there was no question of being maimed: death would be instant. The thought calmed me, and I stepped and slid down the metal steps, a few modest inches at a time. My high-wire act continued for long minutes in the darkness. And then I saw that the fire escape went only halfway down the building, ending abruptly at another closed door. The rest of the way down to the ground, some four flights, was air alone. But luck was with me: this second door had a handle. I tried it and it opened, into a hallway.

Before I entered the door, holding it open with relief and gratitude, it occurred to me to look straight up, and much to my surprise, there were stars. Stars! I hadn't thought I would be able to see them, not with the light pollution perpetually wreathing the city, and not on a night on which it had been raining. But the rain had stopped while I was climbing down, and had washed the air clean. The miasma of Manhattan's electric lights did not go very far up into the sky, and in the moonless night, the sky was like a roof shot through with light, and heaven itself shimmered. Wonderful stars, a distant cloud of fireflies: but I felt in my body what my eyes could not grasp, which was that their true nature was the persisting visual echo of something that was already in the past. In the unfathomable ages it took for light to cross such distances, the light source itself had in some cases been long extinguished, its dark remains stretched away from us at ever greater speeds.

But in the dark spaces between the dead, shining stars were stars I could not see, stars that still existed, and were giving out light that hadn't reached me yet, stars now living and giving out light but present to me only as blank interstices. Their light would arrive on earth eventually, long after I and my whole generation and the generation after me had slipped out of time, perhaps long after the human race itself was extinguished. To look into those dark spaces was to have a direct glimpse of the future. I gripped the rusted railing of the fire escape with one hand and tightened my hold on the open door with the other. The night air clipped my ears. I looked down, a steep drop, and the blurred yellow rectangle of a taxicab sped by, and then an ambulance, its wailing reaching me from four floors below, and stretching out as it headed toward Times Square's neon inferno. I wished I could meet the unseen starlight halfway, starlight that was unreachable because my entire being was caught up in a blind spot, starlight that was coming as fast as it could, covering almost seven hundred million miles every hour. It would arrive in due time, and cast its illumination on other humans, or perhaps on other configurations of our world, after unimaginable catastrophes had altered it beyond recognition. My hands held metal, my eyes starlight, and it was as though I had come so close to something that it had fallen out of focus, or fallen so far away from it that it had faded away.

I WALKED ALONG CENTRAL PARK, WHICH WAS CHOKED WITH the smell of horse dung, past Dr. Saito's apartment building to Columbus Circle, and took the 1 train down to Twenty-third Street. When I came off the subway, instead of going directly home, I crossed the West Side Highway. I intended to see the water, and approached the Chelsea Piers building. Coming around it on the right, to where the yachts and tourist boats were docked, I saw a man in uniform. He raised his arm in greeting. We are just about to leave, he said. I presumed he was in charge of the boat, and I explained that I wasn't part of the party. It's okay, he said. The boat isn't at capacity yet. And you don't have to pay anything; they've covered the costs. He smiled, and added, I can tell you'd love to hop on. Come on! We'll be back in under an hour. I followed him to Pier 66, and stepped onto the long white boat, which was already noisy with college-age revelers. It was almost eleven, and there was no rain. In the brightly lit interior cabin, someone in a waiter's uniform was checking ID cards before letting the students take filled plastic champagne flutes from his tray. He offered me one, and I declined. Most people were watching the view from inside the cabin, as the wind was by now brisk. I made my way to the back deck. There were a handful of couples and some solitary individuals, and I found a place to sit near one of the railings.

The engine emitted a low grumble, and the boat pitched back a little and trembled, as though it were inhaling air in readiness for a dive. Then it pushed off the pier, and soon, the water between us and the docking piers widened, and the chatter of the revelers floated up from the glassed-in cabin. We traced a fast arc south, and the taller buildings in the Wall Street area soon loomed into view on our left. Closest to the water was the World Financial Center, with its two towers linked by the translucent atrium and lit blue by night lights. The boat rode the river swells. Sitting on deck, watching the frothy, white wake on the black water, I felt myself pulled aloft and down again, as if by the travel of an invisible bell rope.

Within a few minutes of our entering the Upper Bay, we saw the Statue of Liberty, a faint green in the mist, then very quickly massive and towering over us, a monument worthy of the name, with the thick folds of her dress as stately as columns. The boat came close to the island, and more of the students had by now moved up onto the deck, and they pointed, and their voices, which filled the air around us, fell echolessly into the water. The cruise organizer came up to me. Glad you came, aren't you? I acknowledged his greeting with a faint smile, and he, sensing my solitude, went away again. The crown of the statue has remained closed since late 2001, and even those visitors who come close to it are confined to looking upward at the statue; no one is permitted to climb up the 354 narrow steps and look out into the bay from the windows in the crown. Bartholdi's monumental statue has not, in any case, done particularly long service as a destination for tourists. Although it has had its symbolic value right from the beginning, until 1902, it was a working lighthouse, the biggest in the country. In those days, the flame that shone from the torch guided ships into Manhattan's harbor; that same light, especially in bad weather, fatally disoriented birds. The birds, many of which were clever enough to dodge the cluster of skyscrapers in the city, somehow lost their bearings when faced with a single monumental flame.

A large number of birds met their death in this manner. In 1888, for instance, on the morning after one particularly stormy night, more than fourteen hundred dead birds were recovered from the crown, the balcony of the torch, and the pedestal of the statue. The officials of the island saw an opportunity there and, as was their custom, sold the birds off, at low cost, to New York City milliners and fancy stores. But it was to be the last time they would do so, because one Colonel Tassin, who had military command of the island, intervened and was determined that any birds that happened to die in the future would not be disposed of commercially, but would be retained in the service of science. The carcasses, each time two hundred or more of them had been gathered, were to be sent to the Washington National Museum, the Smithsonian Institution, and other scientific institutions. With this strong instinct for public-spiritedness, Colonel Tassin undertook a government system of records, which he ensured were kept with military regularity and, shortly afterward, he was able to deliver detailed reports on each death, including the species of the bird, date, hour of striking, number striking, number killed, direction and force of the wind, character of the weather, and general remarks. On October 1 of that year, for example, the colonel's report indicated that fifty rails had died, as had eleven wrens, two catbirds, and one whip-poor-will. The following day, the record showed two dead wrens; the day after that, eight wrens. The average, Colonel Tassin estimated, was about twenty birds per night, although the weather and the direction of the wind had a great deal to do with the resulting harvest. Nevertheless, the sense persisted that something more troubling was at work. On the morning of October 13, for example, 175 wrens had been gathered in, all dead of the impact, although the night just past hadn't been particularly windy or dark.

# ACKNOWLEDGMENTS

Thanks to Elizabeth, Andru, Jean, and Jeremy, who read the text and made useful comments on it. I thank Chimamanda, Siddhartha, Amitava, Femi, Patti, Nanda, Kwame, Hilary, Maria, Madhu, and Carey, friends who helped me write the book. I am especially grateful to Angelika, the source of several ideas and much kindness. My agent, Scott, was an enthusiastic and perceptive champion of the manuscript right from the beginning, and did a great deal to sharpen it. My editor, David, was unfailingly patient and kind, and he turned a wayward manuscript into a less wayward book. I am grateful to my parents and siblings for their love and stories. I am indebted to the many friends I haven't named, and to the strangers who inspired me. Above all, I am grateful to Karen, love of my life and protector of my solitude.

TEJU COLE was born in the United States in 1975 to Nigerian parents and grew up in Lagos. His books include the novels *Tremor* and *Open City*, the essay collections *Known and Strange Things* and *Black Paper*, and the experimental photo book *Blind Spot*. He has been honored with the PEN/Hemingway Award, the Internationaler Literaturpreis, the Windham-Campbell Prize, and a Guggenheim Fellowship, among others. He is an elected member of the American Academy of Arts and Sciences. Cole is currently a professor of the practice of creative writing at Harvard University and a contributing writer to *The New York Times Magazine*.

tejucole.com
Instagram: @_tejucole